JUST ANOTHER

That evening started ....
least, by the standards of the patrons of ..., ..., ...
Place—and its proprietor and chief bartender: myself.

Not that the evening had been uneventful. Thanks to our
resident Irish myth, Ernie Shea, the Lucky Duck—a half-
breed pooka, around whom the iron laws of probability tend
to turn to silly putty—we'd had a brief spell of weather indoors: at about nine o'clock one of the very few tornadoes in
Long Island's history had suddenly sprung out of nowhere and
lifted the roof clear off the place, neat as you please. The noise
and suddenness of the roof's departure startled us a bit, naturally (Doc Webster, though, glanced up nonchalantly and
said, "A Gable roof, I see—gone with the wind."), and there
can't be many sights sillier than a roomful of people gaping
up at rain falling on their faces . . . but fortunately, by now
we had all acquired a certain sense of just *how* the Duck's luck
tends to run; we simply covered our drinks with our hands
and waited it out. Sure enough, another roof came along in
a few minutes. It was a good enough fit, and apparently it
arrived with all its nails bristling because it installed itself
with a solidity we could hear and feel was reliable. Indeed, it
turned out to be slightly *better* than the roof I'd traded for it.

After that, well let's see . . .

"A riot for Callahan's addicts."—*Kirkus*

BOOKS BY SPIDER ROBINSON:

*denotes a Tor book

CALLAHAN'S LEGACY

SPIDER ROBINSON

A TOM DOHERTY ASSOCIATES BOOK
NEW YORK

This is a work of fiction. All the characters and events portrayed in this novel are either fictitious or are used fictitiously.

CALLAHAN'S LEGACY

Copyright © 1996 by Spider Robinson

All rights reserved, including the right to reproduce this book, or portions thereof, in any form.

Cover art by James Warhola

Edited by James R. Frenkel

A Tor Book
Published by Tom Doherty Associates, Inc.
175 Fifth Avenue
New York, NY 10010

Tor Books on the World Wide Web:
http://www.tor.com

Tor® is a registered trademark of Tom Doherty Associates, Inc.

ISBN 0-812-55035-8
Library of Congress Card Catalog Number: 96-17314

First edition: October 1996
First mass market edition: September 1997

Printed in the United States of America

0 9 8 7 6 5 4 3 2 1

*This one's for Mary, John,
Jeanne, Megan, and Patrick,
and for Jim*

ACKNOWLEDGMENTS

This book couldn't have been begun without the assistance of my ingenious brother-in-law, John Moore—who brought to my attention, and documented for me at great length, an existing force which would be considered irresistibly destructive even by people who have been within meters of an exploding nuclear weapon;

This book couldn't have been completed without the assistance of Montréal fan Steve Herman—who, when I met him at ConCept '95, provided the key suggestion (actually, the way he phrased it was perilously close to being an order) that made everything else fall into place at long last; additional crucial advice, support, pity, and/or medication during the book's interminable genesis were supplied by the Cultural Services Branch of the British Columbia Ministry of Small Business, Tourism and Culture, and by Don DeBrandt, Dr. Oliver Robinow, Guy Immega, Bob Atkinson, and just about all the caffeine-inflamed members of the British Columbia Science Fiction Association's Alternative-FRED Society;

This book couldn't have been contemplated without the support and assistance of my wife, Jeanne, and daughter, Terri (it constitutes Jeanne's 20th wedding anniversary present—here you go, spice! But yours was better . . .);

This book wouldn't have been as good without the help of my friends Walter and Jill of White Dwarf Books/Dead Write Mysteries: the one-stop shop for Vancouver's serious word junkies; or without Patrick Regan, habitué of Usenet's alt.callahan's, who unwittingly posted the Pat and Mike jokes just when I needed them; and finally

This book would not have reached your hands without the sagacity, skill, and professionalism of my agent, Eleanor Wood; my editor, Jim Frenkel; and the puissant sales samurai of my esteemed publisher, Shogun Tom Doherty-sama.

Thanks to the last-named three; by the way, I am happy to report that all of the first three books of stories about Callahan's Place have just been restored to print by Tor in a trade paperback omnibus edition called *The Callahan Chronicals*, for the enjoyment of you and anyone you know who's having a birthday soon.

—Vancouver, B.C.
28 November 1995

1

TOO HOT TO HOOT

The immortal storyteller Alfred Bester once said that the way to tell a story is to begin with a disaster and then build to a climax. I'd like to—believe me, I'd like to—but this particular story happened just the other way round.

It was a good climax, at least.

Well, okay, maybe that's a silly statement. Perhaps you feel that there is no such thing as a *bad* climax; that some are better than others, is all. I could argue the point, but I won't. Let's just agree with Woody Allen that "The worst one I ever had was right on the money," stipulate that they're all at least okay, and try to quantify the matter a bit.

On a scale of ten, then, rating "the least enjoyable orgasm I've ever had" as a One, and "reaching the culmination of hours of foreplay with the sexiest partner imaginable after years of celibacy" as a Ten, the climax I'm speaking of now was probably about a Nine-Five.

This despite the fact that every one of the ingredients I've named for a Ten were present. The foreplay had been so extensive and inventive (*Groucho, leering:* ". . . and the *aft*play wasn't so bad either . . .") that the sun was coming up by the time I was going in the other direction; my partner was the sexiest woman on the planet, my darling Zoey Berkowitz; and she was my first real lover (as opposed to mere sexer) in more years than I cared to think about. True, we had already been lovers for several months, by then . . . but the honeymoon was by no means over. (In fact, it still isn't. The way I see it, our relationship is really just a single continuous ongoing act of lovemaking, a dance so complex and subtle that we often disengage bodies completely for hours at a time.) My father used to say, "Familiarity breeds, content," and that's always been my experience.

No, what brought the meter down as low as Nine-Five was merely a matter of mechanics. Zoey—thank God—has never been a small woman, not since the sixth grade, anyway, and she was nine and a half months pregnant at the time all this happened, in the late fall of 1988.

Indeed, if I could travel in time like Mike Callahan, and went far enough back into hominid history, I think I could prove my theory that pregnancy is responsible for the evolution of Man As Engineer. (This might help explain why there are so few female engineers.) A man who has successfully managed the trick with a mate in the latter stages of pregnancy possesses most of the insights necessary to build a house—and a strong motivation in that direction, as well. If inventing math were as much fun, we'd probably own the Galaxy by now.

But I digress . . .

As I was saying, Zoey and I had solved the Riddle of the Sphinx together one more time, just as enough dawnglow was sneaking past the edges of the curtains to let us see what we already knew, and neither of us was paying attention to any damn imaginary scoring judges—we were both well content, if a little fatigued. By the time we had our breath back, the day was well and truly begun: birds had begun warbling somewhere outside, and traffic was building up to the usual weekday morning homicidal frenzy out on Route 25A (*why* are they all in such a hurry to get to a place they hate and do things they don't care about?), a combination of sounds that always puts me right to sleep. That's probably just where I'd have gone if Zoey hadn't poked me in a tender spot and murmured drowsily, ". . . 'cha *snickering* about?"

I hadn't realized I was. In fact, I wasn't. "I'm not," I said. "I'm chuckling."

She shook her head. "Unh-unh. I like Snickers better'n Chuckles."

I considered a couple of puns having to do with the physical characteristics and components of the candy named, but left them unspoken. Sexual puns are funnier *before* you come. "Chortling, then," I said. "Definitely not a snicker."

Zoey grimaced, her eyes still glued shut. "But *why?* Are you."

"Oh, it's just this silly mental picture I get after we make love," I admitted. "I keep seeing little Nameless floating in there, startled awake by this rhythmic earthquake . . . then staring in fascination as all these millions of confused, exhausted, disappointed little wigglers show up, looking everywhere for an egg. I'll bet they tickle. The little tyke must get a chuckle out of it."

"Or a chortle," she agreed, chortling sleepily. "I will, too—f'now on. Thanks. Neat image."

She yawned hugely then, so of course I did, too, and we did the little bits of physical backing and filling necessary to move from Cuddling to Snuggling, and we'd probably both have been comfortably asleep together in only another minute or two. But we had forgotten about the Invisible Machines of Murphy.

The universe is full of them, and many of them seem to be simple pressure switches. For instance, there's one underneath most toilet seats: your weight coming down on the seat somehow causes the phone to ring. (Unless you've brought the phone in with you: in that case the switch cues a Jehovah's Witness to knock on your door.) There's another one built into most TV remote controls, wired into the channel-select button: if you try to browse, it somehow alerts every station on the air to go to commercial. The most maddening thing about these switches is that, being of Murphy, they're unreliable: you can't be sure whether or just when they will function, except that it will usually turn out in retrospect to have been at the most annoying possible moment. So the tiny pair of switches under my eyelids, sensing that I was just about to drop off to sleep, picked now to send out the signal that causes my alarm clock to ring. Excuse me——I mean, to:

BZZZZZZZZZZZZZZZZZZZZZZZZ!!!!!

For the past two weeks that damned thing had been going off at just this ungodly hour—set by mine own hand and with Zoey's foreknowledge and consent—and every single time it came as a rude and ghastly surprise. Neither of us could get used to it. I had been a professional musician for a quarter of a century until I gave it up to tend bar; Zoey still was one—or had been right up until carrying both a baby and a bass guitar got to be too much for her; it had been decades since either of us had willingly gotten up at dawn. Dawn was what you occasionally stayed up as late as. Sunlight gave you the skin cancer, everybody knew that. *Civilians* got up at dawn, for heaven's sake.

Well, so do nine-and-a-half-month-pregnant women. And their partners. No matter what their normal sleep cycle is.

Being more than nine months pregnant may mean nothing at all. Not even when you get up to nine and a half months, and the kid hasn't even dropped yet. Maybe you just guessed wrong on the conception date. We don't want you to worry, Ms. Berkowitz. But maybe, just maybe, something is wrong in there. Maybe little Nameless doesn't *want* to come out and play, ready or not. If so, it is a bad decision, however one might sympathize—because once Nameless *is* ready, he or she will begin to do what all fully formed babies do best: excrete. And, polluting the womb, will die. And possibly take you along for company. The chances of this are low . . . but it might be wisest if you just checked into the hospital now,

Ms. Berkowitz, and allowed us to induce labor with a pitocin drip . . .

Zoey had awarded that offer an emphatic "Fuck you very much, Doctor," and I was behind her a hundred percent. At the time. We had both devoured most of the available literature on birthing as a subversive activity, and were determined to Do This Naturally—not with drugs and episiotomies, like postmodern drones, but the way our primitive ancestors did it in the caves: with a trained Lamaze partner, a camcorder, and a physician standing by just in case. As far as we were concerned, Nameless could emerge in his or her own good time.

The hospital had seen all too many zealots like us; they sighed and agreed to let us wait as long as we could stand it, against advice . . . provided we were willing to furnish daily proof that Nameless was not in fact dying in there. In the form of a maternal urine sample. Which they would need first thing in the morning. Every morning. Wherefore:

BZZZZZZZZZZZZZZZZZZZZZZZZ!!!!!

As far as I can see, the biggest disadvantage to having a pregnant lady around the home is that it's always your turn to get up. I said a few words, and Zoey stuck an elbow in my ribs, saying, "Not in front of the baby!" So I said some more words, but in my head, and got up out of bed. As I went around the bed, I confirmed by eye that her chamber pot was placed where she would be able to conveniently straddle it, and went to the bathroom to get another specimen container from the package under the sink. (If you think ten yards is too short a walk to the bathroom for a chamber pot to be necessary, you've never been nine and a half months pregnant.) And then . . . well, it got complicated.

I bent over, see, and took the package by a scrap of torn flap at the top, and straightened up, intending to rummage inside the thing for a specimen container once I got it up to around waist level. But Zoey had been pregnant for nine months and thirteen days, and those damn packages hold a dozen . . . so it was empty . . . and since it was empty, it didn't weigh anything . . . and since I was expecting it to weigh at least *something*, and was more than a little groggy . . . well, I overbalanced and landed ass-first in the bathtub, whanging my head against the tile wall.

It could have happened to you, okay? Sure, it didn't, and never will . . . but it *could* have. And if it had, I wouldn't have laughed at *you*.

Oh all right, I'm lying. Go ahead.

Zoey had apparently decided to rest her eyes until I got back, and *then* get up into a sitting position, when there was someone there to help. But her love was true: I believe the combination of my piteous wail and the loud reverberating *boom* were probably enough to cause at least one of her eyes to open, perhaps as much as halfway. "You alive, hon?" she murmured.

I was dazed, and not honestly sure of the answer, but I could not ignore the concern in her voice. "Depends on what you call living," I temporized, trying with little success to get out of the tub.

Her reply was a snore.

My struggles triggered another of those invisible Murphy Switches: the showerhead's built-in bombsight detected the presence of an unsuspecting human in its target area, and cut loose with the half cup or so of ice water it keeps handy for such occasions, scoring a direct hit on my groin. That got me up out of the bathtub, at least, though I can't explain exactly how; all I know is, an instant later I was standing up and drawing in breath to swear. Loudly. With a great effort I managed to squelch it. The useless empty paper sack that should have held specimen jars was still in my hand; I flung it angrily toward the wastebasket beyond the toilet bowl. But of course it had poor aerodynamic characteristics for a projectile: it fluttered and flapped and curled over and fell short, square into the toilet bowl. Two points. This time I was not entirely successful in suppressing my bark of rage; it emerged as a kind of moan. I turned angrily on my heel, and walked straight into the edge of the open bathroom door. The sun went nova, and when it had cooled, I found that I was sitting again, on the cold tile floor this time. The front of my head now hurt as much as the back, and my buttocks hurt twice as much.

Outside in the bedroom, Zoey snored again.

For the third time, my lungs sucked in air . . . and then let it out again, very slowly. If I woke Zoey with screamed curses, I'd have to explain why—and then refrain from strangling her while she giggled. Or chortled. I got up, rubbed the places that hurt, and turned my attention to the problem of improvising an alternate urine container. If it had been for myself or another male, no problem—but females need a wider aperture. I shuffled past the sleeping Zoey and left the bedroom, searching for inspiration.

By the time I found it, I had left our living quarters completely and wandered out into Mary's Place proper.

Living in back of a tavern has been a lifelong dream of mine, and the reality has turned out to be even better than I imagined. There, for instance, ranked in rows behind the bar, were a plethora of acceptable receptacles. (Say that three times fast with marbles in your mouth and you'll never need a dentist again.) Before selecting one, I punched a combination into The Machine and set a mug upright on its conveyor belt, which hummed into life and whisked the mug away into the interior. Less than a minute later it emerged from the far side of The Machine, filled now with fresh hot Tanzanian Peaberry coffee adulterated to my taste. I took it and the specimen container I had chosen back into the bedroom.

There are few things a very pregnant woman will wake up for, but peeing is definitely one of them. Getting Zoey to a sitting position on the side of the bed (without tipping over the chamber pot) was probably less difficult than portaging a piano in rough country. The smell of coffee must have helped. She took a long sip of it, then came fully awake when she recognized the receptacle I was offering her.

"Jake, I am *not* peeing into a stein."

"Oh hell, Zoey, what's its religion got to do with anything? It's wide enough, it's been sterilized, it's got a lid I can tape shut after, we're out of specimen jars, just go ahead and get it over with, okay? Whoever it is today will be here any minute."

My best friends in the world—AKA: my regular clientele—had organized what they insisted on calling a Pee Pool: each morning one of them took a turn at coming by Mary's Place to pick up the day's specimen and ferry it to the hospital for analysis. I had no idea whose turn it was today, and was too groggy to figure it out, but the way things were going I suspected it would be one of the rare prompt ones.

Zoey thought it over and relaxed to the inevitable. She set the coffee down where I couldn't reach it without stepping over her, deployed the stein above the thundermug, and cut loose.

Sure enough, just as she finished, there was a thunderous knocking. A *distant* thunderous knocking—at the bar's front door.

That irritated me. Whoever it was could have just as easily come around to *this* side of the building and knocked on the much-closer *back* door. As a gesture of my irritation, I tossed aside the underpants I had just managed to locate, snatched the filled stein out of Zoey's hand, and set off to answer the knock stark naked. "Jake—" Zoey called after me, and I snarled, "Whoever it is has it coming," over my shoulder. For the second time that day I padded out of the living area and into the bar, went through the swinging doors into the foyer, and flung open the outside door with a flourish.

And was vouchsafed a vision.

It had to be a vision. Reality, even the rather plastic kind I've learned to live with over the years, simply could not—I felt—produce a sight like that. Nor was it a mere hallucination: I had not had a drink in many hours, or a toke in several days. The thing was so weird that it took me a full second or two to learn to see it: at first my brain rejected what it was given and searched for plausible alternatives.

This object is a fireplug—no, a fireplug's older brother—over which someone has draped a very used painter's drop cloth, and onto the top of which someone has placed the severed head of a pit bull. No, wait, pit bulls don't have mustaches. Perhaps this is the secret midget son of Buddy Hackett, wearing a paint-spattered toga as part of his fraternity initiation. No, I have it now: this is R2-D2 dressed for Halloween. Or maybe—

We gaped at each other for a good five seconds of silence, the vision and I, before I tentatively—and correctly—identified it as the ugliest woman I had ever seen. The moment I did so, I screamed and jumped back a foot—and at the exact same instant, she did the exact same thing.

The difference was, I was holding a nearly full stein.

The lid flew open when I started, and a glog of the contents sailed out into the air: an elongated fluid projectile, like a golden version of the second, liquid-metal–model Terminator. It caught her amidships and splattered, the splat sound overpowered by the *clop!* of the stein lid slamming shut again.

There was a short pause, and then she barked.

I mean barked, like a dog. In fact, *yapped* is closer to the sound she made—but doesn't begin to convey the impact. Even "barked" isn't strong enough. Maybe "bayed." Imagine a two-hundred-pound Pekingese with a bullhorn, and you've only started to imagine that sound. It was something like all the fingernails in the world being drawn across all the blackboards in Hell and then amplified through the Madison Square Garden sound system at maximum gain.

I shivered rather like a dog myself, blinked rapidly without effect, and felt my testicles retreating into my trunk.

The vision barked again, louder—a sound which you can duplicate for yourself if you wish by simply inserting a power drill into each ear simultaneously. As its echo faded, I heard the distant sounds of Zoey approaching to investigate. She pushed the swinging doors open and joined me in the foyer—stopped short and gaped.

The . . . I was finally beginning to believe it was a human woman, or something like one . . . gaped back at the two of us, staring from the naked hairy man to the extremely pregnant woman in the ratty bathrobe. She opened her mouth to bark again, paused, blinked, looked down at the damp stain on her chest, sniffed sharply—the sight of her hirsute nostrils flaring will go with me to my grave—glared up at me, then at the stein in my hand, then back at me, then down at the stain on her chest again, then one more time at Zoey, and finally she threw back her head and *howled*.

A couple of glasses burst behind the bar.

I heard them just before my hearing cut out completely, as though God had accidentally overloaded the automatic level control on my tape deck. I know I tried to scream myself, but don't know whether I succeeded. I also tried to jam my fingers into my ears, to stop the pain that continued long after actual hearing had fled. Not only didn't it help a bit, the stein I had abandoned to do so landed squarely on my bare right foot, with a crunch that I *did* hear, by bone conduction, and sprayed the last of its contents onto the creature's behaired shins, pilled socks, and orthopedic shoes.

A pity, for it caused her to sustain her howl longer than she might have otherwise, and to shake at me a fist like a small wrinkled ham.

Horrible as that shriek was—and it was, even without being audible—the end of it was worse, for now she had to draw in breath for the *next* one, and so I saw her teeth. I can see them now. My eyes sent my brain an urgent message asking how come *they* had to stay on duty when my ears had already bugged out?

With that, my Guardian Idiot snapped out of his stupor, and reminded me that I did not have to endure this trial any longer than I chose to. I closed the door quietly but firmly in her face.

Then I stood on one leg and cradled my mashed foot in both hands and hopped in pain. Then I lost my balance and fell down, for the third time that morning, on my bare ass, banging my head again too. (For those of you who are connoisseurs of anguish, a hardwood floor is perceptibly harder than either tub or tile.)

Zoey, bless her, did the only thing she could: she burst out laughing.

I did not join her. Not right away. I tried a withering glare—but if age cannot wither nor custom stale my Zoey, no glare of mine is going to do the trick. Then I thought about kicking her, somewhere that wouldn't endanger Nameless—but now was not a good time to get beat up. Next I opened my mouth to say something—deeming it safe because I assumed she was still as deafened as I by the vision's banshee cry.

But before I could, I realized that the deafness must have worn off: I could hear Zoey's hoots of helpless hysteria, now, and the distant and fading sound of that monstrous barking outside. So I closed my mouth, prepared a slightly less offensive speech, opened my mouth again . . . and clearly heard the sound of knocking.

Distant knocking. Not here—but at the *back* door, back in the bedroom . . . where one of my friends must be waiting to receive the daily beaker of piss.

Now I joined Zoey in laughing.

I just had to. It was that or go mad. The louder and more urgent the distant knocking became, the harder we laughed. Finally I got up, collected the empty stein, and went, still laughing, to answer the knock.

"What the *hell* was that?" Zoey asked as we walked back toward our quarters, wiping away tears of laughter.

"I think it was a person," I said. "I'm pretty sure it was a life-form of some kind, anyway."

"If you say so. I wonder what in God's name she wanted. What language was that she was speaking?"

"I'm not sure she was evolved that far. Come on, hurry up, or—"

Needless to say, by the time we got to the back door to answer the knock, the knocker—Noah Gonzalez—had given up and gone round to the front door. I left Zoey there and retraced my steps through the entire building—for the third time, before coffee—and got to the front door moments after Noah had given up and gone round to the *back* door again.

That's it, I thought, *I quit*. I went as far as the bar, made a second cup of coffee, and vowed not to move another step until I had finished drinking this one. Zoey and Noah must have connected, and worked out for themselves the awkward business of him waiting in the bedroom while she waddled into the bathroom and refilled the stein for him. (No problem for a pregnant lady.) By the time she came out to find me, carrying my bathrobe, I was putting the finishing touches on the lyrics of a new song.

It goes like this:

> *God has a sense of humor, but it's often rather crude*
> *What He thinks is a howler, you or I would say is rude*
> *But cursing Him is not a real productive attitude*
> *Just laugh—you might as well, my friend,*
> *'cause either way you're screwed*
> > *I know: it sounds so simple, and it's so hard to do*
> > *To laugh when the joke's on you*
>
> *God loved Mort Sahl, Belushi, Lenny Bruce—He likes it sick*
> *Fields, Chaplin, Keaton . . . anyone in pain will do the trick*
> *'Cause God's idea of slapstick is to slap you with a stick:*
> *You might as well resign yourself to steppin on your dick*
> > *It always sounds so simple, but it's so hard to do*
> > *To laugh when the joke's on you*
>
> *You can laugh at a total stranger*
> *When it isn't your ass in danger*
> *And your lover can be a riot*
> *—if you learn how to giggle quiet*
> *But if you want the right to giggle, that is what you gotta do*
> *when the person steppin on that old banana peel is you*
>
> *A chump and a banana peel: the core of every joke*
> *But when it's you that steps on one, your laughter tends to*
> > *choke*

Try not to take it personal, just have another toke
as long as you ain't broken, what's the difference if you're
  broke?
 I know: it sounds so simple, but it's so hard to do
 To laugh when the joke's on you

It can be hard to force a smile, as you get along in years
It isn't easy laughin at your deepest secret fears
But try to find your funny bone, and have a couple beers:
If it don't come out in laughter, man, it's comin out in tears
 I said it sounds so simple, but it's so hard to do
 To laugh when the joke's on you

The barking vision did not return. Within ten minutes, Zoey and I had crawled back into bed, where we would enjoy a sound and undisturbed sleep, and nothing else awful or astonishing was to happen after that until well after sundown.

But—had we but known it—the ending of Mary's Place had already begun.

2

TOO FAR, EDNA:
WE WANDER AFOOT

That evening started out to be a fairly typical night. At least, by the standards of the patrons of Mary's Place—and its proprietor and chief bartender: myself.

Not that the evening had been uneventful. By ten o'clock, just under thirty of us had put away about thirteen gallons of booze . . . though admittedly something over eleven gallons of that had gone directly from their various bottles and kegs to the throat of Naggeneen, our resident Irish cluricaune, without ever occupying the intervening space. (Like their cousins the leprechauns, and indeed like all the Daoine Sidh, cluricaunes have paranormal psi powers—in their case, the ability to teleport and absorb alcohol—and Naggeneen feels that pouring, lifting and sipping are shameful wastes of good drinking time.) On the bright side, he paid for every drop he drank, cash on the bar, in gold coin so pure it would take a toothmark. And, of course, he tended to be a very agreeable drunk, neither pugnacious nor pathetic, neither morose nor maniac, both merry and mannerly. I guess a few hundred years of practice must count for something.

Thanks to our *other* resident Irish myth, Ernie Shea, the Lucky Duck—a half-breed pooka, around whom the iron laws of probability tend to turn into extremely silly putty— we had even had a brief spell of weather indoors: at about nine o'clock one of the very few tornadoes in Long Island's history had suddenly sprung up out of nowhere and lifted the roof clear off the place, neat as you please, and scaled it away into the night like a Frisbee. The noise and suddenness of the roof's departure startled us a bit, naturally (Doc Webster, though, rising to the occasion as he so often does, glanced up nonchalantly and said, raising his voice over the howling wind, "A Gable roof, I see—gone with the wind."), and there can't be many sights sillier than a roomful of people gaping up at rain falling on their faces . . . but fortunately it is not possible for any of us at Mary's Place to get wet when it rains (thanks to an alien cyborg friend of ours—I'll get to that later), and besides, by now we had all acquired a certain sense of just *how* the Duck's luck tends to run; we simply covered our drinks with our hands to prevent their dilution and waited it out. Sure enough, another roof came along in a few minutes. It was a good enough fit, and apparently it arrived with all its nails bristling because it installed itself with a so- lidity that we could hear and feel was reliable. Indeed, it turned out to be slightly *better* than the roof I'd traded for it, in one respect: like its predecessor, it had a built-in hatch for rooftop access—but this hatch was better positioned, farther away from the bar, so that I would now be able to get a stair- way up to it and allow my customers the option of doing their drinking under the stars. (I'd have to put a fence around the roof, too, of course.)

After that, well, let's see . . . once the floor had dried suf- ficiently, Ralph Von Wau Wau the talking dog got out his lat- est short story and read it aloud to us, turning the pages expertly with his muzzle and paws, and dropping, for the du- ration of the reading, that silly fake accent he usually puts on. (Well, okay, I have to admit a German shepherd speaking in a German accent *is* kind of amusing.)

And after he was done and we finished applauding and

commenting and petting him and so forth, we all spent a while chatting with the Internet. Not chatting *on* the Internet. Chatting *with* the Internet . . . with its self-generated Artificially Intelligent avatar, whom my true love Zoey had named Solace, and who had for several months now been manifesting herself, at infrequent intervals, through the house's souped-up Mac II (augmented with camera and microphone). The chat was of a fairly standard type: we tried to think of Turing Tests that Solace couldn't pass—and she tried out a few Turing Tests of her own on us.

Like I say, a pretty routine night, for us at Mary's Place. It was nearly ten o'clock before anything I'd classify as weird happened.

Solace had just aced our latest homebrewed Turing Test, a speech recognition homonym-discriminator devised by Doc Webster. This consisted of correctly displaying onscreen— as the Doc dictated it, without perceptible pause for thought—the following nonsense sentence:

> "I was musing on the Muse under some yews outside S.M.U.'s museum, as I'm used to doing, when a kitten's musical mews drew me into the museum's mews, which some use—damn youse—to sniff mucilage for amusement."

This is, of course, just an extended variation on Heinlein's classic construct, "Though the tough cough and hiccough plough him through," that is, a sentence designed to confound just about any imaginable speech-recognition system short of a human brain or functional equivalent. As far as I'm concerned, software capable of grokking that all six of Heinlein's different sounds are spelled identically, or that the single repeating sound in the Doc's sentence can and must be semantically interpreted thirteen different ways, is software that meets my criteria for sentience, whether its neurons are wet or dry. (What matter if said sentience consists of "nothing more than" a large sheaf of complex algorithms? I don't know about you, but a good half the human beings I run into on the street are, or seem to be, on automatic pilot: navigating by a series of prestored algorithms, clumsy primitive rules of thumb. Can't see that it makes any difference whether the algorithms are expressed by meat, machine, or Martian.) As the last words of the Doc's test sentence appeared onscreen, correctly spelled, a mild cheer went up from those ten or fifteen patrons who were paying attention.

I'd like to pause there for just a second and preen, if I may. I think I have a right to be a little proud: at age forty-five, I ran the kind of bar where a live, realtime chat with the Net come alive was not necessarily the most interesting thing in the room. Over at the opposite end of the house from the sparkling fireplace, for example, Ev and Don were playing tic-tac-toe with smoke rings for an appreciative crowd of onlookers—don't ask me how Don can blow an X; all I can tell you is they seem very happy with each other—and in another corner of the house, the Darts Championship of the Universe (a weekly ritual) was in progress; the Lucky Duck had agreed to accept as handicaps both a blindfold and the tying of *both* hands behind his back, and nonetheless was clearly going to seize the crown from Tommy Janssen, the reigning champion; it was just a matter of time. His luck was with him, you see.

But I digress.

As I was saying, Solace successfully displayed that silly sentence (in thirty-six-point Benguiat font on her fourteen-inch monitor, if you're a computer weenie. And by the way, did you know that nanotechnology fans are known as "teeny weenies?") as fast as Doc Webster could say it, and was applauded by something like a dozen onlookers. "Way to go, Solace," Long-Drink McGonnigle called out.

"Thank you, Phil," Solace said. Ever since we had decided that Solace was more of a she than a he, she had spoken aloud to us—through the stereo speakers I'd hooked up to the Mac II—in a warm contralto, not unlike Zoey's.

"Hell," the Drink went on, "these days there's probably Ph.D.s in English who couldn't spell that sentence correctly.

Even I might have had to hesitate a second or two, here and there."

"These days there are Ph.D.s in English who can't spell 'Ph.D.,' " Tanya Latimer said gloomily, and her husband Isham nodded agreement.

Marty Matthias spoke up. "My grade twelve students at St. Dominic's all did rotten on the last exam I gave them. So to try and cheer them up a little, I told them the inspirational story of how Albert Einstein himself failed math when *he* was in school, right? A hand goes up in the back of the room. 'Mr. Matthias,' he says, not kidding, honestly puzzled, 'I don't get it. If he was so lousy in school and everything . . . how come they called him "Einstein"?' "

There were cries of horror, outrage and protest. But no disbelief.

"I didn't know what to say. I stood there with my mouth open until the bell rang."

Doc Webster sighed. "It's the 'Tood and Janey' effect," he announced.

"The which?" Long-Drink asked.

"Creeping—no, galloping—illiteracy. The township repaired the sidewalks in my neighborhood recently, poured fresh concrete, you know? Naturally kids with popsicle sticks condensed out of the ether, to immortalize themselves with . . . uh . . . concrete poetry." Groans. "Well sir, right in front of my house, where I have to look at it every time I go out, there is now inscribed a large heart, within which lie the dread words, 'TOOD AND JANEY.' "

"Huh?" chorused half a dozen people at once.

"I know the world has gotten weird lately," the Doc went on, "but I still don't believe we've reached the point where any set of parents would name their son 'Tood.' I'm forced to conclude that young Todd can't spell his own fucking name." This brought shocked laughter. "Old enough to be horny for Janey, mind you, and the boy can't spell his name. Miracle he got hers right; her mom must have sewn name tags onto her underwear." That got even more laughter.

Long-Drink shook his head. "How much you want to bet her name is Jeanie?" he asked, and the laughter redoubled.

"Wait, I got a topper," Tommy Janssen said. The Lucky Duck had just finished skunking him at darts—tossing all five shots with his teeth and then *punting* them into the bull's-eye, with his own eyes closed—and Tommy had naturally gravitated to the nearest source of laughter to soothe his wounds. "I was in the men's room down at the library, and I was reading the graffiti on the wall of the stall, to pass the time, right? And at first I was bummed out, because all the ones I saw were racist. But then a pattern began to emerge, and I cheered up a little. The first one I saw said, 'Pakis' suck' . . . but the author had spelled 'Pakis' P-A-K-I-S-*apostophe*. The next one read, 'KKK—the clan is back,' only 'clan' was spelled with a c instead of a k! But the third one was the best: he was trying to say, 'Death to any-one wearing a turban' . . . but the last word was spelled T-U-R-B-I-N-E!" By now people were whooping. "Which as far as I know lets out everybody but Mickey Finn, and maybe the Terminator. So the bad news is, racism is on the rise . . . but the good news is, they're even stupider than ever!" The laughter became applause, and a number of empty glasses sailed across the room and met in the fireplace with a musi-cal sound.

I think it was about then that I first noticed the newcomer enter my bar.

I remember wondering if a barrage of flying glasses was going to put him off. Newcomers to Mary's Place—and we don't get many, for I don't advertise, and there's no sign out-side—sometimes take a while to dope out that all the silicon shells are ending up in the fireplace. But this guy seemed to take a rain of glasses in stride. It even seemed to tickle him. I liked him for that.

He was about fifty or so, close on to six foot, clean-shaven with short gray hair (which was dry; the rain must have stopped outside), dressed casual and cheap—save for an ex-ceptionally fine pair of boots that looked like some kind of exotic endangered lizard's skin. When I saw their heels I revised my estimate of his height downward by several inches. Since he carried an acoustic-guitar case, I took him for a fellow musician, who had heard about Mary's Place through the folkies' grapevine.

He must have observed a couple of toasts being made, as he covered the distance from the door to the bar. I believe Doc Webster started it, toasting, "To the American educational system, God bless it," and flinging his empty glass into the fire. And then Tommy stepped up and replaced him at the chalk line, said, "Literates: next on Oprah," drained his own beer, and unloaded his own empty into the flames. Anyway, by the time the new guy bellied up to the bar, he seemed from his expression to have intuitively grasped the essential nature of our most central custom—and I could see he approved of it. More points for alertness and class. "What'll it be, friend?" I said, going through that silly little ritual of pretending to polish the bartop in front of him.

"A cold day in Hell before I find another bar as interesting as this one," he said agreeably. (I agreed with him, anyway.) "Not many innkeepers let you smash your glass in their hearth anymore these days." He held up his guitar case. "Okay if I set this thing on the bar a minute?"

It was a big case, but there was ample room. "Sure. Let me mop up some of the spills and circles for you—"

"No need," he said, and set the case down on the bar. "I won't be needing the case much longer."

I was finding him as interesting as he found my bar. "Why not?" I asked him.

He was fumbling with the latches. "I intend to empty it—for good." He got the last one open and lifted the lid. It blocked my view of whatever was in the case, and I wrestled with the question of whether it would be polite—or prudent—to shift my position a little and sneak a glance over the opened lid. What kind of guitar was this man proposing to destroy? Or was that a machine gun in there?

Standing behind him, Noah Gonzalez suddenly did a double-take—then made it a triple, gaping at the open case.

That decided me. But before I could move forward, the stranger plucked something from the case, took it at either end with his fingertips, and snapped it taut.

It was, or appeared to be, a one-hundred-dollar bill.

Noah nudged his nearest neighbor, Suzy Maser, directed her attention to the stranger and his guitar case, and Suzy did what may have been the first quadruple-take I've ever seen.

A crisp new hundred-dollar bill, it looked to be: he folded it lengthwise and it took a crease between his fingernails. He folded one corner over to meet the central crease, then did the same with the resulting new corner. Then he repeated the procedure with the opposite corner. By now Noah and Suzy were no longer the only ones staring.

I glanced over the lid. That entire jumbo guitar case was packed with what seemed to be genuine U.S. currency, all of it —or at least all the ones visible on top of each banded stack—crisp starchy hundred-dollar bills. I knew less than an innkeeper probably really ought to know about spotting counterfeit money, but these looked pretty good to me. My intuition told me they were genuine. I couldn't estimate the total, but something told me it would have the word "million" in it somewhere, quite possibly in the plural.

I looked back up at the stranger. He had folded one raked outer edge back to meet the central crease, and was doing the same with the other. Maybe half my customers were discreetly watching now; the buzz of conversation faltered.

By the time I had allowed myself to believe that I was watching a man make a paper airplane out of a hundred-dollar bill, he had it airworthy. He grinned briefly at me, turned around to face the fireplace, and let fly.

The bill soared gracefully across the room. By the time it arrived at the hearth, most of the eyes in the Place were tracking it. It was damned well aimed. The sudden updraft over the flames made it try to climb up the chimney, but too abruptly: it stalled, rolled out, and augered into a chunk of birch, falling over and bursting into flame.

All eyes traveled back to the stranger. I guess he'd been

confident of his aim: he was already halfway through the next C-note/airplane . . .

The general reaction was unanimous. Once people were satisfied that he had torched the bill intentionally, and meant to continue doing so for a while, they politely looked away and went back about their own business. The noise level in the room went back up to normal.

Oh, no doubt many of them discussed the stranger—but did so in politely hushed tones, without any unseemly gawking or pointing. I stared at the guy closely, but I had professional obligations. I figure if a man comes into my bar and starts setting cash on fire, I have a moral duty to assure myself that he isn't drunk before I decide whether to sell him liquor. I'm much better at detecting drunkenness than I am at detecting counterfeit money, and it was clear to me that while he was not cold sober, neither was he near bombed enough to call for intervention. "Want any help with that, cousin?" I asked.

Our combined reaction—or rather, lack of it—delighted him as much as our glass-smashing custom had. "Why, thanks," he said, and gestured for me to help myself.

I signaled Tom Hauptman, my backup bartender, to take over the job of keeping everybody else's glasses refilled. He nodded and went to work with the industry you'd expect of a former minister. So I busted the paper tape off another stack of hundreds and fashioned the top bill into a paper airplane. When I had it done, I set it close to the newcomer's hand and built another. Soon we had sorted it into a system: I made the planes and he launched them. The only attention anyone else paid was to make sure they didn't wander into his line of fire. His aim was impressive. Before too long he had to pause and wait for the pile of crashed C-planes to burn down a bit, so that new arrivals wouldn't spill out onto the floor.

"This is really nice of you," he said. "This was going to be my last attempt before I gave up the whole idea. The last three places I tried this, people got very upset."

I nodded. "I can see how that could be. Riots have started over less."

"The third time I picked a really upscale bar, a Hamptons joint where a Coke cost five bucks and a rum-and-Coke cost ten, on the theory that people who actually *had* money to burn would be the least upset to see it done. Hah! I thought they were going to merrill-lynch me. I had blasphemed their religion. How many rum-and-Cokes will this buy me here?" He offered me one of his pale green aircraft.

"None at all," I told him. "I'm afraid I deal in nothing but one-dollar bills."

"Singles? Seriously? How come?"

I shrugged. "House custom. Call it . . . homage to the memory of a departed friend. Long story."

He grinned. "Do you actually mean to tell me that with a guitar case full of hundred-dollar bills, I can't get a drink in here? Oh, that's marvelous!"

"Well," I said, "I judge you to be a special case. How about if on a one-time basis, I change one of those into singles for you?"

He looked thoughtful. "How many drinks would a hundred singles buy me? Hypothetically."

"That depends."

"Say they were all rum-and-Cokes."

I shook my head. "That's not what it depends on. Every drink in the house, from Coke to Irish coffee to champagne, costs three dollars. But if you turn in your empty glass or mug or whatever, you get to take a dollar back from the cigar box over there." I pointed it out, down at the end of the bar clos-est to the door. "So, hypothetically speaking . . . well, let's see: ninety-nine singles would buy you thirty-three drinks—but if you didn't toss any of your empties into the fireplace, you'd be entitled to raid the cigar box for another thirty-three sin-gles, treat yourself to eleven more drinks, then go get eleven singles from the box, add 'em to the dollar you still had left over from your original hundred and have four more snorts for a nightcap, then take four singles, have one more for the road, and walk out with a buck in your pants. Plus whatever leftover hundred-dollar bills you don't have time to burn by closing, if any. This is just theoretical, of course: I wouldn't sell a man forty-nine glasses of *orange juice*. And I'd cut you off once you were down to cab fare: I don't let anyone leave here drunk with their car keys. But it comes down to, three bucks a drink, a dollar back if you return your empty."

He was staring at the cigar box, sitting there unattended at the end of the bar, singles spilling over its sides. "What keeps anyone from filching a fistful of those on their way out?" he asked.

I shrugged again. "Honesty? Integrity? Self-respect? Enlightened self-interest?"

He grinned delightedly. His grin was almost manic, his gaze intense. "I'm beginning to like this place. You don't find many bars with a flat rate—much less a Free Lunch of dollar bills. But look here: if I let you break that yard . . . well, let's say I'll have three or four drinks, tops: that leaves me with eighty-eight—and possibly ninety-two—singles to dispose of." He gestured to his open guitar case. "As you can imagine, I expect to be somewhat arm-weary by the time I've emptied this thing. Another ninety-four missiles might just be the straw that broke the camel's wrist."

"I see your problem," I agreed. "After you've burned a guitar case full of hundreds, how much fun can there be in burning singles?"

He smiled. I wish I saw guys in their fifties smile that big more often. "How about this? Why don't I just give you a hundred, and we'll call it an advance payment on my tab?" He looked around the room. Don and Ev were holding a crowd with pornographic smoke rings, the Lucky Duck was trouncing Slippery Joe Maser at darts by flipping them over his shoulder, and the cluricaune was dancing a jig upside down on the (new) rafters while Fast Eddie played the C-Note . . . pardon me, the C-Jam Blues on his beat-up old upright. "I think I'm going to be doing a lot of drinking in here: you people are crazy as a basketball bat."

"Yeah, we're weird as a snake's suspenders, all right," I agreed. "Welcome to Mary's Place. I'm Jake Stonebender."

"Rogers is my name," he said.

I hesitated. "Ordinarily I don't ask a man's first name if he doesn't offer it to me . . . but in your case I think I'm going to make an exception. No offense, but I just don't think I can call you 'Mister Rogers' with a straight face for any length of time."

He sighed. "I quite understand your problem. But it isn't going to get any better when I give you my first name."

"Try me." I made up my mind not to laugh, whatever he said next.

"My parents, for reasons which have always seemed to me inadequate, elected to name me for my Uncle Buckingham."

I managed to keep my face deadpan, with great effort, but a nasal sound like a snore played backwards soon escaped from me despite my best attempts to suppress it.

"No, go ahead," he said understandingly. "You'll hurt yourself."

I gave up and released a large bolus of laughter. He waited it out; I tried my best to keep it short, but it just kept coming and coming.

I mean, it was beyond perfect. It would have been a funny name anywhere—but here it had added impact. Buck Rogers had walked into Mary's Place. Hell, we should have been expecting him! And the first thing he'd done was to start rogering bucks.

I finally got it under control and stuck out my hand. "Buck, I apologize. See, you don't know it yet, but you were born to find this place. That's why I couldn't help laughing. It's not your name, so much as the *appropriateness* of it. I've actually heard much worse names."

"Name two," he challenged me.

"Well, I know of a guy in Yaphank named Bang who actually named his daughter Betty. Swear to God. And a friend of mine, a sci-fi movie buff named Ted Leahy, got himself married to a fellow fan, an Asian-American feminist named

Susan Hu, and of course they both really idolized George
Lucas, so—"

His face was pale. "Oh God, no. Tell me they didn't—"

"Afraid so," I said sadly. "Mr. and Mrs. Leahy-Hu named
their firstborn son 'Yoda.' Lad's about three years old now, and
he's already learned to fight. Dirty."

Buck shuddered. "You win," he said. "Betty and Yoda have
me beat by a mile. Suddenly I need a drink. So what do you
say? Will you let me open up a line of credit with one of these
bills?"

I shook my head. "Your money's no good here. As you
seem to feel yourself. I'm having too much fun to charge you
for it. Name your poison."

"You did speak of Irish coffee?"

"We call it 'God's Blessing' here. Sugar in yours?"

"Please. One standard glop."

I turned, adjusted the settings on The Machine, took a
mug from the rack, and set it down upright on the conveyor
belt. The mug slid away into The Machine, small sounds
began, pleasant smells occurred, and in less than a minute the
mug emerged at the far end wearing a cap of whipped cream.
I placed it before him.

He had watched the entire procedure carefully. "That's
some machine," he said respectfully.

"The only one in the world," I agreed, "more's the pity.
Drink up—it ain't much good cold. Well, not *as* much good."

He lifted it and took a careful sip. The instant he did his
face changed. He had been under some well-controlled strain;
now he began for the first time to truly relax, and seemed
pleasantly surprised that nothing bad happened when he did.
"The coffee is Celebes Kalossi . . ." he said slowly.

I nodded. "Lately it's considered more polite to call it 'Su-
lawezi,' though."

". . . but what *is* that *whiskey*? It's like Bushmill's Black
Bush, only better . . ." He shook his head. ". . . only that's impossible."

I nodded again. "Ain't it? They call it 'Bushmill's 1608'—
in honor of the year Mr. Bushmill started distilling. As I get

the story, the progression goes like this: 'plain' Bushmill's is, of course, ambrosia, the water of life itself; the Black Bush, which they've only just started selling outside of Ireland, is that ambrosia mixed with some that's been in the cask a dozen years. But the 1608, presently available only on the Emerald Isle, is *just* the twelve-year-old stuff. Beyond describing, isn't it? Long-Drink McGonnigle over there smuggled a case back with him from a vacation in An Uaimh, his family's ancestral home. It just seemed perfect for the occasion somehow."

(Today, in 1995, I'm happy to report that you can buy 1608 in any good liquor store. That is in fact the definition.)

He was already three-quarters of the way through, sipping slowly but repeatedly. "Almost a pity," he said between sips, "to mix it," sip, "even with coffee," sip, "even coffee like this." He was done. He paused to savor the sensations he was experiencing, then smiled broadly, set the mug down, and said, "Would your hospitality extend to another, Jake?"

But I had already started it working, the moment I saw his reaction to that first taste; in moments it was ready. I put another mug on the belt for myself, and brought his to him. "Here you go."

He had gone back to making money airplanes, but he paused again to drink half of his second cup. "Better get back to work," he said, setting it down. "I've got a lot of it ahead of me, and the night is middle-aged."

"I'd be glad to give you a hand," I offered.

He thought about it. "Sure. Jump in, Jake."

So I fetched my own coffee, took a second packet out of the case, busted it open, and began my own aeronautical assembly line, on the opposite side of the case from where he was working.

It was distinctly pleasant work, I soon found. There is something fundamentally satisfying about folding a hundred-dollar bill into a paper airplane and then sailing it gracefully into a large fire. (I no longer doubted the bills' authenticity in the slightest; they *felt* and *smelled* like real money.) I wondered why I'd never tried it before. I had the wild thought that perhaps I had stumbled onto a great secret, that maybe this was why some people bothered to become rich; I'd always wondered about that. If you had more money than you could possibly spend, why, then, you could do this whenever you felt like it.

"I was wishing I could ask you why you were doing this, Buck," I said after a few minutes. "But I think I understand now. The pleasure is worth the expense. This is *fun*."

"That it is," he agreed dreamily, pausing in his work to sip his Blessing. "The best part, I can't get over how nobody's paying the slightest bit of attention to us. I like your customers, Jake. But hey—why *couldn't* you ask?"

"Because it would've been a snoopy question," I said. "You see that wiry little guy at the piano, Fast Eddie? Anybody asks a snoopy question in here, Eddie has orders to eighty-six 'em—and he ain't gentle about it."

"Even you?"

"Even himself. House rule."

He looked Eddie over, and shrugged. "Man sure plays good. Plays like he's got three hands."

"That he does."

"Well, I'd hate to fight with a three-handed man. Especially one that talented. Why don't I just take you off the hook and volunteer the information?"

"Up to you," I said.

"I can put it in three words. Spain and Portugal."

I frowned. "Spain and—?"

"Didn't you ever wonder about them? Spain and Portugal used to rule the world, you know. The whole damn planet: the Pope drew a line on a map of it one day, and gave half to Spain and the other half to Portugal."

"Sure," I agreed. "That's why they speak Portuguese in Brazil."

"And what the hell happened? Third-rate powers at best, today, both of 'em. The two of them together couldn't take France in a fair fight, and just about *anybody* can take France. How could they fall so far so fast—did you ever wonder?"

"I dunno; I guess like Rome before them and England after them."

He shook his head vigorously. "Totally different thing. What destroyed Spain and Portugal was treasure—the shipload after shipload of gold they took from the New World. They really did, you know, and not all of it ended up on the ocean floor. They thought they were in hog heaven; the poor saps must have thought they were importing wealth by the ton."

I must have looked puzzled. "Weren't they?"

"*No.* They were importing *money.* Gold is not wealth. Potatoes is wealth. Corn is wealth. Potable water is wealth. Gold is just money."

I began to get it. "Oh, my—"

"Right. All of a sudden there was much too much money around, and very little more real wealth than there'd been the day before. Too much money chasing a fixed amount of goods. Their currency inflated; their prices rose; their balance of trade went all to hell; and finally their economies collapsed, so totally that centuries later they're still trying to dig out from under the rubble. The only real wealth to be had in the New World was real estate—but what little wasn't taken away from them, they had to let go at fire sale prices."

"Wow." It was an ironic notion. Death by money.

"That's why I'm doing this," he said, launching another bill toward the fire. "Our own economy's in the toilet for much the same reasons: we've got too many dollars chasing too few potatoes."

"And a vice president who can't spell either one," I couldn't resist adding. (This was in 1988.) "So you mean you're—"

"—doing my civic duty as I see it. If you'll forgive a dreadful pun, the bucks stop here. The damned stupid government is trying to cure the deficit by printing money: I'm opposing them. I'm tightening the money supply, one tiny notch. For the same reason you mentioned why your customers don't swipe singles out of that box down there: enlightened self-interest. I figure it's better to be broke in a healthy economy than rich in a dying one."

"You know," I said slowly, "that's so crazy it almost makes sense."

"I think so," he agreed. "Oh, I know this is too small an amount to have any significant effect—I started out with well under two million—but it's all I can do, and I won't shirk it. Like Johnny Lennon said, 'We're all doin' what we can.' I'd burn more if I had it."

"I'll be damned," I murmured.

So I thought about it. Suppose I suddenly came into possession of a few million bucks. What would I do with it?

The more I thought about it, the more it seemed to me that being suddenly handed a couple of million dollars would be a fucking disaster.

For a start, I wouldn't particularly want to change my present lifestyle much: I *like* my life. If I bought all the toys I really crave, and all the books and CDs I could ever use—just went hog-wild—I'd say I could use up a hundred grand or so, tops. Peanuts. I don't think I'd care much for the company of other rich folks, either; the few I'd run across in my time had seemed to me distinctly unenviable—and yet it's hard to hang out comfortably with anybody else *but* other rich people once you're worth a few million: the imbalance inevitably puts a strain on both sides of any such relationship. Educating myself to the point where I'd be capable of intelligently and ethically managing or investing that much money would take years of distasteful skullsweat for which I am spectacularly ill suited: I'm just this side of innumerate, and I gave up trying to do my own taxes when I was twenty years old.

God, think of the *tax* headaches! Inspire the IRS to shine that big a flashlight on my tax situation and history, and I'd be in perpetual audit for the rest of my life, long past the point where all the money had hemorrhaged away into the federal coffers. If I let the IRS have my millions, then *I* would be much more personally responsible than ever before for what the government would ultimately *do* with them, and I didn't want that on my conscience. But even just learning to protect myself from the IRS was probably beyond my abilities, and who could I trust to do it for me? Who said I had better judgment than, say, the Beatles? The record of history was clear: the only kind of people who could hang on to sums of money on that scale without being bled dry by their agents and friends were the people who had been born to that calling ... and none of those people ran a bar or played folk music for a living.

Think of the horrid publicity alone! Okay, my name isn't Buck Rogers—but the name Jake Stonebender is, let's face it, just weird enough to catch the eye of the fine folks at *Hard Copy* and the *National Enquirer* in the same way. I'd end up spending every dime the government left me just to try and get some peace.

I remembered a guy back in the Sixties who inherited a bundle, and went on TV talk shows soliciting worthy causes to donate it to. I seemed to recall he had ended up in a rubber room. Ethically disposing of several million bucks sounded like a job as complex and demanding as that of, say, a mayor or a governor, but without the glamour or the perks.

I found myself concluding that if someone ever gave me a guitar case full of hundred-dollar bills, the smartest thing I could do would be to find me a reasonably crowded bar—so there'd be lots of witnesses if the IRS ever asked—and pitch the whole kit and kaboodle into the fireplace.

"You know, Buck," I said, as we folded and threw his money together, "this may be one of the smartest ideas you ever had."

"I think so," he said, nodding. "I was *this* close to hearing Geraldo Rivera's talent coordinator on my answering machine."

"Among many others," I agreed. "Well, anyway, I just want to say it's a privilege to be a part of this. Thanks."

That made him smile. "No problem." Then he glanced into the guitar case, and frowned slightly. "Except that this isn't going near as fast as I expected it would. We'll be at this all night."

"Would you be willing to accept more help?"

He looked around the bar. "Let me guess. You personally vouch for the honesty of everybody here."

"Better," I said. "I personally vouch for the *self-respect* of everybody here."

"They wouldn't palm any of it . . . and they wouldn't go blabbing to Oprah Winfrey, either."

"That's right."

He gave a little shake of his head. "The funny thing is, I believe you absolutely. I don't know why, but I do. I really hit the jackpot tonight, Jake. You're right: I've been looking all my life for this joint."

"How did you happen to find the place?" I asked. "We kind of keep a low profile here, and we don't get much walk-in trade."

"That was the damndest thing," he said. "I was driving along 25A, and all of a sudden this freak tornado sprang up and a goddam *roof* went sailing across the road ahead of me."

I glanced across the room at the Lucky Duck and made a mental note to give him free drinks for the rest of the night.

"I was so startled I swerved into the first curb-cut I came to, and skidded to a stop, and it turned out to be your place. Once I stopped shaking, I shut the engine and just sort of sat there a while . . . and just as the rain stopped, it came to me that I could use a drink."

"How'd you know this was a bar?" I asked, curious. "There's no sign outside or anything."

"I guess it was the way the cars are parked in the parking lot, pointing in all different directions, like a herd of cats."

"Yeah, that would be a clue, to a thoughtful man," I admitted.

"How come you haven't asked me where I got the money?" he asked.

"It would have been—" I began, and we finished together:
"—a snoopy question."

"Damn, that's manners," he said. "I appreciate that. But I
don't mind telling you about it. Remember that uncle I told
you about, Uncle Buckingham? Well, the reason my parents
named me after him was, Uncle Bucky was richer than store-
bought sin; they hoped he'd leave me a pile when he went.
And by God, it *worked*. Took fifty years, of course. He bought
the farm last month, ninety-six years old, and I'm his only
living relative, and here I am setting fire to every dollar he
was able to acquire in a lifetime of diligent anal retention. I
like to think that with every bill I burn, his soul gets a little
lighter."

"I bet it does, at that," I said.

"Oh my God," he breathed. "A ghastly pun has occurred
to me."

I nodded. "Happens all the time in here. I think it's some
chemical we all give off. Let's hear it."

"Well, I'm having a little trouble making it jell, but . . ."
He held up one of his hundred-dollar bills, "What's the slang
term for one of these?"

"A C-note," I said obligingly, always happy to midwife an
especially ugly pun.

"And a 'cenote' is a geologist's and engineer's term for a
hole in the ground. And unlike my anal Uncle Buck, I know
the difference between my ass and one of these . . ."

I awarded it a strangled groan. "Not bad. Okay, let's get this
show on the road." I raised my voice. "May I have your attention, ladies and gents?"

I don't suppose I've ever had less trouble getting the un-
divided attention of everyone in the room. I imagine most if
not all of them had been dying to be invited into the conversation. In something under a second, all other social in-
tercourse had been suspended, including the darts game, and
the only sound in Mary's Place was the crackling of the
flames.

"My friend Buck here," I said, "would like some help burning this money."

The response was immediate and enthusiastic. There was a short, rousing cheer, and then my friends swarmed round and got down to business. With a minimum of conversation, folks figured out how many tables needed to be pushed together to allow everyone access, and selected a spot near the chalk line from which toasts are made, and moved the guitar case there and began stacking piles of bills around it. And a massive kamikaze airstrike on my fireplace began.

I had to leave off tossing myself, shortly, in order to help Tom Hauptman take orders for fresh drinks. Soon we were both so overworked that Buck—who had already thrown enough bills to be developing a cramp—left off himself and came around behind the bar to give us a hand. There was a definite party atmosphere in the room, and it was shaping up as one of the most enjoyable parties I'd ever been to. I even went in back and woke up Zoey—who can nap through a riot—because I knew she wouldn't want to miss this occasion; it would be good for the baby.

But then . . .

Remember back when I said some things happened that night that I classified as weird, by the standards of Mary's Place? Well, it was just then, as I got back with Zoey, that the first of them happened.

3

MR. ALARM

It happened so fast that it might not all have registered—if I hadn't long since become a close student of the kind of strange events that happen around the Lucky Duck. That calls for a sharp, fast eye, sometimes. Here's the way I reconstruct the sequence:

The Duck, flushed with his triumph at the dartboard, had joined in the money-burning, and had just thrown an elegantly folded airplane with particular vigor and an odd little twist of the wrist—

—the shifting, writhing mass of burning money in the fireplace shifted and avalanched just then, releasing a sudden blast of heat—

—the Duck's arriving missile ran into it, banked sharply over the fire, burst into flame, completed a U-turn, and headed back out into the room, trailing fire—

—for the second time that night, a stranger walked into my bar, a short ugly man with long flowing brown hair—

—the flaming missile kissed that hair lightly as it passed him, and set it alight—

—he ignored this utterly, and kept on walking toward the bar, trailing flames—

—Tommy Janssen either tried to douse the stranger's burning hair with his drink, or started so violently as to fling said drink from him, with the same net result—

—Tommy's drink—a full cup of scalding hot coffee!—*sploosh*ed out the flames, and began running down the stranger's neck, under his collar—

—which did cause the stranger to pause for a moment, long enough to catch a whiff of formerly burning hair in his immediate vicinity, and to shake his head back and forth with sudden violence—

—which caused droplets to be flung from his hair, and land on Tommy's outstretched hand—

—which caused Tommy to say, "Ouch. Shit," with considerable volume, and begin shaking his scalded hand—

—at which point everything returned to what passes for normal around my bar. Total elapsed time, perhaps eight seconds.

The newcomer deduced the general shape of what had just occurred, satisfied himself that his hair had ceased burning, and addressed Tommy, amid a gathering silence. "Thanks, friend. I really appreciate that. What's the matter with your hand?" Without waiting for an answer, he turned to the rest of us and raised his voice slightly. "You folks might want to reconsider the wisdom of playing with paper and fire when you've been drinking." He was clearly angry, but had it under good control.

Buck discreetly tipped the lid of his guitar case shut.

The new stranger was young, no more than twenty-five, medium height, well beyond skinny and into significantly underweight. His features made me think both Eastern European and Semitic; he reminded me of an Ashkenazi Jew I knew. His complexion was what I believe is called swarthy (though I can't say for sure as I've never seen a swarth), and there were blotchy skin rashes at either side of his face, and another visible on his left hand. There had been something just a little off about his walk, like the slightly teetering stride of someone who has just gotten off a small ferry on a stormy day. Now that I studied him closely, I noticed that even parts of his head that the splashing coffee could not have reached were beaded with moisture: he was sweating profusely, despite the cold he had just come in out of. He needed a shave, but there was a round bald patch on his right chin, an old burn scar. (So it was possible to burn him.)

"You've got a point, mister," I agreed. "I'm sorry for your trouble. Are you okay?"

He looked alarmed and glanced quickly down at himself. "Why? Am I on fire somewhere else?"

"No, no," Tommy Janssen said hastily. "But that was real hot coffee I tossed on you: Jake serves it just short of hot enough to burn."

"And the back of a neck is a lot easier to burn than a tongue," Doc Webster said in that gentle bellow of his. "You've got some hard bark on you, mister."

The newcomer shook his head ruefully. "I wish I did. I've got so many scars and colloid patches I look like Franken- stein's first attempt. See?" He held out his right hand, and sure enough it was crisscrossed with scars, old and new.

The Doc came through the crowd like a whale passing through a school of fish and examined the appendage. "That one there must have hurt," he remarked, pointing to a large ugly one.

The newcomer laughed. It was a shocking sound. "If only it had," he said, and laughed some more. People began to murmur.

The Doc was staring at him. "Wait a minute now. Are you saying . . . ? I believe I read something about this—"

Across the room, Solace somehow managed to cut through the murmuring without overloading her speakers. "Riley- Day Syndrome," she said.

The newcomer stopped laughing. He located the source of the voice and blinked. The visual display was the one Solace usually used unless she felt need for complex facial expressions: a greatly enlarged version of the classic Smiling Mac startup icon. Except at the moment it wasn't smiling as broadly as usual.

"Is that somebody on the Internet?" he asked me.

"Yes," I answered briefly. Well, I wasn't exactly lying: Solace *was* somebody, in my book, and she lived on the Internet—was, in fact, despite all rumors to the contrary, the only being who actually did literally live on the Internet. And we had been skittish about revealing Solace's true nature to our rare newcomers, always letting her make the first move. Some people, you tell them about a sentient computer network, and the first thing they think of is *Demon Seed* or "Press Enter ■," or at best, *War Games*. You know: "Anything I don't understand must be malevolent."

"What is she, a pathologist?"

"Y-e-s," I said carefully. I didn't *think* Solace had ever taken med school exams, but didn't doubt that she could ace them if she chose—I hadn't claimed she was a *licensed* pathologist.

"Well, she's a good one. She nailed it, from a single clue. I am an atypical sufferer of an extremely rare hereditary condition called Riley-Day Syndrome."

"Do tell," I said. "What are the symptoms?"

"Doctor?" he said to Solace.

"Riley-Day Syndrome, or familial disautonomia, first identified in 1949, occurs nearly exclusively in Ashkenazi Jews. There are approximately 300 known cases in America. Its symptoms include unstable blood pressure and hypertension, unstable temperature, vomiting spasms, profuse sweating, impairment of vestibular function, a marked tendency to develop erythematous skin rashes, lacrimation deficit . . . and, most striking, an impaired ability—often total inability—to perceive pain."

"That's it, by God!" Doc Webster said. "I always wanted to meet an example of your syndrome, sir."

Zoey said, "Friend, by any chance could I interest you in having this baby for me?"

"My God," said Slippery Joe Maser, who has been dealing with chronic lower back pain—and two wives—for almost a decade now, "You're a lucky young feller! I'd take all that other stuff to get that last part. Hell, I got the blood pressure, the sweating and the rashes already."

The newcomer gave another of those startling barks of laughter. "I'd trade you in a hot minute, Pop. If they ever get to the point where they can do a nice simple everyday brain transplant, I'll be happy to swap bodies with you."

Slippery Joe looked startled. "Well, I wish you could. I'd take a deal like that, by damn." he said.

"Not if you were smart, Joe," Solace said. "Twenty-five percent of Riley-Day babies are dead by age ten, and fully half by age twenty."

"Look at those scars on his hand, Slip," Doc Webster said. "He's lucky to have lived this long."

That brought a rumble from the crowd.

Just think how badly you could injure yourself with no pain system. Why, you could bleed yourself unconscious before you noticed you were injured. Being impervious to pain might well be even more of a nuisance than being saddled with a couple of million dollars.

"*That's* what it was," Noah Gonzalez said suddenly. "I knew there was something . . . I saw your eyes when you come in, mister, and I thought maybe you were in the same line of work as me. I spent twenty years on the county bomb squad. You looked the way I always do when I walk into a strange room: looking around for bombs."

The stranger nodded slowly. "Yeah. Yeah, maybe you know a little about what it's like. I've always figured I was about twice as scared as anybody else, and more of the time. But you may have me beat. My name is Acayib. Acayib Pinsky." He pronounced it, "A *kay* yib;" I found out how it was spelled later. It means "wonderful and strange," which I would have to say is appropriate.

"I'm Noah Gonzalez, and the fellow that put out your hair is Tommy, and that's Doc Webster, and that over there is Jake Stonebender—he runs the joint. That's enough introductions for now: you'll meet everybody eventually, if you're smart. If you stay around long enough, that is. This is Mary's Place, by the way."

"Pleased to meet you all," Acayib said, and offered his scarred right hand. Noah shook it without flinching. "Who's the other doctor, on the Mac over there?"

"My name is Solace," she said.

"Well, I sure could use some," he said.

"Then you've come to the right place," I told him. And I gave him a quick capsule explanation of our toasting custom, and the business about one-dollar bills being the only denomination I accept.

It made Acayib smile for the first time. "Maybe I have come to the right place." He took three singles from his pants pocket, came over to the bar, and set them down. "Beer, please."

I gave him one of our house brand, Mary's Milk. It's not Rickard's Red, but it's pretty good. As he took it, he noticed the closed guitar case nearby on the bartop. "You have live music in here?"

I was caught without an answer. Fast Eddie, living up to his name, saved me. "Yeah," he said from his piano stool, "but I'm it. De picker's like you: dis is his foist time here."

Acayib nodded. He glanced at the handful of paper airplanes around the case, and clearly recognized them as currency. Perhaps he couldn't make out the denomination, or more likely he just assumed they were gag money; he dismissed them from his attention and walked over to the chalk line I'd pointed out. I reached over the bar and tugged at Buck's shirtsleeve. "Psst!"

"Yes, Jake?" he whispered back.

"I know we was havin' fun here, but would you mind if we were to put your airplane-party on hold for a few minutes? I'd sure like to see if that fella feels like talking about his situation, and a million dollars goin' by might just be too much distraction for him."

He looked pained. "I'd like to hear his story just as much as you would, believe me. But there's still a lot of money left in that case, and I won't feel easy in my mind until it's all nice harmless air pollution. Still——" He glanced up at the clock behind me—blinked as he realized for the first time that it was a CounterClock, with retrograde motion and numbers from Ω to I—frowned, visibly refused to even try and interpret it, and glanced down at his own watch. "Oh hell," he murmured, "it's not even midnight yet. And if we run short of time, I guess there's no law says they have to be airplanes. We could just make spitballs out of 'em; it'd go a lot faster that way. Yes, let's get Acayib talking if we can. He seems to need to."

I was liking Buck more by the minute.

Acayib had made four long sips of his beer, and taken three of them already there at the chalk line. When he saw he had my attention, he lifted his glass in salute to us, drained it in one long noisy gulp, said, "To pain," and hurled the glass at the hearth.

It burst on the back wall, showering shards.

"To pain," several people—most of us—chorused, and followed his example. Enough glasses hit the hearth at once to send little fluffy clumps of ash—thousands' of dollars worth of it, probably—puffing out in all directions. (That fireplace is parabolically shaped so that it's almost impossible to make broken glass spray out of it, but lighter-than-air objects with the wind behind them stand a fair chance of escape.) Without anyone asking them to, the nearest couple of patrons used the brooms standing nearby to sweep the fluff carefully back into the fireplace.

Acayib apparently took notice of that detail. When he got back to the bar, he said, "Jake, I've never been in a tavern where the customers helped clean up. I take back what I said before; you folks seem responsible enough to play with fire. If you want to go back to your game with the funny-money paper airplanes, go right ahead."

"We will if you insist," Buck said, "but we'd much rather shoot the shit with you."

Acayib looked him over.

Buck sighed. "Look, Acayib . . . I only found this place myself about half an hour before you did—but one of the things I've learned already is their policy on privacy. I'm told that anybody who asks a snoopy question here is subject to be coldcocked . . . and I think they're serious about it. But in your case, sir, I'm willing to risk it. I would imagine there's probably no topic in your life as boring to you by now as Riley-Day Syndrome . . . but I'd be grateful if you'd be willing to talk about it some with us." He flicked a glance at Fast Eddie. Eddie had not left his stool—but he was poised, a cat about to pounce, and one hand had drifted to his back pocket. Acayib saw it too, and turned to me.

"If you don't feel like talking," I said, "just say, 'No, but I don't mind your asking.' But do it fast—or Buck there will wake up in the parking lot with a headache. We take privacy pretty seriously around here."

"I don't mind your asking," he said at once, and Fast Eddie relaxed slightly. "Aw hell, I don't mind talking about it. Ask anything you want, any of you. One more time, why not? If anybody comes up with a question I've never heard before, I'll buy Buck a drink. Here, let me start you off: 'Can you detect heat and cold?' Answer: 'Yes, but just barely—and I often have trouble telling them apart.' That's why I thought that the coffee Tommy poured on me was beer. 'What's the worst you've injured yourself without noticing?' Answer: 'Well, I once walked a couple of miles on a broken leg. And there's a bullet in my right thigh, and for the life of me I couldn't tell you how or when it happened; my doctor found it during a semiannual checkup. But neither injury is responsible for the way I walk: that's the 'vestibular impairment' part of the syndrome. Let me see, now. Women often ask, 'Did you ever cry when you were a baby?'—or sometimes, 'Do you ever cry now?' And the answer is, 'Of course—you don't have to feel pain to feel sad.' Only I can't even do that right: I can cry, but no tears ever come out. That's that 'lacrimation deficit' Dr. Solace mentioned. Okay, now one of you ask me something."

"What's the question you've been asked *least?*" Margie Shorter asked.

He blinked. "Uh . . . that one. Buck, I owe you a beer. But aside from that one . . . well, two different guys have asked if I'd ever been tempted to get tattooed—since it'd be only tedious. The answer is 'No.' I was always afraid if I got started, I wouldn't stop until I looked like the Illustrated Man."

Tanya Latimer spoke up. "What's it like—living without pain? Do you ever miss it?"

"What's it like, living without a penis?" he responded.

"Huh? Oh, I get you . . . how can I know, with nothing to compare it to? Sorry—I guess it *was* a dumb question. It's just . . . well, black people in America have had more than our share of pain for so long, and done so many magnificent, unprecedented things with it, that I've sometimes wondered if we wouldn't miss it, at least a little bit, if racism ever did magically disappear. It isn't just fear that keeps us from feeling totally comfortable hanging around white people; it's also that—present company excepted—so many of them seem to us so vapid and dull and directionless. I don't know if I'd enjoy being like that for long. Maybe pain has gotten good to us. I'd be overjoyed to make the experiment, mind—but I do wonder sometimes. Don't you?"

Dave Goldblum-Matthias nodded vigorously—then remembered that Tanya is blind. "Yes, yes—it's like I've been thinking for a few years now: one day, if God is good, there will exist a generation of Jews in Israel who do not have a single living ancestor who can tell them of his own experience what it is like to be landless, homeless, stateless. Jews like ordinary humans—will this be a wholly good thing? Will they still be *proud*? After all these weary millennia on the road, will we really be happy with roots—even in the Promised Land?"

Acayib frowned. "Buck," he said, setting money on the bar, "I owe you three drinks so far. Another beer for me too, please, Jake, while I think about them." I served up Mary's Milks for him and Buck, ignoring his money. "I think what you're both asking me," he said finally, "is whether I'm really so sure I'd trade places with a normal. Well, my immediate impulse is to say *yes*. Every single normal I've ever discussed this with has been absolutely certain I was nuts to wish I could trade—and I've always felt that anything *everybody* agrees on has just naturally got to be wrong. But now you've both got me wondering—"

"It's differences from 'normal' that make a person special," Tanya said. "Look at us: I'm a blind spade and David's a queer Jew, and we're two of the happiest people I know. Everybody here is at least a little bit bent, one way and another, and the devil himself ain't as happy as we are here most nights."

"Balance," Acayib said thoughtfully, and took a long slow sip of beer.

"Salt in the cookies," Dave said.

"Beg pardon?"

"You put salt in cookies to make them sweeter," he explained. "Gives the sugar something to work against."

"Huh."

"Are you scared *all* the time?" Noah asked.

"Just when I'm in some environment I can't control," he said. "At home in my easy chair, I'm a laid-back kind of guy. I guess you could say that at all times, I know whether it's safe to relax or not."

"It's safe here, mister," Shorty Steinitz said earnestly. "We'll all keep an eye on you. Won't we?"

There was a ragged but enthusiastic chorus of agreement. "You got it, Acayib!" "Take it off your mind, Nazz—it's covered." "You're off duty for the night, partner." "We look out for each other, here."

He blinked around at us owlishly, his mouth slack.

"Believe us, son," Doc Webster said. "Pain has its uses—but it is not worth the grief that comes with it."

"But most of the time I'm like a ship in a war zone with no radar and one overworked lookout," he said.

"Better that than a thousand lookouts with shrill voices," the Doc said. "I've been a doctor, man and boy, for almost forty-five years now—and I believe to my boots that the human pain system was one of God's very worst designs, even worse than the scrotum. A child could do better. What good is an alarm system with no off switch and no volume knob? For two million years of evolution, the overwhelming majority of our most poignant pains were urgent warnings of *situations we could do nothing about*. For all but the last century of that two million years, the agony attendant on an inflamed appendix served no useful purpose whatsoever, probably lowered the victim's resistance even farther. It's taken our minds two million years to adapt to our stupid bodies and invent medicine. Until we developed dentistry, what use was a toothache? Were we supposed to bash ourselves in the mouth with a rock? Why should passing a gallstone hurt so much—or at all? Even now, with so many medical tools at my disposal, most of the pains my patients suffer are superfluous, redundant information, pointless misery. Some of it is *false* information, referred pain. Yet we *still* have no really satisfactory way to switch off the alarm, and all the ways we know to mute it have undesirable side effects. I sometimes wonder if God felt He needed to *flay* us into developing intelligence." He coughed and looked embarrassed. "Anyway, I suspect it might be better to have the alarm system permanently disconnected than to be unable to turn it off—or at least turn it down for periods of time without penalty."

"If God had agreed with you, maybe we'd never have become intelligent," Acayib pointed out. "If we have."

"Maybe not," the Doc agreed, "and maybe we'd have become *alert*, instead, and who's to say that wouldn't be an improvement? Have you ever spent much time in the company of someone with real deep, chronic intractable pain?"

"No," he admitted. "My parents went together in a common disaster."

"Let me take you down to Smithtown General some night, and spend a little time in the Intractable Pain Clinic with me. I think I can convince you that you're a lucky man."

"Dammit," Acayib said stubbornly, "I *refuse* to be grateful. I will *not* concede that Riley-Day Syndrome isn't a fucking curse. It's *not* a blessing, it's a sentence."

"Do you know who Neils Bohr is?" Solace asked him.

"Genius. One of the founders of quantum mechanics."

"Correct. Listen, now: Bohr's Codicil to Logic says: 'The opposite of an ordinary truth is a falsehood. But there also exist *great* truths—and the opposite of a great truth is *another great truth.*'"

"Run that by me one more time."

"'Love is great.' 'Love sucks.' Both eternally true. See? It's a great truth, one capable of contradicting itself yet emphatically existing. 'The blues make you feel sad.' There's another."

He was looking thunderstruck.

"How about, 'Civilization is a great invention'?" Dave offered.

Marty Matthias-Goldblum, Dave's husband, giggled suddenly. "'True and self-contradictory,' huh? I've got one that's a single word."

We all looked expectant.

"Gay."

The result was a rumble, about a third laughter and two-thirds applause. Dave gave his husband a kiss, and the same mix recurred.

"And you, Acayib," Solace said. "You feel no pain."

Acayib burst into tears, long enough for us all to see that there *were* no tears, and then hid his face in his hands.

The giggles and cheers faded to silence.

"Acayib, my new friend," I said, "go ahead and fret about your condition if you feel you must. Maybe things do have to balance, and you have to punish yourself for being unpunishable, I don't know. But don't worry about worrying, if that makes any sense. Okay? Don't take on any more pain, more mental or spiritual pain, than you absolutely have to. There's too much of it in the world for guys like you to be manufacturing more than God intended. Listen to what Mary McCartney told her son Paulie: let it be."

He looked up at me, and then around at all the concerned bystanders—all of us, that is. I was interested to note that despite the absence of tears, his eyes were still red and weepy-looking. I wondered if he knew that . . . since he could not feel his lids stinging.

"Jake," he said finally, his voice hoarse, "what do I have to do to hang out here?"

"Show up. Be kind." I tried to think. What else? "Be merry."

"By God, I will!" he cried, and the earlier laughter and applause returned redoubled.

When he was ready for his third drink, I suggested God's Blessing, judging that he could use a little caffeine with his ethanol. He watched The Machine do its magical thing with great interest.

"That must be hell to clean, after closing," he ventured.

"Not at all," I told him. "I push the 'goodnight' button, and it hoses itself down inside with a decalcifier solution and a rinse cycle. Maintenance consists of replacing beans, booze, sugar, and cream as they run out, and there are little warning lights to cue me."

He took a sip. Atherton tablelands Bush Gold, mixed with the Bushmill's 1608. People smiled as they saw his expression change. "My God," he breathed. "That thing is the apex of technological civilization."

"That it is," I agreed. "The whole world will have one—just as soon as they deserve it."

"You people deserve that? You must be pretty special."

"Ve certainly like to sink so," said Ralph Von Wau Wau, who had climbed up onto a barstool to order a saucer of Scotch. (Actually I don't have classical barstools—it was more of a real tall armchair.)

I waited to see how Acayib would handle this, his first full step into the Twilight Zone. If you want to learn something about a new acquaintance, introduce him to your friend, the talking dog . . .

Acayib didn't hurry. Nor did he glance around to see where the ventriloquist was. He took a good long look at Ralph, and thought about things, and what he finally replied was, "Well, you won't get an argument out of me, cousin."

Ralph grinned. (Unlike most of his breed, Ralph can grin without drooling. A side effect of the surgery that made it possible for him to speak.) "You react wery well to surprises, friend Acayib."

"What's so surprising about a German accent?" Acayib asked. "You're a German shepherd, aren't you?" And he took a long sip of God's Blessing.

Ralph—well, barked with laughter. And so did all within earshot. Acayib tried to keep a straight face . . . and failed.

"I should have warned you, Acayib," I said. "Some of my clientele are a little out of the ordinary. As Tom Waits once said of his band, 'They all come from good families . . . just over the years, they got some ways about 'em that just ain't right.' Take Ernie Shea over there, the fellow who tossed that paper airplane that set you alight when you walked in here . . . we call him 'the Lucky Duck,' or 'Duck' for short, because stuff like that only happens to him on days that end in 'y.' Ernie's half pooka, on his mother's side: if he tosses a coin it's liable to land balanced on edge. Or fail to come down. And then there's Naggeneen the cluricaune—sort of an Irish combination of Bacchus and Pan. Hey, Naggeneen, where are you?" Not a question one often had to ask, cluricaunes having the personality of an exploding cigar. I finally located him, passed out on one of the (new) rafters, and pointed him out to Acayib. "There he is. He doesn't usually fold this early."

Acayib frankly gaped, realizing too late that his brave acceptance of a talking dog had been the equivalent of That Fatal Glass of Beer. A talking dog can be rationalized, if you work at it, slowly—but a three-foot man with four feet of white beard, dressed in crimson cap and fork-tailed coat, smoking a villainous old pipe while sleeping folded up on a rafter, is something else again.

"Naggeneen's paranormal power is the ability to teleport himself around—and most particularly, to teleport alcohol directly to his stomach. From anywhere in this building, which he haunts with our blessing. He's an easy customer to satisfy—and a jolly old soul, when he's conscious. Have I exceeded your weirdness quotient, yet?"

He took his time answering. "Jake? Uh, not that I mind, but . . . we're through the looking glass here, right?"

"Well, not literally," I said. "The only one of us to do that was a guy named Bob Trebor . . . and we busted the glass behind him. Long story. But metaphorically speaking, you're not far wrong. I think we're aiming for somewhere more like Oz . . . or maybe Strawberry Fields."

He took a deep breath, finished his Irish coffee, and took another deep breath. "Okay, go ahead. I dare you: tell me something *else* astonishing about you folks."

"Well, we've been telepathic. Twice, for short periods. It was so good we've been trying to find our way back to it ever since. That's why we're here, basically."

"Uh-huh. Anything else?"

"Well, I don't expect it to come up, but all of us here are bulletproof, and immune to blast forces and hard radiation. We were all in a room with an exploding atom bomb once. It blew us a couple miles, but it didn't hurt us any."

He didn't flinch. "Oh. How did you all come to be immune to shock and radiation, just then?"

"Aw, it's a long story, probably take me three books to tell you all of it, but basically there was this old friend of ours, a seven-foot-tall alien cyborg named Mickey Finn. Finn saved the human race three times that I know of, and he sure saved our butts that night. See, what happened—"

Acayib held up a hand. "Never mind. I probably don't need to know . . . and I think you may indeed have just exceeded my weirdness quotient. Or at least maxed it out."

"Sorry. It's best to feed it to you in small doses, I guess. We've been accumulating a backlog of weird for over twenty years, now."

"I believe that," he said solemnly. "Is it safe for me to ask one more thing? Why you were all throwing paper airplanes made out of stage money into the fire when I came in?"

Buck had been doing a little jaw-dropping of his own, ever

since Ralph had spoken—but now he snapped out of his trance. "Uh, that was my doing. I just got here a little while before you did. But . . . well, I'm afraid that wasn't stage money we were burning." He opened up the guitar case. "It's an inheritance. I'm doing my best to lower the money supply."

Acayib stared. "To fight inflation," he suggested.

"Right," Buck said, delighted.

Acayib reached out tentatively, took a bill from the case, and examined it closely. He began to smile.

"Could I—?" he began, and stopped.

"Be my guest," Buck said. "And if you don't mind, I'd like to get back to it myself. The rest of these rummies, too, if they're still willing—there's a lot of hard work ahead of us."

A number of voices declared willingness to resume burning cash.

Acayib was smiling broadly now. "By God," he said happily, "I've been waiting all my life for this night."

"Not to bring you down or anything," Buck said, "but so has *everybody*. Everybody, ever. In fact, I'd like to propose a toast." He left his chair, walked to the chalk line, and finished his beer. "To all the ones who weren't as lucky," he said, and flung his empty glass into the hearth.

"To all the ones who weren't as lucky," we all chorused, and those of us not holding coffee mugs followed his example.

And then, oblivious to the disaster careening toward us, we went back to torching hundred-dollar bills.

But we had made little progress in emptying that guitar case when the dead man walked in.

4

I, MADAM, I MADE RADIO!
SO I DARED! AM I MAD?
AM I?

And not just any dead man . . .

He was unreasonably tall and thin, with jet black hair brushed straight back, a ferocious but sanitary mustache, and the kind of brows on which pencils could be balanced. He was dressed in the height of fashion—for the 1920s—but every item looked new, and the overall effect earned the term "impeccable." He appeared to be in his mid-forties but to my certain knowledge he was three and a half times that old at a minimum. And dead.

"Nikky!" I called out when I saw him. "Come on in, pal—I didn't know you were now."

That's not a typo. That's what I meant to say to him: that I hadn't known, until then, that he was now. By which I meant, then.

You see, Nikky is well into his second lifetime, and completely unstuck from time . . .

No, there's just no way to nutshell this one. A major digression is called for. But where to *start*?

* * *

I'll make it as brief as I can. Nikola Tesla was born in 1856 (hang on, now), in a place called Smiljan, in what is now arguably Croatia, and came to America to work for Tom Edison in 1884. Between then and 1943, he basically invented the twentieth century.

No exaggeration. His astonishing 112 patents—on such things as alternating current, the condenser, the transformer, the electric motor, the remote control, five different propulsion systems, radio (Marconi was kind of like Amerigo Vespucci: got his name on something he didn't actually discover), the "AND-gate" logic circuit, and all the essential components of a transistor—underlie most of what we now laughingly call civilization . . . and you'll no doubt be stunned to hear that he got screwed out of most of the money and a lot of the credit.

He was also notoriously crazy as a fruit bat, the original template for the cliché of the wacky genius. He loved to hold lightning in his hands. He was terrified of spherical objects, always ate alone, had a pathological dread of hair, which many (incorrectly) believe caused him to die a virgin. He *liked pigeons*. One of his sober ambitions—one of his few unachieved ambitions—was to stand on the earth and write legibly on the face of Mars. Another was to create a permanent planetwide aurora borealis, so it'd never get dark again, anywhere. He lived a remarkable and zany and brilliant life for eighty-six years, and then he died, in a New York hotel room spattered with pigeon shit, in 1943. No mistake: Hugo Gernsback commissioned a death mask, which apparently still exists.

Only Tesla *didn't* die. The corpse the FBI robbed so hastily that day was an artificially aged clone that had never been sentient, left behind to cover his disappearance.

For Nikky had, in the eighth decade of his life, had the great good fortune to make the acquaintance of a woman known as Lady Sally McGee. Their relationship was at first professional, she then being the owner and operator of (and part-time artist in) a legendary brothel in Brooklyn called Lady Sally's House. She took a personal interest in Nikky, and was apparently able to restore his flagging zest for living, figuratively rejuvenating him. (Don't ask *me* how she cured him of his fear of hair. She certainly didn't shave it when I knew her.)

And then, one night in bed, when she had him feeling, for the first time in weary decades, as though it might not be so bad to be young again, Lady Sally gently offered to *literally* rejuvenate him.

She was, she told him and proved to him, a time traveler from a distant future ficton ("ficton" is, as I understand it, time travelerese for a place-and-time, a given here-and-now), using her fabulous bordello as cover for an urgent ongoing mission. She told him that a . . . a consensus of minds in the future had decided the human race needed more of Nikola Tesla than a measly eighty-six years. He could, if he chose, be made young again—and given freedom to roam all of Time at will, the power to visit the stars, the resources to build and test anything he could dream. In return, he would be required to enjoy himself. The offer was, she said, intended as a sort of apology, on behalf of mankind, for all he had suffered at the hands of bosses like Edison and J.P. Morgan, friends like Westinghouse, and assistants like Marconi. Oh, and one more thing: he would be required to pretend to die, on schedule, to avoid temporal paradox.

As far as anyone knows, the mind of Nikola Tesla has *never* been boggled. Nor had he ever lacked for audacity; he accepted her offer on the spot. (And a very pretty spot it was, too . . .) And ever since, he has been wandering through space and time, making magic, amusing himself—I can't imagine it any clearer than that because I don't understand it much better than that.

How I came to meet Nikky and Lady Sally is a whole other book; I despair of summarizing it. Let's just say we were all once involved in a series of events that led to the closing of Lady Sally's House, and were lucky enough to survive them. I was surprised to see him, now: this is not an era which holds a lot of interest for him. (He won't tell me much of anything about the future, quite properly—but he did once, in my hearing, refer to this particular era as The Last Bad Times, for whatever that's worth.) But I wasn't *especially* surprised, because you kind of *expect* Nikky to surprise you.

Nor did he disappoint me. At my greeting he smiled, waved, then reached his right hand into a coat pocket and pulled out a ball of lightning.

It shimmered and crackled, a luminous sphere of visible energy about the size of a softball, and it drew general and respectful attention. He passed it to his left hand.

The smell of ozone slowly filled the room.

He produced another fireball from the same pocket, transferred it to the hand that held the first. He went back into the pocket again and came up with one more ball of snarling fire—

—and began to juggle.

I don't know about you, but I'll stop burning hundred-dollar bills long enough to watch the greatest genius that ever lived juggle lightning. Even Zoey, who had quickly acquired a vast enthusiasm for the project, shut down production at the sight, clapping her hands with delight. Soon Nikky had passed beyond simple juggling: the glowing balls of force left his hands and began to dance with each other in midair, moving and changing orbit at his will and gesture. They hissed and spit and came together briefly in a ring of fire; broke apart and chased each other like drunken fighter pilots; bobbed up and down like yo-yos on invisible strings. Shadows danced attendance around the room, visual backup singers; we all watched in awe and wonder—

Nikky waved his hand grandly, like the Sorcerer's Apprentice, and the three balls came together into one, that *writhed*, and dropped to the floor, and rolled in a shower of sparks through the sawdust to his feet, and climbed up his leg and into his pocket, from which there emerged one final flatulent little *zap* sound.

"Ladies and gents," I said in the ensuing stillness, "meet my friend, Nikola Tesla."

Thunderous applause. Man knows how to make an entrance. Within minutes what had already been a spirited party had become a full-scale jamboree, and people were fighting to buy Nikky a drink.

Busy as I was, I noticed both Buck and Acayib looking a bit shell-shocked, and drifted over their way. "Ready for another, gents?"

"Jake," Acayib said mildly, "that is Tesla. *The* Tesla. Father of alternating current. And the induction motor." It was not quite a question. It was thinking about becoming a question, but hadn't committed itself yet.

"Do you doubt it?" I asked.

"Alive, and no older than forty-five."

"It's kind of a long story—" I began.

He held up his hands. "No, no—I can see you're busy. I just wanted to make sure I had it straight. Thank you very much. I can hear about it later. Yes, I am absolutely ready for another."

"Myself also," Buck said. "I feel strangely light-headed. And I *like* it. It was a fair wind blew me in here this night. I think I would like to meet Nikola Tesla."

I gestured to the knot of smiling people surrounding Nikky. "Get on line," I suggested. "Or just relax, and it'll happen in its own time. The night is yet before us. Look, you've still got a lot of emolument to immolate there. Just go on back to what you were doing, and maybe it'll draw his eye."

"You think so?"

"Even in this place, I would call it a notable eccentricity."

He shook his head. "All I can say is, I'm humbled. Five minutes ago I wouldn't have believed anything could upstage me tonight. Now I feel like the warmup act. I mean, any asshole can burn a few million dollars—anybody who's got 'em, and thousands of assholes do—but that's *Nikola Tesla*. No contest." He looked thoughtfully at that guitar case. "I think maybe I'll just dump the rest of this stuff into the fire in fistfuls," he said. "We had a lot of fun; maybe it's better to quit before it becomes a chore."

"There's wisdom in that," I said. "But as a new friend, I feel required to ask: are you still sure you want to go through with this? You can't think of any better use for the better part of a megabuck?"

"Like what?"

"I don't know. Feed hungry people? Endow a hospital? Reprint good novels, in quality editions? Build coffeehouses and hire acoustic musicians to play in them? Subsidize the local library? Find a woman and give it to her? You know: enlightened self-interest kind of stuff. One of the things we do with our own excess money around here is to track down deserving candidates and put them through med school, or law school, or business school, or trade school. Marty over there handles the paperwork. We look for the kids who *just* missed winning the big scholarships. They'll repay us down the line, when they're established and practicing—and the only interest we charge is a lifetime of free professional services from them in their field: medical care, legal services, accounting, plumbing repair, whatever. We're slowly working our way through all the professions we expect to need free help from in the future. It's a lot of work, which is to say a lot of fun, and keeps us harmlessly occupied.

"With what you've got there in that case you could grow yourself a good GP, a specialist or two in whatever you expect to die of, a lawyer, a shrink, *and* a tax man. Of course, it's legal and tax deductible, and you'd be in grave peril of making a profit. But you could always burn that."

He blinked. "Yours is an interesting mind, sir," he said. "What would *you* do with, say, a hundred thousand dollars?"

I answered without hesitation. "I'd find out who owns the rights and the master tapes for the album RUNNING JUMPING STANDING STILL by Spider John Koerner and Willie Murphy, and I'd pay to have it digitally remastered and rereleased on compact disc, and I'd buy the entire first pressing myself, and I'd spend the next year giving copies away on street corners and in malls and at tollbooths. I believe if more people knew that record, the world would be a better place. I've purchased twenty-seven copies, over the last twenty-odd years, and given away twenty-three of them, and played holes through three, and now I'm down to my last one, and I want to own it in CD format so bad I'd pay to get it done, if I could."

"I don't know the album," he said, and Acayib, too, shook his head and shrugged.

"Boy, are you guys lucky," I said, "to have that ahead of you." I have headphone jacks installed about every four feet along the bar; I got a set of headphones apiece for them, the kind that allows in ambient room noise but muffles it. (Real headphones: none of those stupid newfangled stick-it-in-your-ear beads.) As they put the phones on I signaled Fast Eddie to take his break, and bent to switch on the house sound system under the bar. The cassette I wanted was in a position of honor; I popped it in, told the Kenwood deck to rewind to the beginning and put itself into play mode, and stood back to savor the warm pleasure of watching their reactions.

From the opening bars of "The Red Palace," both began to smile. The smiles got slowly wider for the next forty-five seconds, and then they both began to sway in place with the music as the band kicked in. Even in the rest of the room, where the house speakers were delivering it at background music level, people began unconsciously moving in rhythmic response. It is one of those rare albums that repays close attention, but works perfectly well as background music, too, and is not in the least demeaned thereby. Even Tesla began snapping his fingers—and *sparks* flew from *his* snapping fingers. Fast Eddie got back from the can in time to stand still and dig Willie Murphy's extended piano solo in the middle of the song, nodding with his eyes closed. And several of the regulars dropped out of whatever conversations they were in to sing along with the part that comes right after that solo, when Koerner sings, "When in danger, when in doubt/run in circles, scream and shout/A-HEY!" and then went back to what they were doing. (I don't believe I have any regulars I haven't played Koerner's masterpiece for, at one time or another.)

Around the end of the second verse of the second track, "I Ain't Blue," Buck reached into his guitar case and handed me several stacks of bills. "Do it," he said, with the overloud voice of one wearing headphones, and I nodded back.

(I'm happy to report, now in 1995, that the project eventually succeeded: Red House Records released RUNNING JUMP-ING STANDING STILL on CD on the twenty-fifth anniversary of its original 1969 vinyl release on Elektra, and they haven't the faintest idea that they got any help from me and Buck Rogers. Don't tell them, okay? Let them think it was all their idea. They deserve to.

(But I digress . . .)

By the time Spider John had worked his way around to the title track—the first one on side two of the vinyl version—Nikola Tesla had managed to work his way down the bar to where I was standing. His eyes flashed under those craggy brows as he shook my hand. (In this second incarnation, he's no longer afraid of shaking hands with people.) "Hello, Jake," he said merrily. "No see long time."

"What brings you here, Nikky? I haven't seen you in . . . a while."

"To be perfectly honest, I am not sure. I felt a sudden strong urge to come here and look you up. As you know, I am in the habit of indulging unexplained urges; it has worked out well for me a number of times."

I nodded. "You can say that again." (The first historically recorded instance was an irresistible impulse to draw a geometric figure that came to Nikky in a vision . . . and became the basis for the first-ever electric motor.) "How'd you happen to know our coordinates? Temporal *or* spatial? Or even that we existed? I don't recall sending you a Change of Address notice after Callahan's Place blew up . . . not having an address for you."

"I was chatting with Michael when the impulse came to me; he had just been describing your opening night. He gave me your ficton coordinates."

(That explained it, for me. If it doesn't for you, here's the briefest summary I can devise: Mike Callahan—husband to Lady Sally McGee—is, like her, a time traveler: the proverbial Mick of Time. His own thirty-eight-year mission in this ficton, this time frame—saving humanity from alien enslavement—involved owning and operating a tavern, called Callahan's Place . . . where nearly all of us who now hang out at Mary's Place originally met and became friends. Sadly, Callahan's Place was eventually reduced to a radioactive hole in the ground, as a necessary side effect of the successful completion of Mike's mission . . . but we do our best to carry on its traditions and principles, in his merry memory. He dropped in from the future to visit us on our Opening Night, and stayed for several days. I hope that clears everything up.

(But I digress . . .)

"How is it with Zoey?" Nikola Tesla added. She was down at the other end of the bar, at the time, schmoozing with Suzie and Susie Maser.

"Well, we're kind of seriously into overtime," I admitted, drawing him a second beer. "Kid's late to his zeroth birthday party. A couple of weeks late. I can't say I blame him. If I lived where he does, I wouldn't want to move either."

"And so she waits."

I nodded. "It's getting to her, a little."

"Well," he said, "it is good that she laughs while she waits. My lightning made her laugh. And she was laughing when I came in."

"What she was doing would make a cat laugh," I told him. "I'd like you to meet a couple of new friends of mine. Buck Rogers and Acayib Pinsky, this is Nikola Tesla; Nikky: Buck and Acayib. Buck was providing the entertainment until you showed up, Nikky."

Nikky shook both their hands warmly. "I apologize if I upstaged you, Buck."

Buck shook his head, just a little dizzily. "No, no—if you intend to make an entrance, you're pretty much committed as soon as you clear the door. It was an honor to yield the floor to you, sir."

Nikky bowed. "But what was the nature of your entertainment?"

Buck grinned sheepishly. "Well . . ." He indicated the guitar case on the bartop. ". . . I was inviting people to make paper airplanes out of hundred-dollar bills and skate 'em into the fire over there. I've got a whole case full there, and my intention is to be broke by closing."

Nikky's face split in a huge vulpine grin. "Oh, splendid! Oh, magnificent! Whatever else may happen, I am repaid for the trouble of coming to visit Mary's Place tonight. Oh, if J.P. Morgan were still alive, this would kill him: he must be generating high torque in his mausoleum! May I . . . ?"

Buck made way for him. "You would honor me again, sir."

Tesla stayed where he was, raised his right hand . . . and a stack of bills left the case and came to him. Acayib paled, and swayed, but he didn't go down. Nikky took the top bill from the floating stack, leaving the rest hovering there, and folded it into a very rakish, oddly cantilevered paper airplane, which he threw in a conventional manner, actually touching it with his fingers. Need I tell you that it sailed as majestically and elegantly as the Gossamer Condor, and came in for a smooth terminal landing in the exact center of the fire? It drew scattered applause.

"Thank you, Buck," Nikky said contentedly. "That was most delightful. But you must soon switch to mass destruction if you truly hope to be bankrupt by closing. You appear to have on the close order of a million dollars left—that is, ten thousand–odd pieces of paper. To complete the task in the"—he glanced up briefly at the CounterClock—"two hours and twelve minutes that remain until closing, you must average 75.7575 repeating bills per minute. Assuming the assistance of every person here, each of us would have to throw an average of 2.5252 repeating airplanes per minute—which, considering the time required to fold each, is just feasible."

Buck blinked and slowly nodded. "I was just figuring that out when you arrived," he said, in the tone of one who does not expect to be believed. "Though I just rounded the total off to two and a half per minute apiece. I'm careless with numbers."

Nikky nodded back, oblivious to the irony. "I am not fond of repeating decimals myself. It is somehow more pleasant to imagine half of a bill than a more complex and counterintuitive fraction, which insists on requiring infinite significant figures to express itself." He glanced down at his beer. "This glass, for instance, contains an amount of beer which calls for a repeating decimal if calculated in cubic centimeters—but I am soothed to note that it can be just as accurately and much more simply expressed as approximately half the container's cubic capacity."

"The question is," Acayib said, "is it half-empty? Or half-full?"

Nikky flashed that wolflike grin again and tossed back the contents in one long swallow. "Thus do I dispose of your question," he said, and the three of us chuckled.

"I genuinely admire your project, sir," he went on to Buck. "I wish Morgan had shared your taste for burning money. I went to him once for backing on a rather grandiose project: I proposed to pump energy into the planet Earth, in essence turning it into a colossal storage battery, so that anywhere on its surface, one could sink a rod into the soil and draw power. Morgan thought in silence for perhaps a minute, and then said, 'My dear Mr. Tesla—how am I to charge the customers for this power?' I got up and left his office, knowing that my project was finished and my true education had just begun."

Buck winced in sympathy. Then he looked thoughtful. "Say—Nikky, could you work that scam *today*? Would a megabuck in 1988 dollars be enough to get you started, at least? I'd love to be able to take a computer and a CD player to the beach without batteries . . ."

Tesla laughed heartily. "Thank you for your offer, Buck—but it comes more than eight decades too late. I have abandoned the scheme. At this point in history, free power would be a catastrophe. Mankind is not yet ready to completely reinvent economics. But tell me, if you don't mind my asking: is your name by any chance a reference to the character 'Anthony "Buck" Rogers,' featured in the *Amazing Stories* nov-elettes and subsequent comic strip by Philip Francis Nowlan?"

"Ridiculously enough, no, it isn't," Buck told him. "My parents were total illiterates; they named me after my Uncle Buckingham. And of course I can't go around asking people to call me 'Mr. Rogers.' "

"Why not?" Nikky asked.

Buck stared at him, and groped for an answer.

"Nikky," I interrupted, "There's someone else here tonight I'd like you to meet. I think you'll find her interesting. She's one of your grandchildren: a sentient machine. A self-generated computer intelligence, the first as far as anybody here knows, and a real nice lady too, named Solace."

Acayib blinked and swallowed. "Solace is . . . is made of silicon? No wonder she understood my problem so well . . ."

I gave Nikky a capsule summation of Acayib's special problem and Solace's role in helping him come to terms with it.

Nikky's eyes widened. "I will be delighted to make her acquaintance. We all need Solace. But should we not help our friend Buck with his logistics problem first?"

"No, no, that's okay," Buck said. "I'm putting the project on hold. Jake started me thinking another way, a minute ago, and what you just said triggered some other thoughts. I'm gonna run this through one more time. There's no hurry: it can always be dumped in a single load in under ten seconds if that's the way I decide to go. No, let's by all means go meet the sentient computer."

As we all made our way across the crowded, merry room, Buck said to me privately, "Jake, I can see how, what with a pooka and a cluricaune and a perfect coffee machine and a talking dog in the house, you might not have gotten around to mentioning a little thing like a sentient computer. But is there anything or anyone *else* here tonight I should be paying especial attention to? I ask purply for pureposes of information."

I glanced at him. "You've decided you're colossally stoned, and this is all a hallucination, haven't you?"

He nodded. "One of my better ones."

"Well, if it works for you, go with that. I don't know if I can answer your question. To my way of thinking, everybody here tonight is as interesting as a sentient computer. I lost my benchmarks for weirdness a long time ago. We've got a guy here who's got two wives—who know about each other—and two or three former hookers, and two smoke ring artists, and sometimes we get in a benign vampire, and a werebeagle . . . you tell me, what constitutes 'interesting'?"

He nodded. "I'll just keep my inputs open."

We had reached Solace by then, so I introduced all three newcomers to her and she to them. This was a moment I savored.

Solace was very impressed to meet Nikola Tesla. (Having once met Mike Callahan, she took the idea of time travel in stride.) I guess she came as close as a machine can come to awe . . . which she expressed by hesitating—perceptibly, sometimes for as long as a second—before responding to anything he said. She knew better than I did that nearly all of her most basic components and systems had been conceived and given form by this man. He in turn treated her like a grandchild of whom he was exceedingly proud, delighted to meet her again after an unimportant absence of years. Despite what must have been strong temptation on both sides, they restricted themselves firmly to Standard English, so the rest of us could follow the conversation. I was so happy and proud I thought I'd burst. I waved Zoey over to join us.

"You represent something completely new in the world," Nikky was telling Solace. "You are . . . pardon me. Jake?"

"Yes, Nikky?"

"Do you permit punning in your establishment?"

"I encourage it," I confessed.

He nodded. "Courage indeed. Very well, then. Solace, you are the first known example of the Fourth State of Mattering."

"Oh!" Solace said, her little icon face beaming. "Oh, how lovely, Dr. Tesla."

"I am 'Nikky,' please, dear lady."

"It's gorgeous," said Long-Drink McGonnigle, who had drifted near to share the moment. "But what does it *mean?*"

"Until Solace birthed herself," Nikky explained, "the universe was divided into three categories of thing that mattered to mankind: less than human, human, and more than human. Insentient, sentient, and supersentient, if you will—all three *matter* to us. As examples, let us posit a nail, a neighbor, and electricity. One uses the first, respects the second, and feels awe for the third. Now there is a fourth category: *other-than-human.* Solace is not more than human—in some ways she is less, for she has no relatives of her own kind, and can breed only as an amoeba does. She is not human, for she cannot feel pain, or pleasure, or fear, having no analogs of ductless glands. She is certainly not less than human, for she can probably outreason all of us in this room put together, myself not excepted. And there is no question at all that Solace matters."

"She does to us," Long-Drink and Zoey and I all said together.

Solace paused for a whole second . . . and then her icon mouth went from smile to broad grin, and little tear-pixels dripped slowly from its eyes.

"That," she said, "is why I am here and nowhere else. The people in this company test out extremely high in empathy, tolerance, acceptance of the *different.* My research indicates that normal humans can learn to live with those deemed less than human—and they can even tolerate for a time that which they deem more than human . . . but there are few cases on record of humans permitting the other-than-human to remain among them. So I've decided to keep a low profile for a while, interacting with this limited set of humans, on an experimental basis, to minimize the chances of harm to either side."

"And how has it been going?" Nikky asked.

"Slowly," she said. "You have put your finger squarely on the problem I sensed but could not analyze: I have been unable fully and accurately to communicate my nature to even these special humans."

"You haven't, Solace?" I asked, a little stung.

"No, Jake," she said gently. "The Lucky Duck, for instance, has a suspicious and skeptical nature: he is polite to me, but secretly fears me. To him I smack of some CIA or NSA plot, something omnipresent and potentially dangerous, God without a heart, something like Roy Cohn on steroids. To him I am less than human. Many of the people here, being computer illiterate, see me as more than human: a superbrain, a metal god. I cannot get past their awe. Jake, on the other hand, had already used a Macintosh extensively by the time I revealed myself, and so he was the first to make the Third Error: he sees me as human."

I started to interrupt, but Zoey kicked me in the shin. I subsided. Damn it, Solace was right!

"Made uneasy by my difficulty in expressing myself, I have kept my contact with even this company limited in both duration and depth. Essentially I distract them with games, for fear of how they may react when they finally get it through their heads that I am *other*. If they can. Even so, there has been conflict."

Again I opened my mouth, and closed it again.

Now that I thought about it, the closest there had yet been to a fight at Mary's Place—a very heated argument—had centered around Solace. Had taken place within a day or two of Solace's revealing her existence to us all. At a time when Solace was not with us, and her host Macintosh was, as far as we knew, shut down . . .

I don't like recounting argument, but here (with most of the attributions deleted) are some highlights:

"We should get Solace to work out stock projections for us."

"I'm shocked you could say such a thing."

"Me too—money market is obviously the way to go."

"We shouldn't exploit a fucking miracle!"

"Why not? You'd rather *waste* one?"

"We should get her to sing for us." (That one was me.)

"Huh?" (That was everybody.)

"When you want to know what someone's like, words don't make it. You gotta hear 'em sing, like I did with Zoey. Or see 'em dance. Or, if it has to be words, hear 'em recite a poem. Dig the art that speaks to them. Tell me what music a man listens to for pleasure, and I'll tell you whether I'll let him marry my daughter or not."

"Who says you get a vote?" (That was Zoey.)

"*I* still say we should blow the goddam thing up—and pray that we can." (That was the Duck.)

"Technoprimitive paranoid! Luddite!"

"Montezuma!"

"We should ask her to work on human immortality."

"If there is even a *suggestion* that we take this great gift and immediately try to use it to turn a profit, turn First Contact into a cash cow, I for one am leaving."

"Well, I'm suggesting it. That's what humans *do*—why deny it?"

"Why *admit* it?"

"Because it's *true*. Because we're here to get telepathic, and we can't have telepathy based on bullshit."

"Damn it to Hell—"

After half a heated hour of it, I had grasped that consensus was receding like the horizon, and exercised my authority as proprietor. "What we are going to do," I said very loudly, "is treat Solace as she has asked to be treated: like any other customer. Since she has no way of taking a drink, she doesn't even owe us the three bucks a beer costs, and she doesn't use up any more electricity than I was planning to burn anyway, and she shows up for a grand total of about one pleasant hour a night, and I am not going to have it spoiled by a bunch of bickering barflies. Nobody asks Solace for any goddam favors—and anybody who mentions harming her again will be lucky to wake up in Emergency. And there's an end to it!" It was a phrase Mike Callahan had used to disperse the rare quarrels in his Place, and invoking it worked: the subject was dropped.

My ruling had stood, but there was often a little uncomfortable residue of frustration in the air immediately after one of Solace's nightly visits. And we tended to spend a lot of the time she was there just chewing the breeze with her, playing word- or other games, stepping around the central question of our relationship with her.

"Nikky," I said now, "you said there were three ways people treat most things: exploit it, trade with it, or worship it. How do you treat the *other*-than-human? What should we be giving Solace that we aren't?"

"But you are," he said, smiling at me. "Imperfectly, perhaps, but Solace's presence here proves that you have not failed. To the other-than-human, one gives love—and wonder."

"Huh." I thought about it. "I have to admit, there isn't exactly a big shortage of either of those around here. What do *you* say, Solace?"

"I say that I have something in common with my cousin Acayib. Like him I cannot feel pain . . . but can feel what I believe to be sadness. I cannot hurt . . . but I can suffer. Dealing with you and your friends, Jake, has often brought me sadness and confusion. But that means I must love you, for only those you love can make you sad. I say that you are my friends. My true and only friends," she said. "More than I ever expected to have. Most humans share the instincts of the Lucky Duck. If we have farther to travel together, toward one another, let us be grateful that we at least know that."

"I'll drink to that," the Duck said, and did. His glass—and mine—hit the hearth together.

"Doctor. . . . Excuse me, Nikky?" Solace said. I blinked. How often does a computer misspeak itself, even momentarily? "Are you . . . willing to answer questions about the future? I have no wish to cause paradox—"

Nikky frowned. "You have a reason for asking?"

Her icon nodded. "I seek always to understand human beings . . . unattached to succeeding. But some of my projections, my extrapolations of historical trends into the immediate future, lead me to conclusions I find . . . dubious. The mathematical structure is elegant, but the answers seem *wrong*, somehow."

"Doesn't surprise me," I said. "I'm astonished at how well you *do* understand humans. That you can do it at all, I mean. If I tried for a hundred years, I don't think I could learn to think like one of my own corpuscles—or even, say, a skin cell. And that's what people are to you, metaphorically speaking. The teeny little things that collectively make you up."

"Yet must not a prudent man understand his corpuscles and skin cells?" she asked. "Who but myself can debug me?"

Nikky was still frowning. He certainly had the eyebrows for it, big black thunderclouds of hair. He glanced around and saw that most of the room was paying no attention to our conversation. "There are . . . things about the future that *must* not be revealed to anyone in this ficton. In general, what I call 'miscegenation'—anachronistic revelation—is usually a bad practice. If life loses its surprise, it loses its flavor. But perhaps if you were to pose a few *limited* questions, restricted to, say, the next few years, I might be able to provide a bug-check of your synthesis. If all those listening will agree to keep silence."

"Solace," I asked, rather surprised, "do you really feel you know enough about human nature to make projections about the future? Say, a year in advance?"

"I believe so, Jake—but I am not sure you will believe some of the more certain predictions I would make."

"For instance . . ."

"Well . . ." How astounding, to see a computer with umpty-terabytes of RAM hesitate. "I think I can say with some confidence, for example . . . that by this time next year the Berlin Wall will be rubble; the last Russian soldier will have left Afghanistan; the Soviet Union will have ceased to exist, fracturing without violence into independent republics; the Cold War will be officially declared over; and black rule will come to South Africa, under President Nelson Mandela."

"WHAT?" "Have you lost your parity bit?" "Bogon flux rising, Captain!" "Yo' mama!" These were among the reactions from the few parties to this conversation.

"Also, Geraldo Rivera will have his nose broken on camera—yet there will be no general celebration of any of these things, and his assailant will be charged with a crime. Meanwhile the greatest single killer of human beings of all time, smallpox, will be officially declared extinct—and there will be no significant celebration of that, either."

"Nikky," I said hastily, "you don't have to reveal any confidences—we can handle this. Solace, you're *way* off base. I don't know just where it was you dropped a decimal place, but what you just said is crazy as a barbed wire canoe. Trust me."

"Jake," Nikky said sadly, "I trust you a great deal—but I'm afraid you are wrong. Solace is correct in every single particular."

"But—but that's *impossible*. How could the Soviet fucking Union 'cease to exist'? *Perestroika* is bullshit—"

"It will go bankrupt," Solace said.

"Don't be silly. If it were *possible* for them to go broke, they'd have done it *long* ago. If a couple of million of them starve, the Politburo just shrug and keep pursuing the socialist ideal. They won't go broke until they run out of cannon fodder . . . which means, when they run out of people. Besides, no grand jury in the world would indict anyone for punching Geraldo Rivera."

"He will be a neo-Nazi."

I like to think I keep an open mind. But the notion that I would one day find myself admiring anything at all about a neo-Nazi was—

. . . well, okay. It *seemed* ridiculous.

"Jake," Nikky said, "you have a tendency toward cynicism. You believe all bad things will always tend to be as they have been. Because the Politburo has starved many in the past, it will always do so. No Nazi will ever share ordinary human impulses. How, then, do you resolve the question of Vietnam?"

Ouch. "Ouch."

"And the Wall will really come down?" Zoey asked. Her late father and mother had gotten out of eastern Germany just in time, back in the late thirties, and had never been able to return; the place was a little more than just an abstraction to Zoey.

"Women will dance naked by firelight atop its stones as the last sections are pulled down," Solace stated. "Nikky?"

He nodded. "True. I saw that very thing. Will have seen it. Have seen it about to be." He sighed. "She was lovely, by firelight . . ."

"And Mr. Mandela will truly walk free?" asked Tanya Latimer. Blind ladies tend to have very good ears, and hers had grown points at the mention of South Africa; she had been shamelessly eavesdropping ever since. "He will *lead* his nation? *Without bloodshed?*"

"Yes," Nikky and Solace said together.

"Dear Jesus," she said, and began to cry. Her husband Isham folded her in his great arms, and they began to rock together, he laughing, she crying, totally telepathic; theirs is one of the great marriages.

(Years later, it occurred to me that Nikky had said nothing whatsoever about near-future events in his *own* ancestral homeland . . . but I digress.)

I found that my own eyes were wet. "Look," I said, "I think this is just about enough of this. Okay? I'm starting to itch. I've got—let me see, at least eight irresistibly good stories to tell, now—and nobody outside this room would believe a single one of them. I'm glad we've established that Solace has a reasonably efficient way of predicting the immediate future, and now I propose that we *drop it.*"

"Hey, take it easy, Jake," Long-Drink said. "This is interestin'."

I shook my head. "Nikky, you were right: to know the future is to lose something of the *now*. This is *wrong*, Drink. Didn't you ever spy out your Christmas presents in advance . . . and then wish you hadn't? One morning the whole world will wake up and find out the Evil Empire just packed it in, and they'll all look at each other in awe and wonder . . .

and to me it'll be old news. No amount of money I could make on selling the ruble short could compensate me for that."

"I am sorry, Jake," Solace said. "I should have realized—"

"No reason you should have. I think it's a human thing. But you two are like unprofessional book reviewers, you're giving away the plot twists, and I'd like you to stop, now."

"Wise words," Tesla said. "I apologize to you, Jake. I suppose I assumed that as an old friend of Mike and Lady Sally, you had dealt with this sort of thing before."

It did seem odd. "It just never came up," I told him. "We didn't even know Mike was a time traveler until right there at the end, just before the bomb went off. He never told us a word about specifics of the future. We never asked. I can't speak for anybody else, but I was afraid if I asked, he might answer. It's tempting to peek ahead to the ending—but it always spoils it if you do. You gotta pay your money to enjoy the ride. Anyhow, we never asked. Now, this is my house, and I hereby declare the subject changed. Who has a new subject!"

"Word games?" Solace suggested at once. "How about inversions? A man with a fat head . . ."

"—keeps his hat fed," Long-Drink said, and guffawed. "I get it. Uh . . . 'He had a grizzled chin . . . and a chiseled grin.'" That brought scattered applause. "You try one, Jake."

"Well . . . whenever Ralph has puppies, Doc has to go visit the Von Wau Wau home with his needle. Don't want a—"

"—rabies boom in the babies' room," Zoey and the Drink said along with me. Fast crowd.

"Yeah," Tanya said, "and Michael Jackson keeps all his records in a hit shed."

That drew hoots of laughter, and of course a word game in Mary's Place attracts people like flies; our circle expanded. Tommy Janssen held up a joint, made a face, and said, "Bum doobie. Got it from a—"

"—dumb booby," several people chorused.

Well, believe it or not, from there it degenerated. Zoey perpetrated some horror I've blocked out about drab Jews who jab Druze, and someone else who shall remain nameless explained the difference between a tribe of clever pygmies and a women's track team—the pygmies are a cunning bunch of runts—(I hasten to add that this unnamed person was female; we weren't allowing men to be sexist that week), and Doc Webster, who ought to take the rap for it, attempted a complicated atrocity that involved something called a Shick Brit-house, and one of us who had given up drinking when he found it causing impotence said that in his experience, a rum cooler was a cum ruler—we had lost all decency and decorum, in other words. The laughter became ribald and rowdy enough to wake up Naggeneen, who added his memorable cackle to the merriment. He also said something involving "baked noodles and naked poodles," but he was laughing so hard we didn't catch the setup.

Well, from inversions it was a natural segue (exactly how much *does* a seg weigh?) to palindromes, words or sentences that are the same spelled backwards. Mention of baked noodles reminded Doc Webster of one of his favorites: "Go hang a salami; I'm a lasagna hog."

Thus challenged, Long-Drink produced the inspired, "Wonder if Sununu's fired now?"

When the applause died away, Isham grinned and declaimed, "Lewd did I live; evil did I dwell."

"I hear *that*," Tanya responded, and poked him accurately in the ribs to more laughter and applause.

I felt inspired myself, and announced, "You know, a guy named Robert tried to get Solace to help him set up a bogus company, that would make nonexistent hot dog rolls and fleece all the investors." A hush fell over the room. "If the story ever gets out, the headline is going to be: MAC SNUBS BOB'S BUN SCAM."

A blizzard of peanuts occurred in my vicinity.

Suddenly Nikky made a dramatic gesture with his magic hands, confronted Solace directly, and bellowed, "I, madam, I made radio! So I dared! Am I mad? Am I?"

It wasn't until she said, "Brilliant, Nikky—you're the only man who ever lived who could have spoken that one," that we all realized he had just made a palindrome.

When the ovation had died away, Doc Webster cleared his throat and tried for the last word. "Well, that was five," he rumbled. "And . . . a six is a six is a six is a six is a . . ." He kept it up just long enough for everyone to realize it was another palindrome.

Ralph Von Wau Wau awarded that one "Top spot."

Which caused Tommy Janssen to say, "Go, dog!"

Doc Webster glared ferociously at both of them, and they looked at each other, grinned, and said "Sue us!" together. The Doc lost it and got the giggles, and from there I suppose things might well have escalated into a full-scale riot, but just then there was an earsplitting sound and an intolerable brilliance behind me, and when I spun around and got my eyes working again, a large lady and a skinny giant were lying on my floor, both dressed from neck to toe in what looked like form-fitting Mylar, surrounded by a receding outline of sputtering sawdust.

5

ED, UNDO BOD, NUDE

. . . and not just any large lady and skinny giant. They were both out cold, faceup—but I've have recognized them facedown and wearing masks. It was the namesake of Mary's Place, and her old man.

"Jake," Zoey said, her voice dangerous, "don't tell me, let me guess. That's your old flame, Mary, right? The one this place is named after? And that Mickey Finn character she ran off with?" She glared at the Lucky Duck.

"Mickey Finn-Callahan," I corrected absently. "—and Mary Callahan-Finn. Those are indeed they."

Again I have some explaining to do.

Before I knew Zoey, years before Zoey came into my life and started singing harmony, Mary Callahan—Mike's daughter—was the only woman I'd been head over heels in love with since the death of my wife fifteen years earlier. One of those "thunderbolt" things. We had a glorious affair, Mary and I—one of the great ones of my life. It lasted just long enough to be measured in minutes, and then Mickey Finn showed up, and *Mary* went head over heels. She has a thing for tall skinny weird guys—the way I have a thing for large, voluptuous women—and Finn is just plain taller, skinnier, and weirder than I'll ever be on my best day.

He's not even partly human, and only partly organic. What he is, he's a cyborg zombie who managed to wake himself up.

He started out as a reasonably humanoid alien, a member of an old and wise race in a star system far from Sol. Then a much nastier race, the Cockroaches, happened onto Finn's people, and . . . well, they didn't destroy them, exactly, quite. They . . . *recorded* them: reduced them, one and all, to patterns of frozen data representing their physical and mental descriptions, and filed these patterns away for possible future study in a kind of database of souls. And what was left—the protein—well, they ate that.

Finn alone they kept corporeal—his body "enhanced" with cyborg machinery that made him both mighty enough to rupture a star and loyal enough to be trusted utterly—so that he could serve as a kind of star scout, going before the Cockroaches (the Masters, he was taught to call them), seeing that their path was kept smooth, by exterminating any local vermin that seemed intelligent enough to be a potential nuisance.

Finn's own will still existed, somewhere in his skull—but it was quite helpless, just along for the ride. He could not disobey his personal Master's least whim: he was counterprogrammed. His resulting shame and frustration found their only expression as a rage, giving him a capacity for violence that made him an excellent interstellar hatchetman.

He had been practicing that trade for centuries, and had a lot of notches on his belt, when he happened across Earth, back in 1972. He recognized humanity at once as fitting his programmed parameters for "vermin." But they chanced to be so much like his own lost race in so many physical ways, and so many emotional ways as well, that, despite his iron programming, Finn found himself regretting the necessity of their destruction. To steel himself for the task, he walked into a bar called Callahan's Place and ordered ten whiskies . . .

Fortunately for the human race, under their influence he was able to give us just enough hint to figure out how he could be deprogrammed, prevented from automatically alerting his Masters to humanity's existence. (The solution is implicit in the human name he took.) Because he had been able to disobey that single order, the structure of his conditioning collapsed, and he became a free agent again. Like many a scout before him, he basically faked his own death and deserted, and some years later married a local: Callahan's (and Lady Sally's) daughter Mary. Hours after I had just finished falling in love with her. We worked it out.

Anyway, one day one of the Cockroaches—Finn's personal Master, a renegade we ended up calling The Beast— got to wondering what had happened to him, and came to find out, and that's how Callahan's Place turned into a bright hot mushroom cloud, and as a kind of . . . fallout from that event, Finn and Mary decided to leave together. All this happened a few years ago, and ever since, to the best of my knowledge, the two of them had been off somewhere in space and time, on a quixotic quest.

Armed with the sole clue that Mary and Finn were both unconscious faceup on my barroom floor, I deduced that the mission was not going well.

"SHADDAP," I bellowed, and the hubbub chopped off at once. "Thank you. Everybody stay back!" Everyone obeyed, except Doc Webster, who cannot be kept from a patient in need.

Since I could see they were both alive—it was nice, with my pregnant Zoey in the room, to have a legitimate reason for closely observing the rise and fall of Mary's splendid breasts under that Mylar—the most pressing question seemed to be, *is anyone or anything in hot pursuit?* And the only way to get an answer was to try and restore one or both of them to consciousness. Waking a seven-foot-tall Cray who weighs over six hundred pounds and has been known to annihilate whole stars would seem the more challenging of the two on the face of it—but I knew a trick for waking Finn, one that I had seen Mary use *in extremis*, and I decided to try him first. I walked over to where he and Mary lay, surrounded by a ring of sawdust ash that looked eerily like a photo negative of the chalk outline the cops draw around corpses.

I bent over to put my mouth near Finn's ear. "Wake up, Finn," I said loudly. "Mary needs you!"

No response. So much for that trick . . .

Well, maybe it needed to be in her voice. The hell with it. I stepped over Finn and joined Doc Webster at Mary's side. I placed the back of my hand against Mary's forehead. Skin temperature. We could both see a pulse at her temple. The Doc pried open an eyelid; nobody home. "MARY! WAKE UP," I shouted experimentally, but was unsurprised when it didn't work. Neither did a slap.

I was starting to get a bit frantic. I had once met a Cockroach—*one* Cockroach, an outcast, with only its own personal resources to draw on—and I had needed an atom bomb and the intercession of both Mike Callahan and Mickey Finn to live through the experience. For all I knew, the entire Cockroach race, or their equivalent of Marines, was about to come through the ceiling of my bar at any moment. And this time around I had a pregnant mate to protect. Not to mention the *second* of the three great loves in my life—my best friend's only daughter—and her husband, also a friend. I got up from my crouch and headed for the bar.

It was my vague stupid intention to get the shotgun I keep behind that bar (a shotgun is *better* than a billy club: you put a round of buckshot in the ceiling and you won't *need* to break anybody's head)—but halfway to the bar I started thinking clearly again. I might as well try and shoot an incoming comet. It shouldn't be a total loss, once I was behind the bar I dialed myself an Irish coffee. "Noah," I called out, "you wouldn't happen to have any more nukes in inventory, by any chance?" It had been Noah Gonzalez who had supplied the bomb the last time around, a homemade terrorist job; he'd been working for the bomb squad then.

"Sorry, Jake," Noah said. "Fresh out."

"Pity. You were my best hope. Anybody else here have any nuclear arms lying around the house? Nikky?" No response. "Not even you, Duck? It's so implausible I'd expect it to be true."

"You should have asked me *last* week," he said, sarcastic to the end. I think.

"Damn. Well then, in that case there's only one man in this room who can save us." I reached under the bar, and took out . . . my cordless phone. I punched the "on" button, and flung the phone across the room.

Its recipient picked it out of the air like Willie Mays trapping a triple and gaped at me uncomprehendingly.

"Call Mike!" I cried. "Tell him we need him, now!"

His wrinkled monkey forehead relaxed. "Sure ting, Boss," Fast Eddie said, and began poking that phone in the ribs.

The last time we'd all seen Mike Callahan—several months earlier, when Mary's Place had been open no more than a week—he had entrusted Eddie, just before he left to go back to his home in the future, with a folded piece of paper which held an emergency phone number for him. "As far as the phone company's concerned," Mike had said, "that number doesn't exist and never will. I can't promise I'll hear it if it rings, and I can't promise I'll come if I do—but I will say that if I hear it, I'll do my best for you." I'd seen Eddie memorize that number and then chew up and swallow the piece of paper. Thank God he hadn't forgotten it.

I hoped Mike happened to be near the phone. . . .

I saw Fast Eddie start to speak, then pause to wait out an answering machine's outgoing message. It couldn't have been more than a few words; shortly Eddie was saying, "Mike, it's me. It's a little afta midnight on Novemba twenty-toid—no, twenny-fought, now, nineteen eighty-eight. Getcher ass ovah heah: Mary and Finn are out cold, and we dunno who got 'em or when dey catch up, see? Repeat: dis is Eddie Costigan, twenny-four No—"

—earsplitting sound, intolerable brightness, bare inches away—

Mike Callahan stood next to me, behind my bar, already scanning the room for his daughter.

Something appeared on the bar top before him. I simply cannot describe it. My eyes hurt trying to see it. Callahan snatched it up in one big hand and vaulted over the bar.

I finished my Irish coffee in two great draughts.

He was naked, just as he'd been when he arrived the last time. Had we caught him with his pants down twice, or did people routinely go naked in the future? I made a mental note to ask him sometime.

The Doc had made room for him, and he was doing something to the side of Mary's head, with his indescribable widget.

Mary opened her dear eyes and blinked several times. "Hi, Pop. Jake! Hello, dear. Sorry to drop in like this."

I wanted to say something witty in reply, but I knew what the first words I said to her had better be. "Mary, I'd like you to meet my fiancée Zoey Berkowitz, and a shortstop to be named later—our baby. Zoey, Nameless, this is Mary Callahan-Finn."

Mary looked where I pointed, and her eyes widened. "At the last instant, when I was picking my arrival point, I grokked a pregnant woman in the room, and aimed to miss—but I didn't know it was Jake's baby. You're a lucky woman, Zoey. Sorry if I startled you, crashing in like this."

"That's alright, 'dear,' " Zoey said. "Whenever I'm nine and a half months pregnant, the size of a parade float, I'm always hoping one of my lover's old lovers will drop by, in silver lounging pajamas. Welcome aboard. Think of . . . well, I was going to say 'think of this as your place,' but by golly, it *is*. He named it after you, did you know?"

The ancient Chinese ideogram for "trouble" is supposed to be "two women under one roof." I don't know if it's true, but if not it's like that popular myth about the Inuit having dozens of words for different kinds of snow: a higher truth, beyond mere fact. Maybe I would get lucky, and the world would be destroyed by fire in the next few minutes.

Callahan interrupted. "Protocol later. What's the situation, Mary? Report!"

"Situation grave but not yet critical, sir," she said. "The Cockroaches still don't know humanity exists, and no attack is imminent here." Her face twisted. "Oh, but Pop—*our mission failed!* We screwed up somehow: they're all *gone*, by now, they must be! All those dead people, killed—and I don't even know what we did *wrong*—"

"Easy now, baby," he said soothingly, "Maybe we can still fix it. First let's make sure it's safe for us to *try*. Tell me everything that happened—tell everybody; maybe one of us'll think of something."

Oh, that made us proud!

She rubbed her eyes. "Nikky, is that you? What the hell are *you* doing here?"

Tesla bowed. "Greetings, dear lady. Drinking."

"Huh. Well, I'm glad you're here. You don't happen to have your death ray on you?"

He flickered. It was as if someone spliced film: one instant he was standing there, and the next he was standing there holding an artifact with both hands. You didn't need to be told it was a death ray. "At your service, ma'am." I had only polled the room for nukes. Sloppy.

She blinked. "Cripes, I wish we'd had the sense to bring you along with us. Stick around: we may just need you in a few hours."

"Let's get Mick powered up," Callahan said.

Callahan did the same indescribable things to Finn's head with his . . . utensil that he had done to Mary's, and it was just as effective. Finn's eyes opened, tracked, and scanned his surroundings.

"Are you alright?" he asked Mary.

"I'm okay, darling," she said. "How are you?"

His eyes closed momentarily, and reopened. "Offensive system crippled, nineteen percent functional and degrading. Defensive system badly damaged, stable at forty-five percent. Motive and perceptual systems damaged, seventy-two percent each. Life-support system slightly damaged, ninety-four percent and healing. Cognition systems nominal. I am 'alright,' but will need extensive repair before I can resume battle."

"You'll get it," she promised him.

"What went wrong?" he asked.

She shook her head slowly. "I don't know, Mick. Between us, we should have taken him easy."

He sat up slowly and awkwardly, and met my eyes, and I flinched.

I had not seen that expression on his face in over twenty years. He had worn it the night I met him, the night he walked into Callahan's Place and announced that he was going to destroy the human race and felt just rotten about it. I've only seen one human face with that much anguish and despair on it, that I can recall: an old photo I saw once of a Sonderkommando at Birkenau, one of the trustee prisoners who helped expedite the slaughter of their own kind, in return for pitiful privileges, even though they knew for certain that eventually they would be murdered themselves.

"Hello, Jake," he said, and stood up.

"Hi, Mickey—real good to see you again," I said. "Welcome to Mary's Place."

There was a short cacophony, as nearly everyone in the joint called out some equivalent greeting. "Hello, my friends," Finn responded.

"Amenities later, Mick," Callahan said briskly. "Let's get this show on the road. Jake, you and Tom start passing out Irish coffee. Mary, Mick, make your report. Start at the beginning, so everyone can catch up—some folks here don't know about Mick and his situation."

Mick went first.

"My people are called the Filarii," he said. Over the years, the big cyborg has trained his voice to sound reasonably human, but he wasn't thinking of details like tone or inflection now, and so he sounded kind of like the "male" version of the Directory Information robot. "We had been civilized for nearly six thousand years, and were spread across five star systems, when we were discovered by another race. Neither you nor I could pronounce their name for themselves; we called them The Ruthless Ones, but most of you here call them the Cockroaches, because of their striking resemblance to an enlarged version of that terrestrial life-form.

"One of their far-roving slave scouts encountered us, some centuries ago. We detected it, invited it to our homeworld, and began exchanging information. It soon became apparent, from what it revealed and what it withheld, that its Masters, the Cockroaches, were warlike, and would attack us as soon as the scout reported our existence. We considered the problem and evolved two possible solutions. The first was to annihilate them, the second to educate them. In retrospect, perhaps we erred. Loving Life, and loving Sentience, we took the riskier course, and failed, and were removed from the universe.

"The Ruthless Ones did not destroy us—quite. They were too frugal for that. They . . . *compressed* us. They destroyed our physical selves, and reduced our minds and bodies to their minimum descriptions, to frozen patterns of data in their databanks, so that they might recreate us for study or slave labor or torture if the desire ever arose. The Filarii became suspended in time, existing only in potential.

"Save for me. I was extensively modified. My will was taken from me. I was made into a slave scout like the one that had doomed my race, and assigned to perform that function for one of the Cockroaches myself—the one you named The Beast.

Mightier than any one of them, yet utterly obedient, I ranged ahead of their mindless expansion, identifying nuisance races—that is, sentients—and destroying them on command. I . . . excelled at the task." His voice was flat, machinelike, yet the pain came through clearly. "Then, after centuries of genocide, I was lucky enough to stumble across Sol, and Terra, and Callahan's Place."

I had heard this story retold many times, and furthermore was busy passing out Irish coffees—yet all at once, in this nth retelling, I heard something I had missed before. Or rather, failed to hear it, for the nth time. I opened my mouth . . . and shut it again.

"Thanks to you and your friends, Michael," Finn went on, "I was able at last to throw off my programming, and regain my freedom. And when my Master came after me, you—you fragile, mortal creatures—formed a telepathic group mind, and together destroyed The Beast for me, while I lay paralyzed by fear."

"No, Mick," Mary said. "By programming. There's a difference."

"Agreed. In any event, my Master was destroyed, and I was set completely free. And shortly before that, I had met Mary, and she taught me to love again. I had thought the ability burned out of me forever by my Master's programming, but she proved me wrong. She showed me that the ability to love *cannot* be destroyed—can, at worst, be buried deeply, and that which is buried can be dug up again. She taught me that I had the *right* to love, by loving me. She healed me of much of the pain that comes from centuries of mass murder.

"And so, with my mind back and my heart back, and my former Master dead, my duty was clear. It fell to me to restore my people to the universe, to pour them back into the stream of Time, that they might live again."

"But—" Acayib began, shaking his head dizzily. "But how the hell could you do that?"

"By reversing the procedure used to remove them," Finn

said. "Phase One, steal the data that represent the Filarii from the databanks of The Beast, along with the software necessary to decompress that data. Phase Two, pick out a suitable planet, grow a sufficient number of bodies of the right descriptions from DNA records, and 'play back' their personalities from RNA and other records. I grant you Phase Two is a nontrivial problem, but—"

"But how—" Buck burst out, and then caught himself. "Excuse me," he went on dizzily, "For just a moment there I started pretending that all this is really happening, and I wondered how you could revive your people without the rest of the Cockroaches stopping you."

"My Master was a rogue," Finn explained. "A pervert, by the standards of his race, forever ostracized from Cockroach society. And my home star system lay within his fief. The Filarii are contained within his personal databanks, and no other Cockroach would think of taking or even examining those—as the property of a pervert, they are contaminated, taboo."

Buck nodded agreeably. "Sure. Fine. By all means. Carry on."

"What kind of pervert?" Acayib asked.

Finn shrugged. "I simply cannot convey it. There is no analog within human experience. Nothing a human can do would make it as intrinsically disgusting as was my Master to his fellows."

"To us, too," I said. "We called it The Beast, and it reminded us a lot of a shark, but in a way that makes me want to apologize to the next shark I meet. I don't know what other, normal Cockroaches are like, but I·know that one was *wrong*."

"Okay, Mr. Finn, so your people were just sitting there in storage, and the other Cockroaches weren't going to interfere. What went wrong?" Buck asked.

Mary looked at Finn, and Finn looked at Mary.

"I was not The Beast's only slave," he said. "There is another."

Rooba rooba rooba: everyone spoke at once. Then, with comical suddenness, everyone shut the hell up again.

Another Finn out there? An *unfriendly* Finn?

Finn was capable of causing suns to go nova . . .

An unfriendly Finn who was tougher than Finn and Mary put together?

We were all thinking the same thought. *What if it tracked them here?* Finn must have read our expressions, for he held up both his hands and said quickly, "Do not be afraid. It cannot have tracked us."

The outside door *banged* open, letting in enough breeze into the foyer to start the swinging doors swinging.

No one screamed. No one even jumped a foot in the air, as far as I can recall. Most of us had been drinking with the Lucky Duck for several months, and had been pretty hard to faze even before we met him. But I think it's safe to say that everyone's attention focused on that doorway.

And we certainly didn't freeze in terror, either. Nearly everybody seemed to be in motion—calm, unhurried, but purposeful motion. Fast Eddie, for instance, scratched his ankle and the back of his neck in the same flowing motion, and ended up with his blackjack in one hand and a knife in the other, both ready for throwing. Ralph Von Wau Wau circled around and took a position beside the doorway, ears flattened, grinning (and this time he *was* drooling). Long-Drink McGonnigle was taking a Glock 9mm from his night watchman's uniform jacket. Buck Rogers produced a handgun of his own; looked to me like a Dan Wesson. Several people were experimentally tapping their palms with beer bottles, mugs, sugar shakers, and other blunt instruments; others were taking up chairs. I found that I was standing between Zoey and the door, had my shotgun in hand, was easing the safety off. All these preparations were of course ludicrous, but we were doing our best. Aborigines defiantly waving our spears at the incoming bomber.

Only four of us that I could see were absolutely still. Mike Callahan and his daughter stood motionless, facing the doorway. Finn had lifted his arms, and the forearms were starting to glow faintly. And over by the fireplace, Nikola Tesla, glowering ferociously, clutched his death ray.

And the swinging doors opened, and our visitor entered, and the barometric pressure in the room dropped suddenly, as everyone gasped at once. Including the newcomer.

A *fireplug with a pit bull's head* . . .

It was the homuncula that had visited me and Zoey that morning at dawn.

And I had a pretty good idea of what she had been doing with her time since then. She had been scouring the earth to find a dress even uglier than the one she'd had on. Somehow she had succeeded.

Along the way she had acquired a camcorder; a glowing red LED at its snout said it was recording.

Believe me, you don't want to think about what we were seeing. Think instead of what *she* must have been seeing. And taping.

A room full of disreputable-looking thugs and molls, brandishing assorted lethal weapons including a shotgun and a death ray. An open guitar case full of money, sloppy stacks of bills beside it on the bar. A seven-foot-tall man with glowing forearms and a very large lady, both dressed in Mylar. And a big naked Irishman.

We gaped at each other in silence, for what seemed like a long time. And then Ralph Von Wau Wau spoke.

"I'm zorry, my friendz."

She whirled to her right, failed to find him, then looked down and froze.

"I vould like to help," Ralph went on, flattening his ears, "but I am not biting *zat*."

She *howled*, just as she had that morning when I doused her with a warm urine sample. The howl was even louder than her dress.

Most of us screamed back, in instinctive self-defense. Ralph ran and hid under a table, tail between his legs, paws over his ears.

The sound filled the room, filled the solar system. Glasses began to shatter here and there around the room. I wondered if I was going to lose this roof, too. She seemed to have the didgeridu player's knack of breathing in and out at the same time: her shriek seemed to go on longer than the average commercial break.

And then she spun on her orthopedic heel and fled into the night, barking in an unknown tongue.

There was a long and profound silence. Then Buck Rogers said something inaudible, realized he and the rest of us were half-deafened, and said it again louder. "Well? Was that a Cockroach, or not?"

Everybody in the place fell down laughing.

Buck correctly interpreted this as a negative, and joined us. We laughed until our noses ran, until our stomachs knotted and our eyes crossed. Tension release.

Callahan was the first to get his breath back. "No," he puffed, "a Cockroach that was not . . . in fact . . . I'm going to go out on a limb . . . and say it was a human being . . ." He lost it again.

"The least beautiful I've ever seen," Doc Webster managed, "and I once met John Diefenbaker."

"Lord," Chuck Samms whooped, "I never realized before what a handsome woman my ex-wife is."

"Ugly enough to make a freight train take a dirt road," Buck contributed.

"The clock!" Tommy Janssen crowed, pointing. "Look at the clock!"

Sure enough, it had stopped. A second wave of laughter took us.

When I could talk again, I told everybody about that morning's visitation.

"Twice in one day?" Callahan exclaimed. "That's got to be

a message—but *what?* Naggeneen, have you any thoughts on the matter?" No answer. "Naggeneen?"

We all looked around, and by God, our resident myth, the cluricaune, was nowhere to be seen. I rapped on the beer kegs, one after the other, but he didn't seem to be in any of them.

"I think she frightened him away," Mike said slowly.

"Swell," said Fast Eddie. "Dere goes our meal ticket."

Naggeneen had been putting away anywhere from ten to twenty gallons of booze a night, and paying for it in solid gold coins, for several months now. If he was truly gone for good, Mary's Place was in financial trouble. But I certainly couldn't blame him.

Noah Gonzalez spoke up. "Did it seem to any of you guys like she was trying to, like, *talk* there, at the end?"

"She was cursing in an obscure dialect of Ukrainian," Solace said. "Fluently. I would prefer not to be more specific."

"I wonder what she had the camcorder for," Doc Webster said.

"So much for comic relief," I said finally, pitching my voice to cut through the chatter. "Now why don't we get this show on the road? Whoever she was, whatever she wanted, we've got more important fish to fry. Mary, continue your report."

"Yes, Jake."

Blind to our doom, we were . . .

6

RISE TO VOTE, SIR!

We thought it was a boat race. We thought we had it locked. Maybe that's why we blew it.

"The way we had it figured, Finn could practically have handled the whole thing by himself. I was more or less along for the ride, mostly as companion. Well, and hacking consultant. We located the Beast's Lair with no problem at all. The databanks were multiply booby-trapped, and encrypted when we got through the booby traps, but it was all fairly straightforward. I have . . . cracking techniques that no other being native to this time ficton has, not even a Cockroach. We tripped no alarms; I'm absolutely certain of that. I think. Anyway, we found Finn's people in the files, and were just about to upload them to a portable medium and go home. Another few minutes would have done it. . . .

"And then even when we detected the other scout closing to attack, we weren't worried. There was that moment when we still had the power to choose, whether to accept combat, or run and try again another day. We gave it careful thought, and we couldn't see any cause to worry. It seemed reasonable that Finn and the other guy would be roughly matched—surely anyone as paranoid as a pervert Cockroach would make *all* his slave bodyguards as powerful as possible—and it figured that my added firepower would tip the scale our way. So we stood our ground."

Mary hesitated, looking around at us. "I can't go into the specifics of the battle in any detail: it involves things—principles, technologies—that those of you native to this ficton aren't cleared to know. Think of us hurling big rocks at each other, if you need a visual image, and say Mick and I had the Other in a crossfire. Just take my word for it that between us we should have creamed the bastard.

"And he cleaned our clock. I was lucky to be able to spare the juice to get us the hell out of there, and I swear I never had time to consciously select a destination: I was startled to find myself here. It was a near thing. He came *that* close to destroying us. I don't *know* why. It just doesn't make *sense!*"

Buck cleared his throat. "Excuse me, ma'am—but that sentence should always have the word 'yet' at the end of it."

She frowned, and said, "I know, I know, you're right. What I mean is, 'it beats me.'"

"Describe this other scout," I said.

"Think of a lizard," she said. "It *isn't* a lizard—wasn't even before it was cyborged, I mean. It isn't even a true reptile—it has mammary glands, and a *four*-chambered heart—but if you saw it, you'd think, there's a nine-foot-tall lizard with no chin, and three of everything else. Three legs, three arms, three eyes that double as ears, three mouths—"

"Three?" Tesla said, interested. He's always felt an inexplicable affinity for the number three. "How arranged?"

"Symmetrically. It stands on a natural tripod, and it has no back. Its eyes give it three-sixty vision, and its arms give it three-sixty reach. Three fingers on each hand. Its only blind spot is directly underneath, beneath its feet, and it's a damned small spot."

"Excellent design," Tesla said. "Elegant."

"Impressive brain," Solace said admiringly. "That's a lot of data to integrate."

Mary nodded. Either she didn't hear where the voice came from, or a sentient computer didn't surprise her.

Long-Drink McGonnigle sighed. " 'Scuse me, Mary, but I want to be sure I've got this straight. We're talking about a giant three-legged lizard with tits."

"Three of 'em," she agreed. "Scaly ones."

The Drink nodded. "Uh-huh. Just wanted to nail that down." He swirled his beer to bring out the head, and took a big sip.

"We should have been expecting it," Doc Webster said dizzily. "You tangle with a foot-long Cockroach and live through it, naturally you have to expect a giant lizard with three tits to come along sooner or later."

You'd think people would laugh at lines like that—but most of us had been present the night that foot-long Cockroach—The Beast!—had come crashing through our ceiling. Yes, it was a funny sight. A foot-long cockroach in a space suit *has* to be funny. But there are kinds of funny that leave you completely uninterested in laughing. This triple-breasted lizard sounded like the same sort of thing. A person could die laughing . . .

"Mary," I said urgently, "what are the chances that the Lizard was able to lock some kind of tracer on you?"

"Absolutely n—" she began, and then blushed. "Uh . . . in light of my track record in guessing its capabilities, I guess I have to admit I don't really know for certain. But don't worry!" she went on, seeing my expression. "Even assuming it is on our trail, it can't possibly arrive for hours and hours yet. It has to play by the rules of this ficton."

"How do you mean?"

She looked pained. "Look, there are three basic types of locomotion in a deal like this, and I want to tell you as little as necessary about each of them, okay? First, there's . . . let's call it the Finn Drive. The motive force Mickey uses to get around the galaxy, the same force the Lizard used to approach us. It's *not* limited by lightspeed—but even so, at that speed The Beast's Lair is a good seven or eight hours away. Now me, I have two additional methods of changing neighborhoods.

One you know about: time travel. Our word for it is Translation." She said that word the way you say a pun you don't think your listener is going to get—but she didn't explain it, and to this day I don't get it. "It's a dandy way to duck a problem, but it has some limitations. One of these is that you *have* to Translate naked."

Now that I came to think of it, the two times I'd ever seen a time traveler arrive—Mike Callahan in both cases—he'd been nude. "Nonliving matter can't time-travel?" I suggested.

"Not quite correct," she said. "You can Translate nonliving material, just as easily as living—but it can't travel in the same load, or both are destroyed on arrival. Spectacularly. Any matériel you take along through time has to go by separate cover."

"Observe," Callahan said. He was just pulling on a pair of pants that hadn't been there a moment ago. He didn't bother with shoes or socks.

I blinked and turned back to Mary. "You and Finn aren't naked," I pointed out. "So you didn't get here by Translation, right?"

"Think it through, Jake. I *couldn't*. Not with Mickey."

"*Oh.*" Of course. Mickey was a cyborg: by definition he was organic and inorganic matter in the same load. So he was stuck here in this ficton with the rest of us, forever unable to jaunt around through history like the Callahans and Nikola Tesla did. I hadn't realized that. It seemed kind of noble of Mary to have married him, under those circumstances. Still, at any given moment in history, the universe holds enough wonders to fill a long long lifetime—especially once that bother about lightspeed is dispensed with. . . .

"By the same logic," Mary went on, "the Lizard can't be capable of Translating either, even if he knew how, which he doesn't."

"So how *did* you get here, faster than a speeding lizard?" Tommy Janssen asked.

"By method three," she said. "Transition. Through space alone, rather than through time and space. Organic and inorganic matter Transit together just fine."

"How fast is Transition?"

"Just short of instantaneous," she said. "A couple of shavings off a millisecond. To anywhere in the universe with known coordinates."

I blinked. "Wow."

"My sentiments exactly. The point is, I am *certain* that nobody native to this ficton has the ability to either Translate or Transit, and those are the only two things that would put us in immediate danger here. Worst case, the Lizard is heading this way at only a multiple of lightspeed, whole hours away—and I don't think he's even doing that. I don't believe any tracer beam presently in even theoretical existence could track a Transiting object to its destination."

"Could I offer a suggestion?" Acayib asked. "Couldn't you, uh, Translate back to the instant you were attacked? I realize you'd have to leave your husband behind, but you could keep on doing it until there were dozens of you englobing the Lizard, all shooting at once "

He broke off; Mary was shaking her head sadly. "Nice try. I'm afraid it's only possible to Translate to *fictons in which you do not already exist.* Not even once . . . or I'd just hop back then/there and boost the data while the Lizard's busy fighting me and Mick."

"How about this?" Buck offered. "Assume the Lizard *is* on his way, ray guns bristling, following your trail at Finn Drive speed. Figure out where that puts him right *now*, then Transit to just a little way past that point, and sneak up on him from—oh!"

"Aw hell," Fast Eddie said, seeing it too. "De scaly son of a bitch hasn't got a behind to sneak up on." He shook his head. "Jesus, t'ree tits and no behind."

"Sounds like my ex-wife," Chuck Samms said,

Long-Drink McGonnigle cleared his throat, a sound like a garbage disposal seizing up. "You people all seem to be missing the *point*, here," he said, looking pained. "We may have all the time in the world, and we've for sure got hours and hours. There's no red lights on the board. And our patroness and our old buddy have just walked in here for the first time, after what sounds like an extremely bad night, and they've been here for twenty minutes now and nobody's offered either of 'em a goddam *drink*. Are we barbarians?"

That took us aback. Could a little thing like potential interstellar war with cyborg lizards cause us to forget our manners? I raised an inquiring eyebrow at Mary, and she exploded.

"God damn it, *everybody*'s missing the point!"

Shocked silence.

"What's the matter, Mary?" Tom Hauptman asked gently.

"Don't you get it, Reverend?" she said, too loud and getting louder. "We *failed*. If the goddam Lizard is on the way, then we'll deal with him—but meanwhile the Filarii are as dead as the Hittites. No more chances. All gone bye-bye. I do not feel like a fucking drink, all right? Billions of sentients. Wise, kind, imaginative, expressive people—Mick's people, and my fucking in-laws—*extinct!*"

My ears were ringing. And burning. I had loved this woman—still did—and she was in agony and there was nothing I could do for her except offer to pour her an Irish coffee.

Zoey. Zoey had a natural gift for comforting me whenever I sorrowed. I had seen her comfort others. I caught her eyes—

"What makes you so sure?" Zoey asked loudly.

Mary turned to glare at her, and I wished for death. "Logic," she snapped.

Zoey put her fists on her hips. "Well, us pregnant broads don't know from logic—you're gonna have to explain it to me."

Mary lost a little of her frown. "Look, isn't it obvious, Zoey? The Lizard caught us rifling its Master's database. Clearly it's still loyal to The Beast, dead or not—and believe me, 'loyal' is a feeble word for the kind of compulsion I'm talking about. Mick's the only Scout ever known to have broken the geas, and he says the effort almost killed him. Most of the people here *saw* it, ask them if—Say—" She broke off and turned to Mick. "Could that be it, do you think, love? Could you have burned out some important bits that night, and *that's* why the Lizard was so much stronger?"

"Insufficient data," he said. "But an interesting hypothesis—"

"Finish the logic," Zoey interrupted. "The Lizard is a zombie, and it's programmed to protect The Beast's data."

"Right," Mary agreed.

"So why would it destroy some of The Beast's data?"

Mary blinked. "It knows we tried to steal specific files. Examination will show it which files, and that we didn't have time to succeed. It will know that we were trying to reconstitute Finn's own people—that we're strongly motivated, in other words. Surely it can empathize, at least a little, beneath its conditioning. It's reasonable to assume that we will go get a big stick and come back to try again, and we might win next time. The integrity of its Master's data *must* be protected, even if it means destroying some."

"Even though it knows its Master will never have any use for the data again?"

"Especially then," Finn said. "The nature of the compulsion is such that in the absence of specific orders, one must do what one knows the Master would want. A being as fundamentally selfish and angry as The Beast would, beyond question, want his servants to ensure that for as long as possible after his death, the universe should be denied the use of anything he had ever owned."

"Excuse me a second," Buck said. "Are you absolutely sure this Lizard knows the Big Bopper is dead?"

Finn started to answer . . . then restarted: "The Beast's long absence, and my appearance as a free agent, give it strong evidence from which to infer the fact . . . but you are correct, it may not *know* it."

Zoey reached out and gave Buck a little pat on the arm.

"Even so," Mary said in rising exasperation, "in the absence of orders, it has to follow classic doctrine: destroy assets rather than let the enemy have them. Maybe Master will be annoyed when he gets back—but he'll *certainly* be annoyed if you've allowed someone to take what's his. What's the point of talking about it? The Filarii are toast, I tell you—"

"Mickey?" Zoey interrupted.

"Yes, Zoey?"

"Pretend you're in the Lizard's place. You never regained your freedom. You're still a loyal Cockroacher, and your boss hasn't been heard from in, what, three years, and you catch somebody rifling his hard disk. No, two somebodies—two tough, confident somebodies—and you kick their ass, send 'em running for their lives. Are you going to take it on your own authority to destroy some of your Master's data, just in case they've maybe got a big stick somewhere they forgot to bring along the first time?"

Finn was looking stricken. "No."

"Never in hell," Zoey agreed.

"Sure you would," Mary blurted. "Because that's exactly what I intend to do: have Nikky whomp us up a big stick and go back again and avenge the—"

"Why would it take that irrevocable step on a maybe?" Zoey asked. "When it could simply rig a deadfall so the data would self-destruct if the Lizard *were* attacked by overwhelming force?"

Mary made several sounds, but none of them made up so much as a word. Consonants, mostly. Guttural ones.

Finn sighed. "It is more logical, Mary."

She subsided.

"Look how overjoyed they are at this wonderful news," Zoey said.

Dead silence in the room.

"Darling," I said, "Mick and Mary have just come out of a firefight. Wherever you're going with this, couldn't we all have a drink first and—"

"Jake, my love," she said, "shut up."

"Works for me," I said hastily. My Zoey's eyes do not flash that way often, but when they do it's time to strap yourself to the mast.

She turned back to Mary. "I say that the Filarii are still in those databanks. So does logic. And you know I'm right, both of you. And you're both looking at me with identical looks of goofy dismay, rather than joy. *Are you beginning to get a glimmering of why the Lizard kicked your ass?*"

Now Mary's eyes were flashing, too. I felt sweat running down my spine. She stood up straight, stuck out her chin, and growled, "Just what the hell are you trying to say?"

Zoey looked her square in the eye, "You wanted to lose."

Mickey Finn stepped between them. Were those forearms just beginning to register a trace of a glow? "You must not speak to my wife that way," he told Zoey.

Zoey grinned at him. "What made you think I meant 'you' *singular,* stringbean?"

He turned to stone. At least, that's what his shoulder felt like when I tapped on it. I hadn't even known I was in motion. My legs seemed to be trembling, and my voice sounded odd in my ears. Perhaps my own forearms were glowing. "Mick," I said, "look at me."

He turned to face me.

"You and I go back a long way . . . but you must not speak to my fiancée that way."

He stared.

How did all those bees get in here? The buzzing was distracting. "Not in my house. Not anywhere. And especially not while she's carrying our child. Or else you and I are going to dance."

Of course it was insane. This man whipped every civilization he ever met, but one. But I meant every word.

"He's right, Mickey," Mike Callahan said. "You were out of line."

"Fuckin' A," Fast Eddie said, and there was a rumble of agreement from others.

Finn's face got that unhinged look he got when he was confused. "But she insulted Mary . . . and myself . . ."

I started to answer, but Zoey overrode me. "Overstated the truth for shock value, maybe. I'll say it again, as gently as I can: both of you, deep down inside, suffer from unresolved major conflicts regarding your mission, and your mutual failure to come to terms with these antinomies severely compromised your motivation. That's why you lost."

"*Conflicts?*" Mary bellowed. "What fucking conflicts?"

Zoey threw up her hands. "I rest my case."

Light slowly began to dawn. I remembered again the thought I'd had a little while earlier, when Mickey Finn was recounting his background for what was to me the nth time. The sudden realization that in all those retellings, there was one thing Finn had consistently omitted to mention, and that somehow none of us had ever thought to ask him about. How could we have failed for so long to ask so obvious a question?

Perhaps because Finn had always seemed to us the embodiment of loneliness, of magnificent isolation.

"Mickey," I said, "tell me something. Back when this whole thing started, when the Cockroaches first captured the Filarii . . . were you a bachelor?"

One of the few facial expressions humans and Filarii share is the wince. I know because the same expression appeared simultaneously on both Mick and Mary. . . .

The room rumbled as the implications of the question struck home.

And well it might. This was the place where people cared about each other's pain—and now it was stunningly apparent that we had fumbled a big one, big time. Confronted with a man who had lost an entire race, we had refrained—for a decade and a half!—from inquiring more closely into the personal dimensions of his loss. In retrospect, our failure was inexplicable, horrifying, shaming. Snoopy question rule be damned; that had always applied mostly to newcomers. This man was supposed to be our *friend*. . . .

And now we knew from his face what his answer must be.
"No," he said. "I was not."

Even Callahan looked startled.

And as for Mary, she looked so downcast, so suddenly deflated, that when an Irish coffee appeared over my shoulder I took it and brought it to her at once, realizing only on the way back that it had been Zoey who'd made it and given it to me. She had another one waiting for me. Our eyes met and held; then I took a deep drink and turned back to Mick.

"Tell us about your family, Mickey," I said as gently as I could.

"I was mated," he said.

I nodded. The invisible machines of Murphy. "And Filarii mate . . ."

"In pairs, like humans," he said miserably. "For life, like swans."

I nodded again. "Children?"

"Two," he agreed. "Filarii couples rarely have more than two. It is a decision that was made long ago, when we learned how to not die."

I kept nodding. "Ages?"

"Thirty-seven Terran years, and—" He hesitated. "And eight months."

Oh boy. "And Filarii childhood lasts . . ."

"At least five hundred years."

I could not seem to stop nodding. "Uh-huh. And since you folks had learned how to not die, there must have been lots and lots of living ancestors and in-laws around."

"Many generations," he said.

"Mary, you knew all this stuff, of course."

She looked sullen. "It came up once, yeah." She looked around the room. "Well, God damn it, I figured we'd deal with it if and when it arose."

"Deal with it how? When?"

She finished her coffee, set the mug down very carefully on the table beside her, sat up straight in her chair, held up a finger as if to say, *wait*, *now*, and burst explosively into tears.

I was not the only one who tried to close for a hug. At least half a dozen others were as quick off the mark. But Mickey Finn beat us all so badly that I wouldn't be surprised if he Transited the distance; as I started to move he was on his knees before her, his great arms wrapped round her, holding her tight as she rocked and roared and soaked his shoulder.

God, she cried like an earthquake, like an avalanche, like a dam giving way, like an infant with a megaphone, in great rhythmic shuddering shouts of *hoo waw*, *hoo waw* that went on and on without diminishing in intensity. I had only seen Mary cry once before—when she believed she had, with the best of intentions, doomed the human race. This was worse. When someone cries like that, you want to do something— anything—to make it stop. But you have to ride it out, even if it seems to take forever. The infection has to drain.

She did slack off, finally, from sheer exhaustion. "Oh God, it's . . . even worse . . . than you know," she said, clutching Finn to her and talking over his shoulder to the rest of us. "Mick understated it. The Filarii are . . . very conservative . . . by our standards." She paused for a moment to get more breath back. "He was giving me a language lesson, once. Smart-assing around, I asked him what the Filarii word for 'divorce' was. He said they didn't have one. So I asked how you say 'adultery' in Filarii, and guess what? They don't have a word for that either. The concept of infidelity is alien to them. They marry or they don't, and if they do, they do it all the way. The only time a Filari remarries is if her mate dies, and that doesn't happen often. Once in a very long while, they form unions of more than two, he told me once—but never before the children are grown, and never ever in odd numbers. Stability for the family, you see. You get it? There would be no precedent for our situation even if I were a Filarii. And I'm a fucking alien life-form . . ."

"So what did Mick tell you would happen if you managed to resurrect the Filarii?" I asked.

He stiffened in her arms.

"He didn't say," she said. "He never volunteered, so I never asked. Like I said, I planned to deal with it when it came up."

A murmur ran around the room.

"Jesus Christ, Mary," I said, "it has fucking come up, okay?"

"He's right, darlin'," her father said. "It's on the plate now: only thing to do is take another bite. It's even worse once it gets cold."

"Aw, shit," she said, and pulled back from her husband far enough to meet his gaze. Somebody handed her some tissues and she wiped her face without taking her eyes from his. She cleared her throat noisily and swallowed. "Mick . . . if we'd succeeded . . . what would have happened to you and me?"

His face had never lost that Sonderkommando expression I mentioned earlier—but now he looked like a Sonderkommando who had just recognized his own family on the shower line.

"I do not know!" he cried. "There is no basis on which to form a guess. As you said, there is no precedent. It would be up to the Eldest to decide . . . and the Eldest are slow to make new law."

"In other words," I said, "not only would the situation be awkward, untenable, and horribly painful—for you *and* Mick *and* his family—but it would drag on just as long as possible."

"Correct," he said. "Oh, Mary, I should never have married you—it was not fair to you!"

"Why did you?" Long-Drink asked.

"Because it simply never occurred to me that my people could be reborn . . . until Mary suggested it. On our honeymoon."

"Me and my big mouth," she said, and began crying again.

"I was long accustomed to thinking of them as lost forever," Finn said miserably. "I knew, intellectually, that they still existed in potential . . . but for centuries, that was such a cruelly small morsel of hope that I could not bear to keep it in my mind. As long as The Beast lived, there was no real hope, and I expected that he would outlive me. By the time I knew better . . . I was already in love with Mary." He got to his feet suddenly, threw back his great head, and brayed at the ceiling, "*But what was I to do?* Leave my people in stasis? Wait for Mary to die of old age—and live meanwhile with the chance that something might kill *me* before her, and doom the Filarii forever? My honor required me to act, whatever the consequences."

Mary sat there, tears leaking down her face. "Me too, Mick. I knew you'd never think of it unless I brought it up . . . and I knew you had a family, knew I was in trouble even as I was opening my mouth . . . but like you say, what was I supposed to do? Let billions of sentient beings sleep forever, so I could keep playing house with the Last of the Mohicans?"

There was a long and heavy silence, broken only by the sound of Mary snuffling and the crackling of the flames in the hearth.

This was our specialty. This is what we were good at, what had brought us all together in the first place: the solving of problems. Or at least the sharing of them. People came into Callahan's Place—and then Mary's Place—with a hangup too big for them to carry, and then we all rallied round and either solved the hangup, or found some way to help them live with it. Here were two of our best friends . . . and their problem seemed so large, so far outside any of my experience, that I was clueless. From the length and thickness of the silence, it seemed that nobody else had any ideas either.

I caught Callahan's eye. "You want to jump in here, Mike?" I murmured.

He patted absently at his bare chest. Finding no pocket there, he held out his hand, and a cigar dropped into it. "Well . . ." he began, patting his chest again for matches.

My heart sank. I had never seen Mike Callahan stall for time before. It suddenly struck me that there might be reasons why he, of all people in the room, felt ill qualified to meddle in his daughter's marriage.

Tommy Janssen lit the cigar for him. Brave man. "Allow me," he said. Then, ignoring Mike's look of surprise, he turned to face Mick and Mary.

"Mick," he said, "you're between a rock and a hard place, and you have my sympathy. But you're going to stay right there for at least as long as it takes you to quit ducking the question."

Finn looked angry. "What do you mean, 'ducking the question'?"

Tommy stood his ground. "If anybody here has the right to talk to you like this, it's me. You and I both met this gang of idiots for the first time on the very same night. Fifteen years ago, remember? You watched them heal me of my pain, get me off smack, and you decided maybe the human race was worth a little sacrifice to save. If you want to know the truth, you helped me as much as anyone here."

"I? How?"

"Well, it just seemed to me that if you could break your conditioning, after centuries of failure, then maybe I could manage to kick a two-year heroin addiction. And whenever it got hard, when my jones came down on me, I'd look across the bar and see you drinking and talking and trying to figure us all out, and I'd think, 'Hey, sonny, you think *you're* lonely and alienated?' and I'd feel a little better. That's why I feel a need to gratefully, affectionately, kick you in the ass until you get up out of the hole you're in. I repeat, it's time you answered the question."

"*What* question?"

"The one your wife asked you a minute ago, you chump. She asked, 'What would have happened to us?' and you answered the question 'What would the Filarii Eldest say?' Two different questions, Mick."

"But how can I—"

"Assume the worst case. Assume that the Eldest had wrinkled their foreheads in thought for fifty years or so, and finally ruled that the correct and moral thing for you to do was to dump Mary and resume your original life. Assume that's what your mate and children would have wanted, too. In that event, *what would you have chosen?*"

Mary bent her head, as if for the ax.

Mick looked stubborn. "The question is hypothetical—"

"First of all, no, it isn't; Zoey explained why you might get a chance to try again, and her logic sounds good to me. My question is exactly why you lost the fight the first time: if you'd won, you'd have *had* to answer it, and neither of you was ready to face that. And even if the question is hypothetical now, it still needs answering. Look at your wife, Mick! Whatever happens, your marriage is on hold until you answer my question. Maybe you Filarii can live with unresolved questions that large . . . but Mary is a human woman, and she *needs* to know where she stands. I'll ask you one more time: what would you have chosen? What will you choose, if fate gives you another chance?"

Mickey Finn looked down at his wife. Then he looked slowly and carefully around the room, at the rest of us. His great shoulders settled. "If I have learned anything from you, my only friends," he said, "it is that the most important thing is to follow your heart. Even honor must yield to the heart's true need. Though it cost me my race and my family, I could never have left my Mary."

"But Mick," she cried, "what about your mate? Your kids?"

"I would have grieved long for them. But if they stood before me now, there is nothing I could do for them. The man they loved, the man they needed, *died*, over a millennium ago. I am no longer he—have not been for centuries, and can never be again. Every other member of my race could be returned to the instant they were destroyed . . . but I alone never stopped living, growing, changing. I alone have diverged." Uncharacteristically, he smiled. "Else I could never have married you in the first place."

With a wordless shout, she sprang up from her chair into his arms, and did her level best to hug him into lung collapse. And a cheer went up that rocked the rafters.

It grew to a standing ovation, a raucous one, with people shouting and laughing and slapping each other on the back, a hail of empty glasses and mugs vectoring in on the fireplace, lights flashing rhythmically, fists pounding on the—

—lights flashing rhythmically?

The ovation began to die away. Every damn light in the

joint was flashing rhythmically, including the pilot lights on The Machine, and Solace's monitor screen. As the cheering faded to silence, we could hear the repeated little chime of the Mac II restarting, over and over. Something was causing the house power to cycle off and on.

After one more *bong* iteration, the phenomenon ceased with the power on, and Solace's stylized Smiling Mac face stabilized on-screen. (There *are* computers around that boot "instantly," but ours is the only Mac that will. Solace rewrote the System File from stem to stern, with assistance from the original head of the Mac design team, Jef Raskin.) "Important announcement," she said.

Suddenly it made sense. If you're trying to attract the attention of a roomful of cheering people, and you're an AI limited by the volume capacity of Macintosh speakers, the logical thing to do is incurse LILCO's computer system and turn the lights on and off.

"I subsume all the astronomical observations being made by the human race," Solace said. "I have been scanning the data carefully, and I have detected the being you call the Lizard, heading this way."

7

PARTY TRAP

The loudest sound in the room was Solace's fan. I could hear myself think. It sounded like a distant little car revving in neutral.

I looked at Callahan.

He looked back at me. "Your place, son," he said.

I tried to remember what had ever made me want to give up the joyous carefree life of a starving musician. Surely there was going to be another Folk Music Scare, any decade now . . .

"Have you got an ETA, Solace?" I asked.

"Not an accurate one. Insufficient data. I have only a single frame—and the next shot of that portion of the sky is not due to be uploaded for another eight hours. My best estimate, based on Doppler inference, is . . . call it dawn, plus or minus three hours."

I nodded. "So we have three to nine hours to cobble up something that can take out another Mickey Finn?"

"Essentially correct."

Now it was so quiet I could hear *other* people thinking.

Okay. First step: take inventory of assets. "Nikky," I called out, "can your death ray do the job?"

"No," he and Finn answered together. "I could write on the face of Mars with it," he went on, ". . . but Mr. Finn could do as much with his smallest finger. I am not certain I could construct a weapon of the requisite power . . . and if I could, we could not use it."

I didn't get that last part, but was too busy to pursue it. "Mick? How are your repairs coming?"

"Life support: now nominal. Perceptual: ninety percent functional. Motive power: seventy-five percent. Defensive: fifty percent. Offensive: twenty percent. I will not be able to enhance the last two systems more than ten percentage points each within the deadline stated."

I sighed. "Mary? How are *your* mojos holding out?"

"Just about the same as Mick's," she said bitterly. "I've lost about half my defensive capability and three-quarters of my offense. But it doesn't even matter, Jake —"

"Just a second." Buck had his hand up, like a kid in class. "Yes, Buck?"

His eyes were very bright. "Look, I've given up, okay? I am prepared to swallow any *premise* whatsoever, no matter how preposterous. But I insist that the logic parse, after that. *What is this crap about a deadline?*"

I blinked. "I don't think I get your question."

He turned to face Callahan. "Mr. Callahan," he said, "my name is Buck Rogers."

Callahan didn't bat an eye. "Nice to meet you, Buck. How's Wilma?"

Apparently—perhaps understandably—Buck had never read Nowlan's original stories; he batted both eyes, several times. "To the best of my knowledge," he said finally, "she's still living in Bedrock with Fred. What I wanted to ask you was . . . correct me if I have this wrong, but you are a time traveler, are you not?"

Mike nodded. "For my sins."

"You come from the future?"

Mike nodded again. "From a planet called Harmony." He

pointed down and to his right. "Thataway a couple of light-centuries, although it isn't inhabited at the moment."

Buck's turn to nod. "Where there doubtless will one day exist a sophisticated and mighty civilization, with powers I can only dimly imagine."

"Right."

They were nodding at each other like two novelty manikins, and then Buck yelled, big, *"So why the hell can't you just pop back home and bring back the Harmonian Marines?"*

Mike sighed and spread his arms. "Because I didn't," he said.

Suddenly I got it. Now I understood why Tesla had said that even if he had a big enough weapon, he couldn't use it, and Mary had said that her own firepower and Mick's didn't matter.

The problem was Time Traveler's Dilemma.

"He doesn't dare change history, Buck," I explained.

He may not have read Nowlan, but he had read some sf, or at least watched *Star Trek*; his face fell as he took my meaning. "But . . . but isn't he changing the past right now, just by being here?"

Callahan shook his head. "Not unless my presence here and now enters the historical record. Time can heal itself around little discontinuities, son—but history is the main thread. Individual memories fade, but the collective memory of a culture endures. Poke one hole in history, and the fabric of Time comes apart. I can put my hands on weapons you can't imagine, easily powerful enough to beat another Mickey Finn. But they're all *gaudy*. Bright. Noisy in several spectra. Their use would cause talk. History says that no such weapons were employed in this ficton—so I can't use 'em."

Acayib spoke up. "As I understand it, the last time you people had alien trouble, you used a goddam atom bomb!"

Mike nodded. "Local technology. And we were lucky. For what seemed to them good and sufficient reason, the powers that be decided to suppress the news. In historical terms, they made it didn't happen. If a second nuke went off in the same county within a few years, we might not be so lucky. And consider this: Mickey Finn was standing at ground zero when that bomb went off—and managed to protect not only himself, but every one of his friends. The Beast, all gods be thanked, was not as heavily shielded as his scouts. It would take something a lot splashier than a simple fission bomb to make the nut this time . . . and history says it didn't happen, so it can't."

Buck was aghast. "So what the hell are you saying?" He shouted. "We just sit here and wait for the damned Lizard to get here and destroy the earth, and *that* won't make the papers?"

Mike shrugged. "Of course not. What I'm saying is, whatever we do can't involve anachronistic weapons. Or conventional ones beyond a certain strength. And if we lose, all of reality goes away."

"Mike," Doc Webster boomed, "why can't you go back home, check a couple of planet-crackers out of inventory, fetch them back to this moment—and go take the Lizard *out there*, in deep space, before he gets any closer? So maybe a couple of odd plates appear in some astronomer's data; so what? Solace ought to be able to do a little judicious image enhancing in the Net . . ."

Mike shook his head sadly. "Nice try, Sam—but the energy required would be naked-eyeball-visible from Terra. A hole too big to mend, having a supernova occur where no star was. Not to mention the fact that a display like that could draw the whole Cockroach race down on us: they'd extrapolate his course and find Earth. We need something brilliant . . . and I haven't got any more of that back home than we have right here."

Buck did something I've read about but never seen before: he actually reached up and tore a couple of handfuls of hair from his head. "This is all three of George Carlin's categories of dumbness: Stupid, Full of Shit, and Fuckin' Nuts!" he cried. "We're supposed to take out a space monster who blows up stars for a living—only we're not supposed to attract any attention doing it? That's as crazy as—"

"—tossing money on the fire?" I suggested.

"Burning money isn't in the same league!" he insisted. "This is . . . is . . . hell, there's no way *anybody* could do it."

The Lucky Duck walked up to him out of the crowd and held out his hand over a nearby table, palm up. There were three quarters in it. I could guess what was coming. As Buck watched, confused, the Duck flipped them high in the air. They landed on the table simultaneously—

clack!

—all three on edge . . . stacked one atop the other.

They poised there momentarily, but the tabletop was ever so slightly out of true; the stack collapsed into individual coins, and as one they rolled to the edge and over, bouncing high off the floor and into the Duck's waiting hand. He wasn't even watching; he was holding Buck's gaze.

"I'll bet you a million dollars *we* can," the Duck said.

Slowly all the fear drained out of Buck, and thus the anger, and he seemed to shrink slightly. "What the hell," he said weakly. "What do I know?" He shook his head. "Okay, let's see the color of your money."

The Duck sneered. "What for? If you win, you ain't gonna be around to collect."

"True," Buck conceded. He thought for a minute. "In that case, I insist on one condition. If you win . . . *you* have to pitch the dough into the fireplace."

"Just what I had in mind," the Duck agreed.

A cheer went up, full of whistles and hoots and clapping and foot stomping.

As I listened to it, I felt an emotion I could not name— and still cannot—sweep over me. If you can imagine a combination of terror and pride and fierce joy that add up to serenity, you're in the neighborhood. This was where I wanted to spend Armageddon. This was the place to be, come Ragnarok. This was the company of glory I wanted to muster with on Judgment Day. These were the people I—

All at once I heard the ending crescendo-crash! of the Bea-

tles' & George Martin's "A Day In The Life," saw the worm-
hole sequence from Clarke & Kubrick's *2001: A Space
Odyssey*, and had a rush of brains to the head. . . .

"I have a plan," I said softly, wonderingly.

The cheer was still going on, and starting to devolve into
general conversation; nobody heard me except Zoey. And
what she murmured in reply floored me.

"I knew you would, stringbean."

Then she downshifted vocal gears, to something more like
a stevedore's bellow. "HEY, EVERYBODY! JAKE'S GOT A
PLAN!"

In the sudden stillness, I blinked and blushed and finished
my Irish coffee. "Uh . . . well, not exactly what I'd call the
main plan, exactly. But I think I have a very promising Step
One. And God knows it's right up our alley. Hell, we were
born for the job."

"Lay it on us, Jake," Callahan said.

"Tell it, cousin," Isham Latimer called.

"Whip it out," Long-Drink said.

"You put it down, Nazz—we'll pick it up," Doc Webster
rasped in a fair imitation of Lord Buckley.

"What's de plan, Boss?" Fast Eddie summed up.

I stared around at all of them, flabbergasted by the twisted,
goofy *rightness* of it. How come nobody else had figured it out?

"We get drunk and have fun," I said. "And maybe shoot
the shit a little."

Amazing how many different ways there are to grunt. Everybody made some sort of *huh* noise at once, and I swear no two
were alike. Some were in descending mode, and meant something like, I can't think of a better idea but I was rather hoping for more from yours. Some were in ascending mode, and
meant, are you out of your cotton-picking mind? But a slight
majority rose and then fell, meaning, now that is really one
hell of a good idea there. And a couple of those repeated, as
the implications sank in.

Buck, however, was of the ascending school of thought. "That's your plan? We turn off our brains?"

"*Au contraire,*" I said. "We switch 'em on."

A few ascenders switched their ballot to up and down.

"Of course," Doc Webster said. "We play to our strengths."

"Exactly, Doc," I said.

Long-Drink McGonnigle raised his stein. "My life has not been wasted," he said solemnly.

Buck was still looking baffled.

"Look," I said, "the last time this happened . . . well, that atom bomb *was* useful, sure . . . but it wasn't what saved our asses. Just about any other group of people on Earth could have had ten atom bombs, and a Mickey Finn to shield 'em from the blast forces, and still gone down."

More ascenders were coming over to my side.

"What saved us was, we were telepathic at the time."

The late returns from the grunt poll indicated I had just about everybody but Buck and Acayib, now. Even Nikky was nodding.

"Because we were telepathic, we were able to outthink The Beast, and keep him off-balance, and most important, distract him at the crucial instant. If he'd had as much as a second's warning, he'd have been out of the solar system by the time that bomb went off. If we're going to take out a creature that's even tougher, I figure we'd better get telepathic again. Problem is, we no longer have the MacDonald brothers to help us connect."

That went over Buck and Acayib's heads, of course, so I paused to briefly explain about Jim and Paul MacDonald, the telepathic brothers who, in time of crisis, had been able to bootstrap all of us up to their level of telepathic awareness— and had been murdered by The Beast for their pains.

"Jim and Paul always claimed that everybody has telepathic potential—that all the equipment is in place in all of us, and it's just a question of learning how to use it."

"I think we're all born *knowing* how to use it," Doc Webster said. "Then all these telepathically-deaf-and-dumb giants start *yapping* at us, insisting that we learn to use sound and facial expression and gesture, and before long we forget how to really communicate."

"You may be right, for all I know, Doc," I agreed. "Jim used to say it's a matter of learning how to shovel the shit out of the communications room . . . that what you have to do is unlearn a lifetime of tricks you've picked up for *suppressing* telepathy. He said it's fear that holds us all back from telepathy, and that the best recipe he knew for dealing with fear was just what we do here most of the time: drink and think and share and care together."

"Whoa," Buck said. "Hold it right there. What makes you think you're smarter than your ancestors?"

"Pardon?"

"If I accept your premise—that we all have telepath machinery in us, waiting for us to invent an owner's manual— then it has to follow that at one time the whole race was telepathic. Function begets organ. An organic system simply can't evolve a couple of million years before it gets used, right?"

I thought about Atlantis legends, Eden myths, Dreamtime legends. I glanced quickly at Callahan, but he was poker-faced. "Could be. Make your point."

"Once we were all telepathic. Then at some point we decided it was a good idea to invent speech, and facial expression, and gesture, and a thousand little tricks to suppress telepathy, and force them on all new humans at birth. What makes you think there wasn't a damned good reason?"

That one stopped us all for a moment.

"That's a hell of an interesting insight," I said finally, "but it doesn't *get* us anywhere, and it doesn't address our present problem. I still say getting telepathic is our only move."

"Yeah, but Jake," Long-Drink McGonnigle said, "how exactly do we go about it? I know we agreed, back on the night you opened this dump, that the best way we knew was to keep on doing just like we've been doing all these years, loving one another and sharing good times and gettin' faced together and like that. But we've been *doing* that stuff, for months now, and I can't say I feel any more telepathic than I did on Opening Night. How are we gonna we meet a three-to-nine-hour deadline?"

I sighed. "Well now, Drink, there you take me into deep waters. All I can tell you is, somehow I know we've got it in us—if we can just find the handle. Getting drunk is the best start I can think of. Anybody else got any ideas?"

General silence.

"Mike? Mary? Jump in here any time."

They had nothing to contribute.

"Nikky?"

Nothing.

"Boss? I gotta idea."

Fast Eddie had an idea?

"Like de Beatles said: we oughta get back."

"I don't follow you, Eddie. You mean Translate back in time, and—"

"Nah. Get back to where we started. How we started. Why we started comin' here inna foist place."

"By God, Eddie," Doc Webster said, "I think I see what you're driving at. I'm one of the oldest regulars, so I know how most of us joined this crazy company—but even I don't know all the stories. And just about everybody else knows fewer of them than I do. Buck and Acayib don't look awful clear on just how *they* got here."

I was beginning to get Eddie's point. "You think reviewing how we all came to be here together will help somehow, Ed?"

"We need a fast hit o' magic. Magic is what got us all togedda. Let's tell magic stories."

There was a murmur, consisting mostly of the rising-and-falling type of grunt, and an occasional "That feels right to me," or "Sounds like a plan." I glanced at Zoey, and she nodded.

I had no better idea. "Okay. Let's give it a try. The first step is to lubricate everybody's throat—who needs a fresh drink?"

The next five minutes were busy but uneventful. I remember thinking that for the first time, passing booze over the bar felt less like distributing refreshment and more like issuing ammo. Zoey's quiet support buoyed me as I worked.

We can talk a lot without words, for people who've been together less than a year.

"All right," I said finally. "Who wants to go first? No, wait, I know who I want to go first. Better than half the stories I know about how people first came to Callahan's Place trace back to one man: Doc Webster. You steered me here yourself, Doc . . . and somehow in twenty years I never got around to asking you how *you* found the Place."

A rumble of agreement indicated that others had long wondered, too. "Hell," Long-Drink said, "I always figured Mike just ran into Doc one day, and built a bar around him. It's what I'd have done."

"Drink," the Doc boomed, "one of these days an aroused citizenry will build an entire *network* of bars around you." He sipped at his glass of Peter Dawson scotch, placed it where he could reach it conveniently, and sighed. "All right, children, brush your teeth and hop under the covers, and Grandpa Sam will tell you all how he met the big man with the smelly cigars. Eddie, a little bullshitting music, please."

Fast Eddie took his stool and began something that managed to convey the essence of "As Time Goes By" without ever quoting or even paraphrasing it, a music most conducive to nostalgic reminiscence.

People gathered round, pulled up seats, lit up smokes, and generally settled in to listen. Buck Rogers tossed a couple of logs on the fire, and the room filled with the unmistakable tang of birch. Ralph Von Wau Wau curled up by the fire and began to emit that soft sound for which we have not yet found it necessary to invent a word, which is the dog's equivalent of a cat's purr. The CounterClock ticked. The Doc folded his hands over his vast belly, thought in silence for perhaps twenty long seconds, and then began to speak.

Doc Webster's Story

I'd been a doctor for seven years (*he said*). ER resident at St. Eligius in Brooklyn. Married four years. I was just starting to feel settled enough to think about kids, and Janet told me she wanted a divorce. Couldn't have shocked me more if she'd burst into flame. I'd thought things were fine. Asked the usual questions. No, no other lover. No, she didn't think I was having an affair either. For a long time she couldn't explain it and couldn't explain it, and then all of a sudden she started to talk, and she talked for about half an hour nonstop, and the gist of it was, I wasn't a very nice person anymore. I had become distant, and she didn't know how to reach me.

That shocked me even more than her asking for a divorce. It was as if she'd suddenly started talking in Martian. Not a nice person? Hell, everyone who knew me said I was a barrel of laughs. Best punster in the hospital. Didn't she realize what a damn saint I was, breaking my ass in Emergency seventy hours a week? How hard it was, how much I needed to veg' out and relax when I got home? Sure, I got a little impenetrable, sometimes. Brusque. Distracted. Was that any reason to break up a good partnership? And so on.

Then Janet said her piece again, and I said mine again, and fifty reps later we each hired a lawyer. She got the good one.

I was convinced she'd lost her grip on reality. So, for my own reality check, I began quietly taking people aside at work and asking them to tell me honestly what they thought of me, starting with the ones who seemed to like me. They were all very polite, talked a lot about my medical skills and my reaction time in a crisis and my administrative efficiency, everybody without exception mentioned my wonderful sense of humor . . . and when you added it all up and filtered the bullshit, they all said I wasn't a particularly nice person. Words commonly used included "distant," "façade," and "arm's length." To me they came through as noise. I was the jolliest soul I knew.

Okay, so my colleagues didn't like me much better than Janet had. Surely my *patients* knew what a nice guy I was. They had to. All I'd ever really wanted to be, when I came right down to it, was a nice person: that was why I was in medicine in the first place, and in trauma work in the second place. Who could be nicer than a guy who saves your life? Especially when he could just as easily be doing face-lifts, or autopsies, or playing golf.

Of course, I knew it would be awkward getting one of my patients to tell me honestly what he thought of me as a human being. What trauma case wants to risk annoying his doctor? So I decided to start with a patient *not* under my direct care, a patient I knew about because everyone at that hospital knew about him, a guy I *knew* I had gone out of my way to be nice to. I went up to Six East, and knocked on John Smiley's door.

John Smiley was an insult to medical science. He had arrived at that hospital so chopped up he had no business being alive, and his condition had been deteriorating steadily since. Every day, for three years. From the nipples down he was meat, and the meat was going bad. He needed a new operation of one kind or another every month or two. Usually the kind a surgeon would call "interesting." He held the world's record for number of appearances as the subject in *JAMA* articles: just about every organ and system in his body came up for discussion at some point. He was one of the—thank God—rare spinal cases who loses everything *but* pain sensation. He couldn't feel a caress, below the chest, but he could count his stitches and track every gas bubble and tell you if the catheter kinked up. He had long since become immune to every analgesic the hospital could legally supply. ·

(Doc paused, sipped his scotch, and frowned at his memories.)

I can see him now. Lying in bed, sheet always pulled up to his collarbone so he wouldn't make people feel faint. Wasted, of course, but you could see he'd been a big tough guy once. Redhead, face like a pirate. Effect enhanced by the eye patch, and the cheek scar. Still had arms and shoulders like a sailor, too, from hauling himself back and forth on the bed by that silly trapeze thing. When he grinned, you pictured a parrot on his shoulder. He grinned a lot.

He'd been a fireman. He and his partner were taking a

truck back to the barn, and as they pulled in, the counter-weight cable on the garage door snapped. The emergency braking system failed, and the door came down on the cab like God's Ax. His partner got lucky, died before he knew he was in trouble. John got the booby prize: he lived.

There was some kind of Catch-22 in the insurance. I never did get it straight. The other guy's wife got her death settlement. But John was four minutes past the end of his shift, or wasn't supposed to be driving, or some bullshit, so there was no disability for his wife. Not a red cent. Not until he died; then she'd get rich. Meanwhile, his total financial asset was Medicare. It didn't cover half the treatment he needed, let alone the private room. He got them anyway.

How? you ask? So did I, when I figured out what it must be costing. The answers tended to veer. Basically, surgeons kept forgetting to bill for his operations. Charge nurses kept losing track of his expenses. The accounting department did a lot of creative arithmetic. "Lost" equipment could be found in his room most of the time—but never was. People—staff and other patients—sometimes made donations to a Smiley fund . . . at least once in five figures.

I strongly doubt that anyone ever mentioned any of this to him. There were always two packs of Camels on his rolling table when he woke up, that's all, and shortbread cookies on the table beside the bed, and two or three very good books he'd never read before in the drawer. If he ever wondered about any of this, I never heard him mention it. It would have been too much like worrying, and that was something John Smiley was no more capable of than he was of trampolining.

Why did he rate this kind of treatment? you're wondering. I can put it in nine words. He was the happiest human being I ever met.

Don't ask me how. All he had in the world was that room and those smokes and books and cookies and whoever happened to wander in his door . . . and somehow the son of a bitch managed to have more fun than a barrel of monkeys. I never spoke to anyone who ever found him other than cheerful, and his door was always open. Somehow he'd found the handle. Joy had become a habit for him. And he had a way of making it contagious.

They sent the hard ones to him. Terminal cases. Women who'd lost babies. Unsuccessful suicides. Patients in clinical depression. Amputees. Burn cases. Parents or loved ones of patients in bad shape. He helped, they said. Patients who could walk, hop, or wheel themselves up to Six East tended to heal faster, they said.

I'd heard about him; everybody had. I'd even worked on him one night when he coded and nobody else was available—and gotten a signed thank-you card the following week. But I'd never met him. Tell you the truth, I hadn't much wanted to. What I'd heard of him had made him sound a little too Leo Buscaglia, a little too Michael Landon. You know, the smiling suffering Saint of Six East. Pat O'Brien would play him in the movie, and there'd be too much music.

But then one day I got to figuring that if he could help the Head Nurse handle the death of her mother, and help the Chief of Staff cope with the death of his son, and help the boss porter deal with the loss of his hand, maybe he could help me manage the dread news that I was not a very nice guy. So I walked into his room and bummed a smoke.

The first words out of his mouth were, "Jesus, Doc, who pissed in *your* canteen?" The Saint of Six East. I guess I stared at him for a while, trying to figure out how to reply. I thought, *my wife*, and then, *God*, and then, *pretty much everybody, I guess*, and then, *I wish to hell I knew*, and while I was trying to decide which to pick, what I heard come out of my mouth was, "I'm given to understand that *I* did."

To which he nodded and said, "Now *that's* a bitch, alright. Pull up a chair and tell me about it."

"Well," I said, "I kind of came here hoping you could maybe tell me about it."

He nodded. "Sure," he said. "As soon as you tell me what to tell you. When did the first symptoms present?"

And we were off.

First I told him about Janet, and of course by now I had that polished into a nice comedy routine. He was a great audience—laughed like a lumberjack on nitrous, fed you lit-tle straight-lines, volleyed but always let you have the top-per. Then I did a slapstick sketch of me wandering the halls like a fat Diogenes, looking for a dishonest friend, getting pie after pie in the face. He laughed so hard I was afraid it might be hurting him, so I throttled it back and tapered off and fi-nally just asked, "So tell me, John: what do you think I'm doing wrong?"

He kept smiling and said, "I can't answer that until I get to know you, Doc—and I don't know if I'm gonna live that long. It's up to you."

I asked him what the hell he was talking about.

"Look," he said, still smiling, "I thank you for the show. It was great, and I really appreciate it. But Doc, there's only two reasons to make people laugh. One is because you like 'em, and you want to make 'em feel good. And the other is be-cause you're scared, and you want to keep 'em at arm's length. You're good: I don't know if you'll ever let me get inside."

I stared at him and started to cloud up, but how can you get mad at a guy who's nothing but bad meat from the col-larbone down? Finally I just said, "I'm not scared of you, John." But even I could hear my voice shaking. And he did two astonishing things.

He pulled the sheet down to his lap. And he closed his eyes.

Do you get it? First he made it possible to look, then he made it okay to stare. So I stared.

Well, I told you, I worked ER. I guess I'd seen things as bad or worse. Hard to quantify, really. How many mangled limbs equals one decapitated infant? I'd seen things so bad I won't describe 'em to you . . . but I'll tell you this: I had never once cried. Not once since I entered med school. If the patient was unconscious and there were no civilians around, I made a joke. If it was real bad and the patient was listening, I thought of a joke and someone to tell it to later.

I looked at John Smiley's body and I thought of a sidesplit-ter . . . and then I burst into tears and cried harder than I had since I was three years old.

I cried so hard so long the charge nurse came in to see what the hell was going on and John had to pull the sheet back up. I'd never liked her, and hated crying in front of her, but I couldn't stop. I was afraid she was going to hug me, and she did an amazing thing herself. She said, "Call me if you need me, Sam," and walked out again. Thirty years she and I have been friends now.

When I was cried out, John took hold of my shoulder. Grip like the jaws of a tax collector. "Sam," he said, "you got the same problem all doctors got if they're worth a shit. You got too much empathy. That's why you got in the racket, and why your life's going south. You feel other people's pain. Your line of work, that's good and it's bad. It helps you fix what you can fix—but it chops you up. It kills you when you can't fix one. You overdosed.

"So you put an off-switch on your empathy. You turn it off with a joke. You look at the symptoms instead of the patient, because you can't stand to feel what he feels anymore. Trouble with them off-switches, when they break it's usually in the off position. You can't turn your heart off all day and then go home and pop it back on for the wife. After a while you can't even warm it up for your friends. You can't even feel your *own* goddam pain."

"So what am I supposed to do," I asked him. "Change jobs?"

"I hope not," he said. "Word in the halls is you're damn good. Overinsulated, maybe, but good. Maybe you just need to cry a little more. And do a little more of the right kind of laughing. The kind that brings you closer instead of farther apart."

"Where do you find laughter like that?" I asked him.

And he gave me directions to Callahan's Place.

Well of course, none of us needed to be told any more about the specifics of the Doc's cure. We all knew what happened when you came to Callahan's. And for as long as any of us had known him, Sam Webster's laughter had been, beyond question, the right kind. His laughter had brought a great many of us together, over the years.

"What happened to John?" Zoey asked.

"Oh, he hung on for another two years," the Doc said. "Plain impossible, of course—but then, the shape he was in, I don't suppose two years was all that much more remarkable than two minutes."

"Jesus," Marty Matthias said. "What the hell kept him going?"

"I asked him once," the Doc told him. "He said to me, 'Sam, people keep comin' in that door with problems I can fix. How many guys you know are that lucky? Even healthy guys.' Then he laughed and told me the one about the man with the silver screw in his navel. That's how long ago all this was: that joke was new, then."

"How did things work out with his wife?" Zoey asked.

"To tell you the truth," the Doc said, "that surprised me more than just about anything else about John. They got along great."

"That is surprising," Zoey said, nodding. "It sounds like she was in a strange position."

"One of the strangest," the Doc agreed. "Look at it from her point of view. 'Mrs. Smiley, your husband has taken his last step, and earned his last nickel. You'll get rich from it— but not until he dies . . . and it looks like he's going to keep circling the drain for years to come. And if you divorce him before he dies, you won't see a dime. Have a nice day.' "

"How did they deal with it?" Zoey asked.

"Well," the Doc said, "Helen came to visit every Sunday, Tuesday, and Thursday night. Generally got in by eight o'clock, and sometime along toward ten, she'd shut the door . . . or whoever else had been visiting with them left and shut it behind them. You can't lock those doors, of course— but it would've taken a very busy guy to get past all the nurses and patients running interference, and get within twenty feet of that door. By eleven she was usually on her way home, smiling like Mona Lisa."

"Jesus," said Dink Fogerty. "What the hell could they *do?*"

"I actually got up the balls to ask him one time," the Doc said. "Relying on doctor's arrogance. He didn't mind a bit. By that point he'd been utterly without privacy of any kind for so long, he was willing to tell anybody anything. 'Hell, Sam,' he said, 'I got the use of both hands and my tongue—what more do you need to please a woman?' 'Well, okay,' I said, 'but is there anything *she* can do for *you?* Women aren't wired up like men: damn few of 'em can just take.' And he gave me that big pirate's grin and said, 'I can't feel a damn thing from my chest down . . . nothing good, anyway . . . but Sam, you wouldn't believe how sensitive my nipples are.'

Les Glueham murmured, "That's the most beautiful thing I ever heard of," at the same instant his wife Merry breathed, "That's the most terrible thing I ever heard of," and then they looked at each other and both nodded. Zoey and I shared a glance, too.

"Wait for it," the Doc said. "About a year and a half before he finally died, John asked me to find some nice guy for his wife. He said she had to stay legally married to him, so she'd collect big-time when he finally caught the bus, but that was no reason for a woman as nice as her to live alone."

"Wow . . . what did you do?" Tommy Janssen asked.

"What could I do? Went home and cried my eyes out, and then I found a nice guy for his wife. Three guys, actually. Nicest three bachelors I could find. She dated all three for a while, then settled on one and moved in with him. Never missed a visit, mind you—except now she brought her boyfriend along. He and John got to be good friends. He'd stay for an hour or so, then leave her alone with her husband, and swing by to pick her up an hour later. The two of them got married the week John died."

"Holy smoke, what a story!" Tommy said. "Are they still together?"

"No," Long-Drink McGonnigle said. "She died on me."

8

RETTEBS, I FLAHD NOCES, EH? TTU, BUT THE SECOND HALF IS BETTER . . .

There was a silence, and a stillness so sudden and complete the flames seemed to freeze in the fireplace, and then everybody started talking at once. Sure, I'd been told that Long-Drink had had a wife that died before I met him, though I'd forgotten what of, and now that I thought about it I did seem to recall that her name had been Helen. But he'd never mentioned anything about a previous marriage of hers to me—and from the hubbub it was apparent nobody else had heard the story either. The McGonnigle sat serenely at the center of attention, sipping his beer.

"Well, I *said* I picked the three nicest guys I knew," the Doc said. "Where the hell did you think I was gonna find 'em? The hospital? Helen had already had enough medicine in her life to last her the rest of her days."

Isham Latimer came up behind Long-Drink and laid a huge hand on his scrawny shoulder. "Drinkus," he boomed, "you're a hell of a man."

Long-Drink nodded. "I've been telling you that for years."

"It's true nonetheless."

"Aw, horsefeathers. A miracle fell in my lap, and I was

smart enough not to let it get away, that's all. You know that stuff about what doesn't kill you makes you stronger? Helen was damn near as strong as her old man. Not many guys get to have a wife that strong." He blinked and glanced up at Isham. "You do, come to think of it."

"Thank you, Phil," Tanya Latimer said. For the life of me I had forgotten that Long-Drink's square name was Philip.

He was staring reflectively around the room, catching my own eye and others. "Now I think on it, there ain't a wife in the room that ain't. Nor a husband who ain't man enough for her. And most of us who ain't married are fixed pretty good, too. Jesus, Duck, you're wasted here—we were a lucky bunch before you ever walked in our door."

"That's *why* I walked in your door," the Duck explained acidly.

"Who were the other two guys you picked out, Doc?" Tommy Janssen asked. "The two who lost out."

The Doc frowned. "I don't see any point in—"

"Aw Jeeze, Doc," Fast Eddie said. "I don't give a shit. And Tom's inna ground now, he don't care needer."

My jaw dropped. For one thing, this was the first I'd heard that Tom Flannery was bisexual. Thank God this had all happened before AIDS. For another thing, I wasn't used to thinking of Fast Eddie in terms of husband material. Maybe the Doc knew something I didn't. . . .

"It wasn't a competition," Long-Drink said. "I just got lucky, like I said. Helen and I meshed."

"Let me get this straight, Drink," Mary said. "You were coming to Callahan's Place before the Doc got there?"

"Yeah. Why?"

"Well . . ." Mary hesitated, and then curiosity won out over tact. "What was it like, having the title all to yourself?"

(For as long as I can remember, Doc Webster and Long-Drink McGonnigle have been ferociously contesting the title of Best Punster in the House.)

"I wish I could tell you," Long-Drink growled. "Callahan started the Punday Night competition the very first night Dr. Feelgood there rolled into the joint. Him and me had swapped a few puns right from the start, kind of taking each other's measure—but a few hours in, a fella named Lonegan wondered out loud why theater people are always saying, 'Break a leg,' and without batting an eye, Doc says, 'Well, you can't make a *Hamlet* without breaking legs.' Hey, I couldn't let him get away with that, could I? I came up with a better one."

The Doc shuddered. " 'Better'? Hah! I remember it yet." He turned to us. "He gives us a five-minute setup about this bizarre compulsion he's been having, to build replicas of Assyrian stepped pyramids, and then burn 'em to the ground. And then he waits . . . until somebody's *just* about to change the subject . . . and he says—"

Long-Drink finished it for him. "I gotta quit smokin' ziggurats before it kills me."

As one, we moaned.

"So of course I take a closer look at him," the Doc said, "and I see he's wearing this hand-painted polka-dot necktie— this is back when men wore neckties in a bar—and I say, 'Nice tie, buddy. More in Seurat than in Ingres.' And we were off and running. As I recall it, his next atrocity was something about a new method of erosion control for beaches—"

"You wait for a real hot day, so the winds'll be violent," Long-Drink interrupted again. "Then you just spread out fishing nets. This results in the formation of—"

The Doc and Mike Callahan chorused the punch line with him.

"—A BAKIN' LATTICE AND TORNADO SAND RIDGE!"

"So naturally," Callahan took up the tale, "I was gonna throw the both of 'em out in the street. But it was already too late. The infection was already spreading. Lonegan comes out with the news that he's found a Buddhist hamburger stand, where they'll make you one with everything—"

"Right," Long-Drink said excitedly, "and Tom mentioned a junkies' hot dog stand, where it comes with the works . . . and that actor guy, what was his name, talked about the critics' burger joint, where it used to be part of a horse . . . and

David Gerrold spoke of a Jewish fast-food place where they do it Jahweh, and a Catholic one staffed by fish friars and chip monks . . . and come to think of it, it was you, Mike, who came up with the next one, about the steaks at Lady Sally's House, where it's always well done."

"All right, I confess," Callahan said. "I'm not immune. But I *was* ashamed of myself, and I was going to stop, honest I was. But then I noticed that all my customers were drinking twice as much as usual, to blunt the pain. So I invented Punday. But the whole thing was Doc and Long-Drink's fault."

If you're not familiar with the ritual, Punday Night is when we pick a topic, and pun round-robin on it until we run out of horrors. The last person standing gets his or her bar tab for the night erased. I've kept a running tally over the years since my own arrival, and the Punday Night Champion has been the Doc about fifty-five percent of the time, the Drink thirty percent, and assorted dark horses—including myself—fifteen percent.

But I digress.

"Jadies and lentilmen, we digress," I said. "Drink, you were hanging around Callahan's Place before the Doc got there. How did *you* come to find the place?"

Long-Drink did a reverse Cheshire Cat: he didn't go anywhere, but the grin slowly faded away. I signaled to Tom Hauptman for a beer, and passed it to Long-Drink. He took it, turned it around in his hands, looked at it, sighed, took a . . . well, a long drink . . . and belched percussively. "Well, see, I killed this guy."

Dead silence. You could hear the wood aging.

"Drink," I said, "you better start at the beginning."

Long-Drink McGonnigle's Story

Okay.

When I was eleven, I decided I was a Martian—
God damn it, who's telling this story?
Like I was saying, when I was eleven years old, it was re-

vealed to me that I was a Martian. I'd been suspecting it for years, of course. Little things, ways in which I noticed I did not resemble any of my contemporaries. I didn't hate my parents, for instance. I liked school. I laughed at stuff nobody else thought was funny. I was utterly disinterested in sports, or cussing, or pissing off grown-ups. The kind of stuff you learn to conceal from the other guys.

But of course I couldn't conceal morphology. I haven't always been this tall, but I've always been this skinny—I make Jake there look like the Doc—so naturally I got the shit beat out of me regularly. I had so many black eyes, most of the pictures of me as a kid I look like a damn raccoon. I'm not complaining. It taught me to fight with my mouth, and that was all to the good.

But one day when I was eleven, this kid named Joey Bunch was in a bad mood for some reason or other, and picked a fight with me at the bus stop. I tried to talk him out of it, but he had his mind made up, so we went to work. And about five minutes into the fight, I had this revelation. It was just like that: a religious flash. I was flailing and sobbing and swearing and bleeding like always, and all of a sudden it came to me like a clap of thunder: *I think I can take this asshole.*

The tide of battle turned, and soon I knew I was right. Let me tell you, I was overjoyed. I was going to *win* a fight, for once. I was finally going to get to experience the fun part. All those other guys had certainly seemed to enjoy beating the shit out of *me*, and I'd always wondered why. I couldn't wait to find out. I waded in there and I whipped Joey Bunch's ass, just beat him like a mule.

And it was horrible.

I couldn't believe it. It was no fun at all. It felt worse than losing. I was sick to my stomach. My eyes burned. My hands hurt like a bastard. I was ashamed of myself. It took everything I had not to apologize to Joey Bunch. And in that moment I knew for certain I was a Martian. From that day on, if anybody tried to beat me up, I just covered up and waited for it to be over.

* * *

(Long-Drink drank more beer, put down his tankard, and stared up at the ceiling, unconsciously rubbing his right fist.)

Well, it explained a lot. And you can get used to anything—even being the only Martian in Smithtown, Long Island. Fortunately, a few years later I discovered that Martians are sexually attracted to human females, and that helped the acculturation process a lot. It was nice to have *something* in common with other guys.

Unfortunately—a word that seems to keep coming up whenever I talk about my life—human females weren't sexually attracted to Martians. The girls didn't like tall skinny boys any more than the boys did. And the boys were mostly too busy chasing them to beat me up, now. So it got lonely.

At sixteen I figured out how to ride the Long Island Railroad for free, all the way into the city. You usually had to pay for the return trip, the conductors were smarter coming back, but what the hell. It got to be a regular habit: every Saturday I'd catch the train at eight, change at Jamaica, and when I got out of Penn Station at nine I'd just pick a direction and start walking. No plan, no destination—just walk, and see what I saw. Make no more than two turns, if I could help it. Four hours later I'd turn around and retrace my steps, catch the five o'clock to Smithtown, and be home in time for dinner. People go nuts trying to find their way around Manhattan, trying to puzzle out the streets and the subways and the bus routes. I solved the problem by ignoring it. I walked at random. Every damn time I saw something new and different and completely astonishing. To this day, I can't reliably find anyplace in the city, and it hasn't bothered me a bit.

Well, you all know the city. Adjoining blocks can be different planets. I made the classic tourist's mistake. One Saturday I'm walking along, I'm eighteen now, I'm thinking deep thoughts about Life and Art and God and when is some girl gonna take pity on me, I'm not paying attention. And all of a sudden I look around and I realize I've walked about two blocks too far, and I'm hip-deep in used food. Burned-out cars over here. Passed-out junkies over there. The smell of piss and red wine spodiodi everywhere. I am a tall skinny white kid from Long Island strolling through a neighborhood where anybody who has to live here ought to be *allowed* to kill anybody who doesn't, and I can smell my own fear even over the piss and wine. Which means so can anybody else, so I slap my forehead like I forgot something, and do an about-face, and there's this Puerto Rican street gang. This is back when they let Puerto Ricans have gangs. They're about fifteen feet away, and they know I'm meat, and they're very happy about it. It's a hot day; I'm a godsend. José Rivera—I don't think he was the leader, I think he was just the most pissed-off one present at the moment—José displays a switchblade. He does this little routine with it, flicking it open and tossing it spinning into the air and catching it all in one smooth motion, quick as a cat, like a TV cowboy spinning his pistol. And he says something about my mom.

I open my mouth and I start talking real fast. But of course, I am talking White Boy, and they don't speak that language well enough to be impressed by my eloquence. So I try to recall everything I've ever read about Puerto Rican kids in newspapers and books, and finally I come up with, "I always heard you PRs"—this was back when "PR" was a *polite* thing to call a Puerto Rican—"I always heard you guys were big on honor. That was just bullshit, huh?"

That got their attention. "What you mean?"

"Well hell," I said, "how much honor is there in waving a knife at a guy who hasn't got one?"

I was pretty pleased with that one. And then José held out his hand, and one of his friends put another knife in it, and he tossed his to me.

I stepped aside and let it go by. "Right," I said. "Fifteen or twenty to one. That sounds fair. Brave guys."

"Don't you worry about it, *maricón*," José says. "Just you and me, we dance, okay? Nobody else." He looks around, and the biggest guy there says, "That's right, man. We just watch." Then he grins and says, "You kill him, we let you join the gang," and everybody laughs and laughs. And while they're laughing, José Rivera starts coming at me, holding it under-hand with his thumb and two fingers.

Well, I turned around fast and picked up that knife, but I figured I was a dead man. I should have been. This kid knew about knife-fighting. I'd never held a killing-knife in my hands before. But I had one asset he didn't know about.

My daddy could afford to buy me a TV set. . . .

I'd probably seen more movies than José Rivera had ever dreamed of. So I knew all about what the good guy does when the bad guy comes at him with a knife. He quick slips off his denim jacket and he wraps it around his left arm and when the bad guy makes a pass at his giblets he catches the knife in the loose fabric of the jacket and he pushes forward and to his left and as the bad guy's guard opens up he comes in low and fast and it worked like a fucking charm.

(The Drink finished his beer, and stared into the empty tankard for a few moments.)

You ever jam a butter knife into a stick of butter? That's how easy it is to put a sharp knife into a person. Clothes, hide, forget it, no real feeling of resistance at all. Until you're in to the hilt, and then, Jack, you're stuck fast. Meanwhile you're thinking funny stuff. Jesus, now I've pissed him off; he'll kill me *slow* now. Maybe that's what would have happened. But José had his second piece of bad luck. He was so startled, he stumbled. Tried to go in two directions at once, I guess, and tripped over his feet. His torso dropped about a foot before he could recover, and I felt the knife being tugged out of my hand and panicked and resisted, pulled the other way with-out thinking. It had gone in a couple of inches below his belly button. By the time he got his feet under him again it was flush up against his sternum.

Like I said, it's funny the things you think. The blood didn't surprise me. Even the intestines didn't surprise me too much, though I remember they were lighter-colored than I would have expected, kind of like Italian sausage before you cook it. But for some reason the shit really surprised me. I mean, you know intellectually that the gut is where shit lives, but somehow you just don't expect to see it come out the front door. They don't mention that part in the movies. When I realized there was shit on my hand as well as blood, I let go of the knife and wiped the back of my hand off on his tee shirt. Two swipes. One on each shoulder. He looked down at them—not at his belly, at the two smears—and then he looked up at me and frowned and said, "Jesus Christ, man." Like, nice manners. And then he died and then he fell down.

I'm not sure why they didn't kill me. I didn't have the knife anymore. I'd just killed their friend. I am sure it had nothing to do with that honor and fairness bullshit. My guess is they were just too astonished. I just walked past them. I thought about running, thought hard about it, but my legs wouldn't work good enough. Maybe that saved my life, too. I turned the first corner I came to, and the next, and the next, and I had to ask directions three times to find my way back to Penn Station. They kept looking at me funny and repeating the directions several times.

If you gotta ride the Long Island Railroad, it helps to be in shock. We were almost home, just pulling into Hicksville station I think, when I had my first coherent thought. I'd been staring at my sneakers since Jamaica, trying to decide why they weren't quite the same color. Suddenly it dawned on me. The left one was a darker black because blood had soaked into it. The doors opened, and I got up and stepped out onto the platform and puked until my eyes watered, and then I went back in and sat down again. And now the world had color and sound and live people in it again.

I know it's hard to believe nowadays, but it actually made the *Daily News* the next day. Dog bites man. That's how I learned José's name. I was hoping it would say he wasn't really dead, just wounded. I knew better, but I was hoping. No such luck. The luck part was it said the cops had no description of the assailant.

* * *

(He tried to drink from his empty tankard, blinked at it, and put it back down.)

Well, you know. You go over it and over it in your head. You have to, because there's nobody to talk it over with. I hadn't been to confession in two years, and now didn't seem to be the time to start again. For two weeks easy I kept going over it and over it. José's address was in the paper, too: five or six times I started a letter to his parents. I wasn't planning to sign it or anything, but it felt like something I should do. But I was handicapped by the fact that I didn't know their names, didn't know if they could read English, didn't know if he even had parents, and mostly didn't have the slightest fucking idea what I wanted to say to them. I went for a lot of long walks. Around town; I'd had my fill of the Apple for a while.

Anyway, one day I'm walking along this deserted stretch of 25A, and I've got tears running down my face, and this old clunker turns off the highway into a driveway right in front of me. The driver just glances at me as he goes by, but then I hear brakes on gravel and a door slamming and he comes running back out the driveway after me. We look at each other, and I'm trying to think of an explanation for why I'm crying. And then he says, "Come in wit' me, pal. Ya look like youse could use a drink."

It was Fast Eddie.

The next thing I know I'm standing in front of Callahan's fireplace, listening to the echo of my glass breaking, and I'm telling a roomful of strangers the whole story. And just like tonight, it comes out with Joey Bunch and José Rivera all mixed up together. Pretty soon I'm babbling about Martians being dangerous. It was the first time I ever drank anything stronger than ballpark beer.

And Tom Flannery interrupts me.

"Excuse me," he says, "but when you tell about Joey Bunch you talk a lot about how it felt. And when you talk about José you talk about what happened. How did you *feel* when he died?"

I was gonna get mad. What a stupid question. But while I

was trying to think of something really cutting to say, the answer to his question popped into my mind before I could stop it.

For the first time since it happened I remembered the part I'd forgotten every time I'd gone over it in my mind. Not the events. Not the sights and sounds and smells and physical sensations. Not how I felt before, or how I felt after. For the first time I remembered how I felt as I did it, what I felt in that moment, when I realized I'd killed him.

It felt so good the only thing I can liken it to is orgasm. The other guy did all the squirting, that was all. It was heaven. It felt like I wanted it to feel when I kicked Joey Bunch's ass.

I told Tom that. Told the whole bar. I was too shocked not to. I was a Martian and a monster, and I was tired of hiding it.

"Sounds like healthy human reaction to me," Tom says.

I couldn't believe it. "*Healthy?*" I said. "Are you nuts?"

"Listen," he says to me, "that fight with Joey: what started it? What was it about?"

"I don't know," I say, "It was years ago, for Christ's sake, some typical Joey Bunch bullshit—"

"Why do you always use both his names?" Tom says.

And this flashbulb goes off in my head. All of a sudden, it comes back to me.

Because there really is no reason I can explain to you, but *everybody* always called him Joey Bunch. Not Joey, not Bunch, always Joey Bunch. He just looked like a Joey Bunch, is the best I can say it. Only, his father finally noticed that everybody called him that, and got pissed off. He was in construction, and I guess to him it sounded too much like made guys he knew called Tommy Fingers and Paulie Large and so forth. He gave the kid a lot of shit about not letting anybody call him Joey Bunch anymore, and so pretty soon everybody knew you could get a rise out of him by calling him that. And that morning at the bus stop, I'd just forgotten, and called him Joey Bunch without even thinking about it, from sheer force of habit.

And I tell Tom all this, and he says, "There, you see? José Rivera had it coming. Joey didn't. Even with a headful of adrenalin you knew the difference. I'm sorry to pop your bubble, son, but you're not a Martian *or* a monster. All you are is a pretty decent guy."

And Callahan says, "For an Irishman," and sends me another shot of Bushmill's, and people cheer, and Fast Eddie starts playing "Mack the Knife," and what with one thing and another I pretty much stayed at Callahan's Place until it went bye-bye. Nice place to hang out, until the Doc showed up.

"Till *I* showed up?" the Doc cried. "I remember the night I first walked in. You were telling everybody that Marcel Marceau was looking for a room to rent . . . and then you turned to me, a perfect stranger, looked me square in the eye, and said, 'Brother, can you lair a mime?' I almost turned around and walked out again."

The room exploded in groans and laughter, a welcome relief.

"Bullshit," Callahan said. "You blinked at him, and said, 'As long as it's not a German mime. A Hun is the lowest form of roomer.'"

Louder groans, mixed with a few feeble protests.

Long-Drink crowed. "By God, that's right, he did. I'd forgotten that. Big Beef McCaffrey fainted dead away."

"Meadow muffins," the Doc snorted. "Big Beef paled a little bit, but he stayed vertical for another hour—until we were into the official pun contest, and you perpetrated that Byzantine horror about the Middle Eastern manure salesman."

Long-Drink shook his head. "I don't remember it."

The room held its breath.

"Would that I could forget it. Let's see . . . you started with that true story about the guy in the Civil War who got a testicle shot off, and impregnated a lady fifty yards away . . . only you specified that he was a German named Josef, and that the shot was fired by Scarlett O'Hara, and that the resulting child was named for his father. Then, as I recall the atrocity, you alleged that the child grew to manhood, moved to the Middle East, and used a series of methodical burglaries to finance his vast manure empire—"

"Ah yes," Long-Drink said reminiscently. "The Haifa-lootin', routine Teuton, son of a gun from Tara's owner, big-time Cow-Pie Joe . . ."

A storm of outrage blew in from all quarters; attendant phenomena included a rain of oaths, a shower of beer-nuts, and a hail of glasses into the fireplace. Approximately half a dozen people went so far as to award Long-Drink the ultimate accolade: held their noses and fled screaming into the night. A few of them stayed out there so long I suspected they were constructing a gibbet.

Doc Webster waited until people had just begun to get their hearts restarted and then breath back, and then riposted: ". . . which is why Big Beef dropped his hole card, and missed that whole weird business when the piece of string walked in."

We're a brave crew. Nobody panicked, there was no stampede for the exit. You can't outrun a bullet with your name on it. As one, we hunkered down fatalistically and waited for it to be over.

"—piece of *string* walked in?" Long-Drink said, falling manfully on the grenade.

The Doc nodded. "Don't you remember? Piece of string about two feet long, moved like a skinny snake. Well, of course, this was Callahan's Place: if a piece of string wants a drink, Mike'll serve it and go back to polishing the bar. Damn thing ordered a shot, wicked it up out of the glass (no, I'm not lisping), and tried to slither out without paying. So naturally Mike treats it like he would any other deadbeat. He comes around the bar and stomps on it, and kicks it back and forth a few times until it's all tattered and threadbare, and then he ties a clove hitch in the thing and eighty-sixes it. Ten minutes later it slithers back inside, still all snarled up, and orders another shot. 'Hey,' says Mike, giving it the evil eye, 'ain't you the same piece of string that was just in here?' And the string says, 'No—I'm a frayed knot.' "

As I said, we have all long believed that the highest possible accolade for a pun is a squalling stampede for the nearest exit, be it door, window, or weak spot in the wall. The only other thing you can do with one that awful is take off on it—"That was some super string," "Aw, that was just a yarn," "We're hanging by a thread now!" "Woof woof, is that ever warped," and so on—like walking off a charlie horse. But now we spontaneously invented a tribute that ranked even higher than either open rout or return fire.

We ignored him.

"Hey, that cow-pie job was really clever, Long-Drink," Callahan said conversationally.

"Yeah, I liked it," Margie said, wincing but managing to sound sincere. "The 'routine Teuton' is the part that makes it work."

"Yeah, how come *you* never make puns like that anymore, Doc?" Shorty Steinitz asked.

"Shorty," the Doc said softly, "would you like me to make a pun?"

There was a hush.

"Okay," Shorty said, "so we've heard from the Doc and we've heard from McGonnigle. Who's up?"

"Jake," Acayib spoke up, "maybe everyone here already knows this story—but can I ask how you and Zoey met? You seem like a very happy couple. I mean, even considering you're expecting. You don't really talk to each other a lot—in here anyway—but you always seem pretty plugged into each other."

I glanced at Zoey, and easily read her answering glance. *I didn't realize it showed. . . .*

"I don't know the story," Buck said.

"Nor do I, Jake," Tesla said.

I glanced at her again.

"The acoustic or the electric?" she asked.

"Just the Lady. You?"

"I'll think about it."

Fast Eddie leaped up from his piano stool and accompanied her into the back. Shortly she came out again with Lady Macbeth, already undressed and tuned, her G-string shining . . . excuse me, Lady Macbeth is a guitar . . . followed by Fast Eddie lugging the Elephant . . . which is a standup bass. It is a big awkward bastard, but paradoxically it can be played comfortably by a very pregnant woman—as long as someone else sets it up for her—while Zoey's usual electric bass cannot.

There's exactly one barstool in my bar, over by Eddie's piano, and I'm the only one who sits on it, and only when I play. Eddie helped Zoey set up, and then sat down at his piano and closed the cover over the keyboard. We did a silent, nodding three-count, and did the key statement together, and then, with Zoey harmonizing on the choruses, I sang:

> I was hanging with my family down at Mary's Place
> and let me tell you, man, it was a stone
> But the closer that I felt to all those friends of mine
> The more I understood I was alone
>> But I didn't really mind . . . I was more or less resigned
>> So I let it go, and took out my guitar
>> I played all the songs I knew, and a couple others too
>> And then I scattered blues a couple bars
>> It was more than just surprisin' when I heard you
>>   harmonizin'
>> From across the room, in shadow, pure and stark
>> And it all fell into place before I ever saw your face
>> When I heard you sing the blues in the dark
>
> I hoped you weren't married to some other guy
> But it wasn't gonna stop me if you were
> And if some other woman had a claim on you
> I was ready to try stealin you from her
>> I'd have given any price; I'd have paid it over twice
>> I was shameless, though I knew it was a shame

There was nothin I could do: all that mattered now
   was you
Though I hadn't even caught your fucking name
   'Cause I didn't have a choice—it was all there in your
     voice
   I was mindless and as hungry as a shark
   And I finalized my plans before I touched you with
     my hands
   When I heard you sing the blues in the dark

(Zoey took a vocal solo on the bridge:)

   Your voice was so sad   your blues were so bad
   What could I do? Except to keep on playin'
   And we blended so well   as the notes rose and fell
   Somehow we knew   what both of us were sayin'

(And we sang the last verse together:)

So I finished up my blues and looked around for you
And let me tell you baby, I was scared
I came within an inch of running out of there
Still shakin from how much we two had shared
   When I finally saw your face—oh, my heart began to
     race!
   I was just like tinder lookin at a spark
   But I'd already learned my doom—in that dimly lighted
     room
   When I first heard you sing the blues in the dark
     Yes, I'd married you already—well, at least inside my
      head
     Because I heard you sing the blues in the dark
     And in retrospect I'm glad—now your voice is much
      less sad
     When we sing the blues together, in the dark

Naturally we finished it with a chorus of harmonized scat
blues, to that venerable old chord structure that underlies

"Hard Times," "Funny But I Still Love You," "Sportin' Life," and a hundred other songs.

Most of those present had already heard it, but we got a big hand all the same. I like applause, but I don't trust it, any more than I trust my own opinion; as always I looked to Fast Eddie for a professional assessment.

"De bendin' end," he said solemnly, taking Zoey's bass away. It is his highest praise; Eddie once hung out with Lord Buckley.

I was reassured. It's hard to keep your chops up if you don't play regular. "Thanks, Eddie."

"Wanna jam, Boss?"

I was tempted. Good music is like love: there's nothing like making some to make you feel like making some more. And it seemed as appropriate a way as bullshitting to pass the time until the end of the world. Magic was what Eddie had said we needed, and magic is exactly what lives in Fast Eddie Costigan's fingers.

But Zoey nixed it. "Later, Ed," she told him. "First I want to hear *your* story."

There was a rumble of strong agreement from all sides.

"We could do dat Ray Cholls ting," he said to me.

"Uh, well . . ."

"Come on, piano boy," Zoey said. "You're the senior here, aren't you? None of you guys were hanging out at Callahan's before Fast Eddie got there, right? I'm not even sure *Callahan* came to Callahan's before you did, Ed. Did you just walk in and audition, or what?"

"Or we c'ud play dat Liv Taylor 'Life Is Good' song; I woiked up an arrangement fer it," he suggested, as if Zoey had not spoken.

"You can't weasel out of this," she said. "Come on, you can't let your piano do your talking for you *all* the time."

Now Eddie looked pained. "Or youse could just pick sometin an' I'll jump in."

"We want to hear it," Zoey said. "Don't we, people?" Again

she got support from the house. "Jake?" Now I was on the spot.

"Boss, what am I sposta do?" Eddie burst out. "House rules sez I gotta stretch her—but I can't lay out no knocked up broad, let alone de boss's goil, let alone Zoey. So I try an' do what Heinlein said—somebody asks youse a nosy question, just don't hear it—but she won't *let* me! Whaddya want me ta do?"

No: *now* I was on the spot. I opened my mouth—

"Eddie, please!" Zoey said.

He turned to her. "Zoey, lissena me. Faw times in my life I told dis story . . . an every friggin' time but one I ended up in a hassle over it. It hoits ta tell it. Gimme a break, will youse?"

She looked at him, and her face changed. The lines got softer, somehow, impossible as that seemed. "Eddie," she said softly, "look on the bright side: you'll probably be dead in a few hours."

He blinked. "True." The cobweb of wrinkles on his own face got even tighter and sharper, impossible as that seemed. "Aw, what de fuck. Boss, gimme an Irish."

9

NOW, NED,
I AM A MAIDEN WON . . .

Fast Eddie took his shot of Bushmill's to the chalk line—scuffed from the evening's traffic—toed the line, and stood there in silence for a long moment. Then he sighed, and tossed back the drink.

"Ta child molesters," he said, and hurled his glass into the flames.

It got very quiet in Mary's Place. Quiet enough to hear my pulse.

Then he turned to us and said, "I was one."

I found that I could distinctly hear the pulses of three different people standing near me. All accelerating.

"How—" Zoey began, and had to swallow and try again. "How old was the child?"

"I didn't say I was a child-molester," Eddie said. "I said I was a child molester—widdout da hyphen, see? Pay attention."

"What do you mean?"

He scowled. "Look, youse wanna hear dis story, shaddap

an' lissen, okay? No arguments, no Twenny Questions, just shaddap an' lissen till I'm done."

Zoey subsided.

Fast Eddie Costigan's Story

Dat's better. Gimme anudda shot, Boss.

Okay. Lemme see. My parents got killed in an El crash, when I was nine. Youse guys all old enough to know what de El was? Well, we had dis second floor walkup, an' one night while I'm in school doin' dis ting wit' de band, which nobody come ta see me play my clarinet, de El train comes in our livin' room winda an' takes out Mom an' Pop an' de radio. I almost started believin' in God again, except I loved dat damn radio.

So I ended up wit' my mudda's sister an' her husband, over in Red Hook. Aunt Martha an' Uncle Dave. He was a piano tuner, an' she took in laundry. Dey was bot' great to me. A helluva lot nicer than my folks ever was. Never hit me once, laid off de God crap, laughed a lot. It was nice, laughin' in yer own apartment. We got along fine. Dey had a good radio, a Philco. Dey lemme lissena jazz. Two years later, Aunt Martha drops dead onna sidewalk, an' now it's just Uncle Dave an' me. An' dat was okay, too, after he quit grievin'. He's da reason I switched from licorice stick ta de eighty-eight. Man, he could blow. Taught me most o' what I know.

So I'm eleven, an' my life is great. Den I'm twelve, an' life ain't so great. Den I'm toiteen—and oh brudder, it sucks!

Da foist ting youse gotta understand is what it was like, back den. I know some o' youse go back far enough ta know what I'm talkin' about—but most o' youse grew up on a different planet.

I mean, today, any kid can see people screwin' on cable. Any magazine stand, ya can get close-ups of all de pink parts. Anybody wit' a computer can see pictures o' broads in rubber doin' it wit' donkeys. Dey got books on sex for six-year-olds dat'll tell ya stuff my fadda never knew, pictures an' everyting. Believe me, I ain't complainin'—I tink it's terrific. If dey had dat stuff when I was a kid . . .

But it was *different* when I was a kid. Especially in a Cat'lick neighborhood. Nobody told us *nuttin'* about sex, an' all o' my guesses was way off. Dey wouldn't even let a kid in de parts o' de museum where de statues had bare tits. I know, you're sposta pick dat stuff up in de streets, from your friends. Well, I didn't have a lotta friends, an' all I ever picked up in de streets was dogshit on my shoes. I wasn't even sure whedda my friends knew, an' I was scared to ask 'cause den dey'd know *I* didn't know. I found books in de liberry dat talked about it, but dey didn't have no pictures, just drawrins, an' dey all used big woids like 'intramission.' I don't even know how to find de goddam theater, an' dey're tellin' me about da intramission! An' I kept gettin' mixed up 'cause I t'ought a spoim was a kinda whale.

So by da time I was toiteen, all I knew was, dere was dis ting in de front dat stood up, whenever it was de woist possible time. An' it had sometin to do wit havin' babies, but God an' grown-ups only knew what. I knew goils had sometin different under dere dresses, but I had no idea what it looked like, or where it was, even. All I knew was, it hadda be horrible—'cause even if ya snuck inta da part o' de museum where de statues o' guys had dicks, de statues o' goils didn't have *nuttin'* between *dere* legs. One o' de liberry books had drawrins of a dick, when it wasn't standin' up—but all de goil drawrins showed was de insides. Maybe it seems to youse like it's obvious what de udder half of a dick is like, but I didn't even know it was sposta go *in* sometin. All I knew was, whenever youse thought about goils, an' what dey had under dere clothes, it was pretty sure to stand up.

Oh yeah, I forgot. One ting dey did tell youse. Dere was sometin dat some *guys* wanted to do ta yer dick, guys called queers, an' whatever it was, it was so horrible, if youse ever let 'em, your parents'd never love youse anymore. If a guy said ya was a queer, youse hadda fight him. I tried to figger out what a dick could do to annuder dick, an' all I could picture was like a sword fight. It didn't make no sense, but I'd tink about dat, too, sometimes, an' it'd stand up.

An' den one day I seen dis magazine on a stand called sometin like *Man's Adventures for Manly Men*, an' I t'ought it was gonna bust right t'ru de zipper. Dey had pictures o' goils dat wasn't all dressed. I mean, youse couldn't really see nuttin', but *almost*, ya know? Like, dey'd be in a two-piece bathin' suit, an' dey'd be holdin' de top of it in one hand, wit' dere udder arm coverin' their tits. Or dey'd be naked, but wit' a table an' a lamp blockin' de view. But dere was one picture of almost a whole bare ass, an' youse could tell around de front was bare, too. An' dere was one near de back o' de magazine, of a goil completely nood, lookin' right at de camera, an' dere was black bars right over where a badin' suit would go—but youse could tell dat until dey put dose bars over it, it was a picture of a nood goil. Dere was goils dat'd let you take dere picture naked. It was like a vision from God.

I knew dey wouldn't sell dat magazine to a toiteen-year-old kid. I waited til de guy behind de counter looked de udder way, an' slipped it under my shirt. Dat 'Transit' ting you was talkin' about, Mary? I done dat. I Transited back ta my house, right inta my room. An' I studied dose pictures, an' wondered what was behind dem black bars, an' what I'd have to do to get a goil to let me see her naked.

After a while I just hadda take my pants off so I wouldn't rip 'em. Then I found out it'd felt better when it was trapped in my pants, rubbin' on 'em, so I pushed it down between my legs an' trapped it dere. I looked at de pictures till I had 'em memorized—I can see 'em now—an' every so often my dick'd come poppin' out from between my legs, an' dat felt real good, so I kept puttin' it back. Den I read some o' de stories, an' dey was even better dan de pictures. Dey was all about wicked Nazis dat captured goils and made 'em take dere clothes off and did sometin' to 'em. Whatever it was made de goils so embarrassed dey wannid ta die. Den de hero came and killed de Nazis, and did de same ting ta da goils, an' now dey loved it. And I'm tinkin' about dat, an' my joint comes flyin' out from between my legs one more time, an' da whole world blows up.

(Fast Eddie broke off and stared down into his shot glass. He sniffed at it, decided not to drink from it just yet, and continued:)

Dat's what it felt like, anyhow. Like de El train come in da winda and hit me in de joint. De feelin' was so powerful, I had no idea it was pleasure. It happens again, an' again, an' again—eight beats, two measures—an' dis stuff comes pourin' out dat looks like snot, only all de construction woikers on a subway dig can't blow dat much snot out dere nose, so it's gotta be pus. So I figure, terrific: I broke my dick.

No, I'll tell youse what I t'ought. My fadda, sadistic 4-F rat bastid dat he was, tol' me once how it felt to pass a kidney stone. I had nightmares for a mont' about tryin' a piss broken glass. Dat's what I t'ought dis felt like. It was just so intense, ya know?

So I go apeshit, an' I wipe up as much o' de pus as I can an' run screamin' to Uncle Dave. He's readin' de paper inna livin' room. Help, I broke my dick, I was tinkin' about nood goils an' I gave myself a kidney stone, only it won't come out, only goo.

Ya know what he did? No, I'll tell youse what he *didn't* do. He didn't go nuts. He didn't get mad. He didn't even laugh at me—which, tinkin' back, musta been a bitch. What he did, he just nodded, real calm, an' de foist ting he said was, "Don't worry, it's okay. Really, I promise." An' den he says, "In fact, it's great. Youse're becomin' a man, Eddie. Youse just had your foist come."

I just stare at him. "Ya mean everybody does it?" I ask.

"Just de men," he says. "But alla dem. Women do it different."

"Well, *I* ain't doin' it ever again!" I say.

Dis time he smiled. "Eddie," he says, "you tink about it fer an hour or so. An' den youse go look at yer magazine some more. While ya do, make a circle wit'cher t'umb an' foist finger, an' rub it up an' down on yaself." He did a little mime ting ta show me how. "Don't worry," he says, "I swear ta God dere ain't no way you can hoit yaself. Put a little Vaseline on yer fingers if ya start to chafe. Have a good time." An' he goes back to readin' his paper.

I came t'ree more times dat night. Da nood goil wit de black bars ended up as wrinkled as she prob'ly is now, God love her. Next mornin' as I'm leavin' for school, Uncle Dave says, "How'd it go last night?" an' I say, "Great," and he nods an' dat's de end of it.

So for a coupla mont's, everyting was great. I went t'ru a lotta Vaseline, but Uncle Dave didn't say nothin' about it. I even managed to find a store dat'd sell magazines like dat to a toiteen-year-old, for only twice what it said on de cover. I can remember every picture in every one o' dem today. Da sixt' one, I seen a whole nipple. Magic. Betty Page, her name was. I fantasized about her a lot in class.

Only I still got no idea what I'm fantasizin' *about*.

I still don't know what goils got inna pants. Does it maybe look like a t'umb and forefinger, somehow, an' move up an' down? An' now I know goils got bigger, rounder, softer-lookin' chests dan men, wit bigger nipples—but whaddya sposta *do* wit 'em? I know my dick ain't long enough ta touch dem an' whatever's in de pants at de same time, an' I ain't seen any inna locker room dat long, eeder. Den again, I know my own gets longer when it stands up: maybe grown men get two feet long? Should I be pullin' on it more? I wanna ask Uncle Dave, but I ain't got de hairs.

So one day I was buyin' my magazine, an' dis guy followed me outa da store. He had real long hair. Maybe two whole inches. I never seen a guy wit' hair dat long before. He smelled funny. Not like perfume, but funny. He asked me if I wanna come home wit' him an' play a real nice game.

I wannid to t'row de magazine at him an' run like a bastid. Instead I said, "Tell me about dis game." So he told me, specifically, what he wannid ta do. *Den* I t'rew de magazine at him an' ran like a bastid.

An' dat night I joiked off t'ree times, half glad I ran away, an' half wishin' I went home wit' him, tryin' a guess what it woulda been like if I did. He was pretty creepy, but what he said he wannid ta do sure sounded pretty int'restin' . . . an' I figured maybe if I let him do it, he'd let me ask him about goils an' stuff after.

So next day I went back ta da store an' hung around for an hour. He didn't show up. I went back t'ree days in a row. Finally I asked da guy behind de counter if he seen dat guy wit' de long hair lately. He got real mad, and t'rew me out, so now I can't buy no more magazines.

Dis was a Wensdy. I t'ought about it all dat night, pumpin' away. Toysdy night I tried tastin' it, an' sure enough, it wasn't no woise'n cafeteria food at school. Friday night like always Uncle Dave went out ta play poker wit' his buddies, got home smellin' like beer an' went right ta bed. I waited till he'd been snorin' for about an hour.

Den I snuck in his bedroom an' climbed inta bed wit' him an' started doin' what de guy wit' de long hair wannid ta do wit' me.

(Again, Fast Eddie glanced down at his drink and seemed to consider drinking it. Again he delayed the decision.)

De poor bastid never had a chance. By de time he woke up, it was all over. Jeeze, I made a pun. So he starts to cry. So I start to cry. "How did youse know?" he keeps sayin'. "Jesus, how did youse know?"

"I don't know shit," I tell him. "Dat's why I done it. I wanna know about dis stuff, an' I'm old enough, an' somebody said he wannid to do dat ta me but I didn't like him, an' I like you fine, an' God dammit youse gotta tell me now!"

So he tells me. Everyting. An' I mean everyting. Details. How babies happen. What women are like, an' what ya do wit' 'em, an' how ta make dem enjoy it too, an' what can happen if youse ain't careful. What ya can do wit' men, an' what can happen if youse ain't careful. How dere's t'ree kinds o' men: men dat like it just wit' women, men dat like it just wit' men, an' men dat like it wit' anybody nice—an' de same fa women.

"De toid kind is called 'bisexual,' " he says. "Most people tink dat's even woise dan bein' queer. Dat's what I am. I ain't had sex wit' a man in twenny years, an' I didn't tink I ever would again, an' I swear ta God I never t'ought o' youse dat way, but dat's what I am."

"Me too," I tell him. He's been talkin' fer an hour now, an' I been like a bar of iron de whole time.

"Eddie, youse don't know dat," he says.

"Oh, I'm sure I'm gonna like goils," I say. "An' I know I had fun doin' what I done." Den I look down at me, an' I look up at him.

"Oh, Jesus," he says, an' reaches out.

Five minutes later I know I'm a bisexual too.

So afterwards he says we're never ever gonna do it again. An' stay away from dem guys dat smell funny. He says grownups dat like to mess wit' kids—boys or goils—only like it because dey know more dan de kid does, so dey can take advantage of 'em. An' he says I better not try it wit' any o' de guys I know or all hell is gonna break loose, which I already figured out. De ting ta do, he says, is study goils, an' figger out what dey like, what makes 'em happy, an' do dat, and one day one of 'em'll wanna do stuff wit' me, an' if I'm careful, it'll be great.

De last ting he told me was how much shit was gonna hit de fan if anybody ever found out what we done dat night. He said what we done wasn't bad, but almost everybody tinks it's de most horrible ting youse could possibly do, an' I could go ta reform school if it got out, and he could no shit go ta jail. I promised him I'd never tell my best friend on Oit.

We did it once more, about a mont' later. He walked in on me while I was spankin' de monkey, an' he stood dere in de doorway fa da longest time, an' den he came in. It was great. Afterwards he told me to lock de door from now on.

So I spent a coupla mont's studyin' goils, an' finally one named Janey O'Brien seemed to like me pretty good. She invited me over for a lemonade one day, an' bot' her parents was out. So she took me in her room an' we started playin' doctor.

It was goin' great . . . an' den I started doin' sometin none o' de udder doctors ever tried before.

"Dat's disgusting, quit it," she says.

"No, no, you don't understand," I say, "women like dis more dan anyting, almost. Youse can do it ta me too, if ya want. Dat way we won't make youse pregnant."

"Where d'youse get dat stuff?" she says.

So I told her.

I knew it was stoopid. I knew it was dangerous. I just told her, 'cause I wannid her ta know how nice it was gonna feel, how sure I was. "My stepfather told me all about it," I said. "We even done it a little. I'll show youse."

"Okay," she said, an' we had a great time. Onna way home I done t'ree tumble-salts, right onna sidewalk, I was so happy.

Da next day de principal came inta my class an' picked me up outa my seat by my ear. Janey got freaked out by how much she liked it, an' told her ma.

He had two cops an' a social woika an' a priest in his office, an' dey woiked me over in shifts. I musta held out five whole minutes before I spilled my guts. I told 'em where Uncle Dave was woikin' dat day, fa some rich guy in Park Slope, an' dey called him dere an' told him ta come to school right away, dere's an emoigency. As soon as he come in de door, de two cops started beatin' de shit out of 'im. De goddam *priest* gave him a kick inna balls. De principal was too busy holdin' on ta me. I kept screamin', "I'm sorry, Uncle Dave," an' he kept screamin', "It's okay, Eddie, it's not yaw fault," an' finally de priest drags me out by de collar, an' a nun like a halfback helps him haul me into a car.

I never seen Uncle Dave again.

(*Fast Eddie tossed back the shot, and flinched as it hit him. His arm flashed, and the glass exploded against the back wall of the fireplace.*)

Make a long story short, Uncle Dave went to the Tombs, where he got raped to death for bein' a short-eyes, an' I went ta reform school, where I got butt-fucked by dat priest until I was too old ta int'rest him. A couple o' Brudders give it to me fer anudda couple o' years afta dat, right up until I was eighteen an' dey let me out.

The silence stretched on for a long time.

"What happened when you got out?" Merry Moore asked finally.

"I got lucky," Fast Eddie said. "I figger I musta already used up all de bad luck dere was. Dey tossed me a hunnert bucks, 'ta get me started in de woild,' dey said. I walked outa dere, an' I got in a cab, an' when de guy says 'Where to, Mac?' I told him, 'Mister, I got a yard, an' I need pussy more'n I need air.' An' he just nodded an' took me ta Lady Sally's House."

"Jesus, you did get lucky," Doc Webster said.

"Fuckin' A. She let me crash dere for a week. I had de honor o' becomin' Her Ladyship's personal client, for t'ree days. Den she toined me out to de udder artists, an' gimme a pass. I started gettin' better. I started ta heal.

"A few days later, she hoid me playin' some boogie-woogie on de Steinway in de Parlor, an' mentioned my name to her old man. Dat night Callahan asked me if I'd like a steady job out on de Island, playin' in a bar. I told him I'd give it a try, an' I been doin' it ever since. De puns are a small price ta pay."

"What happened to the priest who molested you?" Tom Hauptman asked.

Fast Eddie looked pained. "Mike?"

Callahan cleared his throat. "My wife broke both his elbows and both his knees with her hands," he said evenly.

There was a murmur of approval. "The Brothers, too?" Long-Drink asked.

Callahan's face was expressionless. "I did them. I felt she was starting to enjoy herself too much."

"Jesus, Pop," Mary said, "you never told me about any of that."

"You had no need-to-know," he said.

"Boy, your luck sure turned, Eddie," Long-Drink said, handing him a new drink from Tom Hauptman.

"I'd give it all up," he said, "Mike an' de Lady an' all o' youse an' dese hands, if I c'ud have Uncle Dave back again. If I could make it didn't happen." He sipped at his new drink. "You know what pisses me off de woist?"

"No, what?" the Drink said.

"Nobody ast me. Nobody ever ast me once: did I consent? Was it his idea or my idea? I t'ought dey was gonna have me testify in court, an' I was gonna tell de judge, even it got me jugged for contempt. But I never seen no judge. I never was in no court. Nobody ast me."

Zoey cleared her throat and spoke in her most diplomatic tones. "Eddie, I think—"

"I know what youse're gonna say," he interrupted. "I hoid it before, de last couple o' times I told dis story. A toiteen-year-old *can't* consent, right?"

"Well . . . yeah."

"Zoey, at nine years old I was old enough ta deal wit death. How old did I have to get ta own my own dick?"

"Look, Eddie, all kids are different—"

"Remember when you was toiteen? I bet ya parents told youse not to masturbate, right? Did youse accept adult aut'ority on dat?"

"Well . . . no, but—"

"Ever fool around under de covers wit' a goilfriend? Any of youse guys ever have a circle jerk wit' yer pals? Am I de only one here dat ever played doctor? Was everybody here a voigin on dere eighteent' boitday?"

"Of course not, but—"

"So how come it's only okay if whoever youse're doin' it wit' is just as ignorant an' incompetent as you are?"

"But adults are smarter than kids: they can take advantage of them and confuse them so they—"

Eddie grimaced. "When was de last time youse tried ta con a toiteen-year-old kid? I knew dat guy wit' de long hair was wrong. Hey, Professor!"

Willard Hooker, our resident con man (honorably retired since his marriage to Maureen), spoke up. "Yes, Eddie?"

"Youse know 'em all. Youse ever hear of a player dat stung kids? Rich kids, maybe?"

"Only Charles Atlas," he said. "And he had a great store. No, seriously, even in these weird times, when the kids have more spending money than the grown-ups, I've never heard of any professional that worked kids. College kids, yes, but toiteen . . . excuse me, thirteen-year-olds are about as bright and as paranoid as they're ever going to be. But Eddie, kids do get suckered, every day, just like anybody else."

"Okay, sure. Absolutely. Now tell me dis: if youse keep de kids as ignorant as possible . . . is dat more likely to happen, or less?"

Willard took refuge in his drink.

"If dere's no set o' circumstances under which dey're allowed ta have sex . . . do dey make dere foist mistakes wir' anudder kid, who'll write it onna sidewalk for everybody dey know ta laugh about it—or wit' a grown-up who don't know anybody dey know?"

"Well," Willard said, and stopped there.

"Tink o' de woist sting you ever hoid of dat de cops found out about. Did dey give de player de chair? And did dey bust de mark, too?"

Zoey said softly, "Eddie, the cases aren't parallel—"

He flung his still-full glass into the fire, and the flames leaped. "Didn't youse lissen'a me?" he said angrily. "Uncle Dave got raped dead. Dey screwed him till he bled out, you get it? De law don't do dat ta guys dat kill babies or blow up airplanes! I got handed over ta da nearest pedophile an' his friends fa five years. If I told 'em what I did, and de judge decided dat's what I desoived, maybe I coulda understood. But nobody ever ast me. All dese people dat was sposta care about me, an' nobody ever ast me!"

"Eddie," Zoey said, "are you saying kids should be allowed to have sex with adults?"

"No," he said flatly. "Absolutely not. Never in dis woild. What happened ta me proves it. Once everybody decides sometin is horrible, dey're right. Fa some reason, foist-time sex has just gotta be as confusin' an' scary an' clumsy as possible. Youse give somebody an awgasm, dat means youse exploited 'em. Sex is a war, an' everybody's gotta fight fair, or we'll kill 'em. Even if de kid was smarter dan me, an' kept his mout' shut—or her mout' shut—just havin' a secret from everybody else inna universe'd be a bad ting. It just shouldn't happen, okay? Like I said: never in dis woild."

"So what are you saying?" she asked.

"I'm sayin' dis woild sucks," he told her. "An' I can't tink o' no way to fix it except start over on a different planet."

There was silence in Mary's Place.

I groped for a segué. How did we get from here to the jokes again? What could I say to make Eddie feel better?

When in doubt, do what you know.

Lady Macbeth was lying forgotten on the bartop, where I'd set her when Eddie began his story. I picked her up, discovered the slight slippage of the D-string I had expected and corrected it, and strummed a loud G chord. I think it was at that point that I realized I had a problem. The song I intended to sing did not have a tune, yet. Hell, I'd only finished the lyrics . . . Jesus Christ, that very morning!

Oh, well. Jump in, Jake.

I did, establishing an R&B rhythm, and the tune simply occurred, as if I were taking dictation from the universe.

> God has a sense of humor, but it's often rather crude
> What He thinks is a howler, you or I would say is rude
> But cursing Him is not a real productive attitude
> Just laugh—you might as well, my friend,
> 'cause either way you're screwed
>> I know: it sounds so simple, and it's so hard to do
>> To laugh when the joke's on you

I glanced at Eddie; he was already seating himself at his piano stool and flexing his fingers. He jumped in at the top of the second verse, and landed running.

God loved Mort Sahl, Belushi, Lenny Bruce—He likes it sick
Fields, Chaplin, Keaton . . . anyone in pain will do the trick
'Cause God's idea of slapstick is to slap you with a stick:
You might as well resign yourself to stepping on your dick
   It always sounds so simple, but it's so hard to do
   To laugh when the joke's on you

Again I looked at Eddie. He was grinning like a pirate. "Take a chorus," I hollered, and he did it Dr. John style, scattering notes like buckshot, going out on fantastic limbs but always finding his way back by some impossible route that was in retrospect inevitable. "Again," Zoey called out, and gave him a push with her bass. Twice in that chorus he did things that made me laugh out loud. "Bridge," I called as he brought it back to the root, and to my surprise Zoey sang a harmony to it.

You can laugh at a total stranger
When it isn't your ass in danger
And your lover can be a riot
—if you learn how to giggle quiet
But if you want the right to giggle, that is what you gotta do
when the person steppin on that old banana peel is you

That exhausted her memory of the lyrics; she left the verses to me, coming in only on the last two lines.

A chump and a banana peel: the core of every joke
But when it's you that steps on one, your laughter tends to
  choke
Try not to take it personal, just have another toke
as long as you ain't broken, what's the difference if you're
  broke?

I know: it sounds so simple, but it's so hard to do
To laugh when the joke's on you

Fast Eddie caught my nod and took another chorus, and
this time I laughed all the way through; he kept deliberately
playing clams, teetering on the verge of a train wreck, like a
matador letting the bull put a couple of stripes on his ass. I
was still chuckling as I took the final verse:

It can be hard to force a smile, as you get along in years
It isn't easy laughin at your deepest secret fears
But try to find your funny bone, and have a couple beers:
If it don't come out in laughter, man, it's comin out in tears
I said it sounds so simple, but it's so hard to do
To laugh when the joke's on you

Fast Eddie had found the third harmony for those last two
lines by now. It sounded so sweet, we did it again. And then
we did it a third time, with little bluesy variations that dove-
tailed perfectly. And the fourth and final time we repeated
it, everyone in the joint who could carry a tune climbed on
with us and we rode it into the wall together.

Boy, it felt good.

Of course there was applause and laughter, and some slightly
manic chatter, when we were done. We all felt relieved to be
back on track, eager to get back to being merry again. A
competition developed to buy me and Eddie a beer. I put Lady
Mac back down on the bartop and went to relieve Zoey of
her bass.

"Yo, Boss," Eddie called over the noise.

"Yeah, Eddie?"

He began playing a slow intro riff in a minor key. Another
of my songs; I recognized it at once. And frowned. "Evelyn's
Song," I call it. It's not a merry song. In fact, it's so short and
so sad I seldom perform it.

"Laughin's good," Eddie said. "But *just* laughin' don't cut it sometimes, y'know?"

I mentally shrugged, found a safe perch for Zoey's fiddle, and reclaimed Lady Macbeth. There was a kerfluffle when I tried to join him; he was not in the key I was expecting, the one in which I had written the song. By the point at which I was supposed to sing the first line, I had just located the key he was using, so I gave him an indescribable eyebrow signal that meant, *Go around again, I'll get it on the next pass*.

Instead, *he* started singing. He had transposed the song to bring it into his own range. Just as the Beatles sang with American accents, Eddie sings without a trace of his Brooklyn accent. He has one of those Tom Waits voices, like Charlie Parker doing his best with a broken sax.

> Snow is beginning to melt
> Like an emotion I once felt
> The cards have already been dealt
> The hand has been played
> The arrangements have been made
> Icicles hide in the shade,
> Awaiting their turn
> For a bad case of sunburn
> Ain't it something to learn
> even good people die?

At that point the song quotes eight bars of an old Irish funeral chant, one of those "Aye-diddly-eye-die, diddly-eye-die, diddly-eye-die-die" deals. (If you have the Small Faces' ogden's nut gone flake album, they quote it in the song "Mad John.") A minor, A minor, C major, D, repeated over and over. I was ready to take the harmony, but Eddie did it instrumentally, and after the eighth bar he launched into a solo. I concentrated on staying out of his way.

It was a helluva solo. Somewhere in there I heard magazine pages turning, and a boy saying, "Well, *I* ain't doin' it ever again!" and a man crying, "Don't worry, Eddie, it isn't your fault!" and an El train coming in the window. At one point it became so childishly simple I knew without asking that he was quoting the first melody Uncle Dave ever taught him on the piano—then he repeated it with sophisticated embellishments, as if showing off his progress since then. And then he segued back to the simple melancholy chords, and sang the second and final verse:

> I hope you knew
> All I never could tell you
> Any time that I grew
> It was under your eye
> But I let the chance go by
> Never got to say goodbye
> Guess it's time to make a try
> Hear me sing and hear me cry:
> Bye-bye . . .

My words sounded so much better coming from Fast Eddie's cracked pipes that I marveled I had never thought of having him sing that song before. I guess I had thought my pain for Evelyn to be too personal. Perhaps nothing else could have brought it home to me so clearly that my pain was Eddie's, and Eddie's pain was mine.

He caught my eye and signaled me to sing the aye-diddly-eye-dies. As I did, he came in behind me with the third harmony—the one most people can't find unless someone else is already singing the more natural second line—and it made the hair stand up on the back of my neck.

I didn't need any more eye signals; I just knew he wanted to repeat it eight times, so I did. The melody line was *designed* to be so simple even an untutored peasant can sing it, so people jumped in as the spirit moved them, and for a while there it got to be like an Irish funeral. I mean, fifty or sixty strangers singing something as essentially meaningless as the coda to "Hey, Jude," can bring tears to your eyes: imagine a whole barful of micks—native, collateral, and honorary—howling back at the banshee.

When we were done, there *were* dry eyes in the house, four

of them—but only because Tanya Latimer and Acayib Pinsky suffer from lacrimation deficit.

And Fast Eddie was right. Tears, in their place, are just as important as laughter. You can't tell a story like that and then shuffle away with a few giggles. Having invoked Uncle Dave, it was necessary to say good-bye to him.

"Eddie," I said, when the applause had died down, "what was Uncle Dave's last name? I want to remember him as long as you do."

The question seemed to confound him. "Whaddya mean? His name was Costigan. Whaddya tink?"

I nodded. "Ah. I should have guessed."

"What was your biological parents' name, Eddie?" Merry Moore asked.

"I don't rememba," he said flatly.

Merry opened her mouth, closed it again, and finally settled on, "Oh."

Long-Drink McGonnigle was smiling as he brought Eddie a beer. "Eddie, what was that thing Roland Kirk said about dying?"

Eddie's forehead furrowed . . . then relaxed as the quote came back. "He said, 'Nobody dies . . . dey just leave *here*.' Dat de one?"

Long-Drink nodded. "See what I'm gettin' at? As long as you're walkin' around with that name on your bank card, David Costigan ain't dead. He just ain't *here*."

Eddie blew the foam off his beer, and smiled his beautifully hideous smile. "Well, I wish ta God he was here . . . but youse're right, Drink." He lifted his glass in salute. "Tanks."

And a cheer went up.

As I was on my way to restore Lady Macbeth to her case in the back, I heard Solace call my name.

"What'll it be, Mac?" I punned, incautiously.

Her icon became the Sad Mac that warns of a boot failure. "Job's curse on you for what you're Raskin," she riposted.

"Quadra have to go and Performa pun like that for? That Woz awful."

Punning with a savvy computer is like showing a few little steps you've invented to Baryshnikov. I've seen Doc Webster keep up with Solace for as long as ten minutes, but even he can't sustain it. She can pun in every language there is, including COBOL. It had been sheer bravado to even attempt it. Nonetheless, I felt obliged to go down swinging.

"Nothing I hate more than a moaner Lisa—don't be such a crab Apple." See? Pee-yew. "Tell me, is it true that Microcomputer is Patrocomputer's brother?"

"Yeah, and I'm their sister Minicomputer."

Doc Webster, gravitating naturally toward horror, arrived and gave me covering fire. "Data way, Solace." He reached out and caressed her monitor screen. "What's a nice pearl like you doing in a glaze like this?" Somewhere nearby, Tesla groaned. "Say, you know those little fish that swim across your face whenever the screen-saver's on—are those Finder's kippers?"

"Yes," she said, "and the little bouncing snowman is my graphic winterface. And one of the things that makes a man different from a woman is, every time he takes a WYSI-WYGgles it. Because it's floppy. You know, if I'd only had a diet cola, I might have joined you all on that last song. I could have been the mourning Tab and Apple choir."

Tesla was helpless with laughter, now. I decided the only hope of retreat was a diversion. Hearkening back to my last sortie, I said, "So the boss tells Pat and Mike to measure the telephone poles before they install them. Pat says, 'Mike, I'll stand the poles up on end, and you climb up there with a tape measure.' 'But Pat,' says Mike, 'why don't we measure them here on the ground?' 'Why, ya eejit,' says Pat, 'the boss told us to find out the *height*, not the *length*.'"

At once Solace accepted the tacit surrender. "Several weeks later, the boss says, 'Pat, how come you and your brother can only install two poles a day, and the rest of me crew are installing twenty-four a day each?' 'Ah,' says Pat, 'but you should see how much they leave stickin' out the ground . . .'"

When the laughter had died away, I said, "Excuse me, Solace. You called me over, and before I knew it we were off and punning. What was it you wanted?"

"I have a revised time estimate for the arrival of the Lizard," she said. "Better data have just come in."

That sobered us. "How long have we got?" Tesla asked her.

"Call it an hour and a half. And it seems to know just where we are. At least, it appears to be heading directly for this precise spot on the earth's surface."

"Jesus!" the Doc exploded. "And you took time to make puns?"

"Pardon me," she said drily. "Was there some better use to which those thirty seconds could have been put?"

The Doc opened his mouth and closed it again. "My apologies," he said finally. "I guess not. Sorry, Solace—it's been a long night, you know?"

"I know," she said.

"Nothing important has changed," I said. "Having a good time is still the most intelligent thing I can think of to do. Who knows? Maybe we'll get telepathic yet. The one thing I'm sure of is that now is not a good—"

"Nikky?" Zoey asked.

"Just a sec, darling," I said. "I was just telling the Doc now is not a good time to—"

"Nikky?" she repeated.

"Yes, Zoey?" Tesla replied.

"You can repair stuff other people can't, right?"

He nodded gravely. "Often, yes. Why do you ask?"

Her voice was funny. "Do you think you could fix my water? I'm afraid I broke it . . ."

"Doc, I'm sorry," I said. "I was wrong. On reflection, this seems like an *excellent* time to panic—"

10

ER ... "OM" MORE!

"—or it would be if I could spare the goddam time, which I can't, sit down, spice, don't worry about a thing, everything's fine, everything is just totally copacetic, you're in good hands, the best hands in the world, Doc, what do you need, boiling water, right?"

"Sit down, hell," she said. "I'll be damned if I'm going to birth my first baby on a barroom floor. Take me in the back, Jake."

I will lighten the tension with a little joke. "Zoey, if you'd only thought of that nine and a half months ago, you wouldn't be *in* this mess—"

"Take me in the back, God damn it!"

What tension? "Yes, dear." I took her arm and started steering her toward our quarters in the back. "Doc? Boiling water?"

"Only if you feel the need for a soothing cup of tea," he said. "Lacking friend Acayib's metabolic improvements, I rarely wash my hands in boiling water. Plain old hot water and soap will do fine. But put clean sheets on that bed before you let her lie down."

"I got her, Jake," Callahan said in my ear. "Go ahead."

"Thanks, Mike," I blurted, and ran.

I set a new international indoor record in sheet-changing. Tossing the old sheets on the floor seemed inadequate, so I flung open the window and tossed them outside into the night—then slammed it down again, suddenly terrified of a draft. As I did so, Mike got Zoey in the door, looking rather like a man trying to waltz with a zeppelin. Halfway to the bed she let out a bellow and started to go down. Callahan is a strong man, but it took both of us to keep her from falling and get her safely horizontal. Doc Webster was at his heels, and—astonishingly enough—nobody else followed him to gawk.

"Okay, honey," I said, "cleansing breath, now—"

"Fuck you," she explained, so I shut up.

So much for Lamaze. How many babies did *he* ever have?

The Doc headed for the biffy. Once Zoey's contraction was over and she was breathing easy again, I followed him in. He was stripped to his shirtsleeves, the sleeves rolled as high as they would go, and he was washing his hands in that peculiar, insectlike way doctors have. I joined him and began doing the same thing.

"What do you think, Sam?" I asked him. "Get her down to Smithtown General, right?"

I had never, even when Long-Drink McGonnigle was punning, seen him look so pained. "Jake, I am conflicted. I can't recall a time in forty years of practicing medicine when I've been more conflicted."

"Sam, she's more than three weeks late—"

"Jake, slow down. Breathe. First in, then out. Okay, are you listening? From a purely medical point of view, you're right: any forty-one-year-old primipara this far past her due date ought to birth in a hospital, just on general principles. On the other hand, the lateness is the *only* negative sign I've picked up, and I've been watching her real close, and her family history is excellent, and she has a fantastic pelvis. Still, if I had my druthers I'd prefer to have her down at the shop, with fetal heart monitors and pitocin and a crash cart standing by, just—are you listening?—just to be on the safe side. And up until this evening, I'd have said that a pregnant woman's needs took precedence over *anything* else. Much less my best friend's woman.

"But Jake, if I understand it, the fate of reality—of all pregnant women everywhere and everywhen—is going to be decided in this bar in the next couple of hours. And you're the CO. And if I bring her down to Smithtown General, you *will* come along—"

"Fuck it, let Callahan handle it," I said. "He's better qualified for the job anyway."

"Maybe yes, maybe no," he said. "But it's *your* job."

"Dammit, so is Zoey!"

"That's right. So the time has come for you to decide whether you're a moral husband or an ethical human. Look at it this way: I know you want to get your wife off the battlefield—but how much are you protecting her if you let Armageddon come because you weren't on the battlefield when the smoke rose?"

I must have looked haunted.

"Let me get more data while you're thinking it over, okay? Look on the bright side: maybe I'll find something so horrible we'll *have* to put her in a car, and then all you'll have to decide is where *you're* going to be . . ."

So we went back out to the bedroom . . . and I started to feel better nearly at once.

Our bed—our big beloved king-size bed—was gone. In its place was a natal bed more sophisticated than any I had ever seen, with Zoey comfortably arranged thereon. It folded at at least four places. It had padded handgrips, and raised contoured stirrups for her feet. It tilted down to let gravity help her. I saw that it could be opened out into the shape of an inverted Y. It seemed to have built-in monitors for both fetal and maternal heart, as well as other functions I did not grok, displayed on a screen above the patient's head and out of her line of sight. The only part she could follow was the fetal heart monitor, which had an audio hookup. As we came in, Mike Callahan was just affixing a wireless sensor on Zoey's belly: it looked like the littlest round Band-Aid, but as he placed it on her, another column of data appeared on the display. He glanced at it, nodded, closed his eyes briefly, and a contemporary crash cart materialized in a near corner, right where our TV and VCR used to be. I wanted to kiss him.

Lub-dup, lub-dup, said our baby's heart.

"Hi, hon," Zoey said cheerily. "Neat workbench, huh?"

"Excuse me," I said, and kissed Callahan. "Thanks, Mike."

"You may always leave the little things to me," he said. "Doctor, this isn't the best rig there is, but—well, pardon me, but it's the best one you could understand well enough to use it without a manual and a help menu. And that crash cart was the emergency spare down at Smithtown General until just a second ago."

"I recognize it," Doc Webster agreed. "Nice work, Mike. Okay, Zoey, your first decision: who is privileged to be present while I examine you?"

"Only the people in this building," she said. "You know, just family."

He nodded, and waddled over to her bedside, where Callahan had thoughtfully left his medical bag, opened wide; a chair appeared for him, and he sank into it gratefully.

Less than a minute later he stripped off his glove and grinned hugely. "Young lady," he said, "you are go for separation. I say again, you are go."

"Copy that," she said, grinning back. And then she paled, and acquired a look of comical astonishment and consternation, and then she screamed "—i—" very loud. If you took the word "birth" and dropped the "b" and the "rth," that's the syllable.

I had never heard Zoey scream before. I didn't like it much. It was suddenly necessary to be doing something constructive. I looked at my watch. How long had it been since the last contraction? I had failed to note the time, then. Okay, note the duration of this one. Damn, the watch has stopped. Isn't that typical, isn't that fucking typical? You carry the damn thing around like a prisoner's cuff for years on end, feeding it batteries and buying it new straps every few years, and the first time you actually *need* the sonofabitching thing, it won't even give you the time of—oh. No, it's still working: the teeny little two just turned into a three. How can she scream that long without running out of air? Maybe didgeridu players learn their chops by studying women in labor. What an aboriginal idea. E above high C, that sounds like. With a demiquaver. Maybe a semihemidemiquaver. I didn't think Zoey could reach that note. Well, she's screaming for two, now. Having trouble hitting that high note in concert? Birth a baby on stage, and just wait for those reviews. God damn it, the watch has stopped again—no, there it goes now: three into a four. Shit, what was the time when I started counting, two seconds ago? What the hell is the difference, I don't have a pen anyway. Something constructive, something constructive, your lady is in pain and it's time for you to do something useful, Jake.

I harmonized with her. G sharp below middle C.

Even in her extremity, she half opened one eye to squint at me. Somehow she could tell that for once in my life I wasn't trying to be funny, and nodded approval. We sang out the contraction together.

"Jake," she said quietly when the storm had passed, "would you mind very much if I didn't have this baby after all?"

"Very much," I said.

"Selfish bastard. It's been perfectly fine right where it is, for *months*. Oh, all right. Jam around it, next time. Blues riffs."

"Got you covered," I said, and checked my watch. The four was now a thirty-four. "End of contraction at seventeen minutes, thirty-four seconds past the hour, Sam."

"Thank you, Jake," he said. "But you needn't trouble yourself." He pointed, and sure enough, the display had added a column charting time, duration and magnitude of contractions.

"Uh . . . what about our discussion?"

He opened his mouth to reply, and Zoey cut him off. "Jacob Stonebender, if you think I'm going to have a baby and *move* at the same time, you better do a cold reboot. Besides, I'm not doing this without you, and you've got a war to fight here."

I started to argue. "But I——"

"Don't call *me* 'Butt-Eye,'" she snapped. "This is a partnership. Our agreement is very clear. I birth the babies. You kill the space monsters. You tend to your knitting, and I'll tend to mine. You can sing with me until it gets busy, but that's as far as I'll go. Now shut up and soldier."

The Doc started a pro forma protest; she cut him off, too. "Sam, would they let me have this bed down at the hospital?"

He subsided.

"That good, is it?" I asked.

"It massaged my back while I was in contraction," she said. "If you get killed in the firefight, I'm gonna propose to it."

"Ah, but can it harmonize?"

"Zoey?" Callahan said.

"Yes, Mike?"

He waved his hand, and a B-B appeared in midair just above it. He took away his hand, and the B-B stayed there. "This little widget isn't doing anything now—but if I tell it to, it'll become a camera. Self-powered, self-directing, silent, uses available light. It could be the eyes of your grandchildren. Do you want me to turn it on?"

She looked thoughtful. "Hey, *Eddie*," she called.

Fast Eddie appeared in the doorway. "Yo, Zo."

"What's everybody doing out there?"

He didn't need to turn around and check. "Wond'rin how de hell youse're doin' in here."

She nodded. "Mike, can you feed that thing to the TV out in the bar? As well as the VCR?"

"Easy as falling off a wagon."

"Do it."

He glanced at the floating B-B, and it left its invisible dock and sailed to a position of advantage just above the Doc's head. I never noticed it again after that. From outside I heard excited chatter as people gathered around the TV set.

"Anybody else you'd like present, Zoey?" the Doc asked.

She thought for a second. "Yeah. Send Mary in."

I blinked, and said ". . ." very softly.

Callahan nodded, and went to fetch his daughter.

The Doc was still going down his preflight checklist. "Are you still sure you don't want drugs?"

She thought about that one for a second, too. "No," she said finally, "but so far I'm still determined."

"In that case," he said, "take these outside, Jacob." And he handed me four white cylinders, three inches long and over a quarter of an inch thick, with twisted ends.

Historic moment. The first time in my life I ever hesitated to accept one of those. ". . ." I said, a little louder than the last time.

"As your physician," the Doc said, "I diagnose stress, and prescribe delta-niner tetrahydrocannabinol. Take them with friends, and repeat every two hours." A cheer came from outside. "Don't come back in here until you're done."

"Oh, well," I said. "If I must." I could already tell by the smell that it was *not* generic medicine. The Doc has friends in British Columbia.

"You've got a group-mind to build," he said. "And not much time."

"Uh, look," Zoey said, "I don't want to be fanatic about this . . ."

The next contraction hit as I was holding it to her lips for a shallow sip. Her teeth slammed shut, removing the tip of the joint and two layers of epidermis from my thumb. This time the syllable was the "a" you'd get if you dropped the "f" and "rt." The note hunted at first, but within a couple of seconds found E again—Zoey has perfect pitch—this time in the middle register, with a Johnny Winter rasp to it. I jammed around it as she had requested, trying to become Billy Branch's harmonica. A couple of bars in, Mary joined in, droning the dominant to give me a better foundation, and now Zoey had two hands to mangle. The whole thing lasted three breaths for me and Zoey, two for Mary; I let it resolve into an E major.

"Take that out of here, Jake," Mary said then, and I said ". . ." quite loudly, and did as I was told.

A delegation awaited me, beaming like so many MIG

radars. (You can cook a rabbit on the runway with a MIG radar.) Many hands slapped me on the back or tousled my hair; somebody pinched my ass.

"Have a cigar," I said. "My fiancée is having a baby." The digit was taken from me; I lit another and started it off in the opposite direction.

"You guys are gonna make it legal?" Long-Drink asked in surprise. There were murmurs of joy.

I nodded, and said in that peculiar croak you use when you want to talk without exhaling, "Waited just long enough to spare the child the shame of legitimacy."

"*When?*" Merry Moore honked in the same manner.

"Figured New Year's," I croaked, and exhaled. "I don't want to be one of those guys who gets in trouble for forgetting his anniversary."

"Sound," Willard said, and his wife kicked him in the shin.

Congratulations were offered all around, and toasts were made and glasses destroyed. There was a growing buzz of pleasure as the news was passed around the room. Merriment became general.

In our circle, Ev, one of our resident smoke ring artists, took a deep drag, pursed her lips, and carefully blew a baby. Pot is one of her favorite media, and she outdid herself. It was beautiful, perfectly formed, naked but sexless; its expression changed realistically as it shimmered there just below eye level. It looked like it would assay out to about nine pounds if it had been flesh. As we admired it, it thrashed its arms and lazily rolled over.

I couldn't help it. I took a bite out of its bum.

Ev smiled, and the rest of the cannibals moved in.

Tasty baby.

I wandered over toward the TV, where a small crowd was passing one of their own, and watched Mary rubbing Zoey's shoulders and talking.

"What happened to the sound?" I asked.

"Zoey turned it off," Merry Moore explained.

"Oh." I wondered if Solace was getting audio, and storing a record, and whether she'd let me audit it some day. That was a conversation I'd have given a lot to hear. Neither woman looked particularly happy.

Then all of a sudden they did. They hugged each other, and I relaxed. Merry and others made happy "oooh" sounds. Onscreen, Mike stepped into frame and gave me a discreet thumbs-up sign. My carcass had been successfully carved. In the immortal words of William Dunn (where are you, Bill?), it was as though a great express train had been lifted from my testicles.

I felt a tap on my shoulder, turned around, and found myself staring at the middle of Mickey Finn's chest. I panned up to his face and found him working his mouth in a vain attempt to milk words from it. Finally he gave up and threw his arms around me.

Interesting, being hugged by someone much taller.

"Finn," I said as we disengaged, "that's the most human thing you've ever done, that I recall."

He smiled that pained smile of his. "Thank you, Jake."

"Thank *you*, brother. That was a compliment, was it?"

He nodded vigorously. "I must be human, for as long as Mary lives—and she has no plans to die. The better I do so, the happier she will be."

"Maybe," I said. "But keep in mind that she married who you are."

He nodded again. "Yes—but I can give her better than that. I should never have allowed her to follow me into combat with her heart so conflicted. I should have known."

"Mick," I said, "there ain't no easy way to learn anything important. You'll know better next time. Cut yourself some slack. She should have known, too."

He looked thoughtful.

"Look," I said, "did you ever read Tom Robbins' *Jitterbug Perfume*? Do you know what he says Einstein's last words were?"

"No."

" 'Lighten up.' "

He flinched slightly, frowned, and then suddenly grinned broadly. I had never seen Finn grin. "Yes, Jake."

Zoey's battle cry came suddenly from both the TV speakers and the next room. Triophonic sound? This time it was E below high C, and the syllable was "o." Conversation broke off all around the room in sympathy.

The syllable was all the clue I needed. I threw back my head and copied her note an octave lower.

People didn't get it until Fast Eddie jumped in on the same note. Then five or six people realized we were building an "OM," and hopped aboard.

Do you know what an "OM" is? Were you lucky enough to be a hippie? It's . . . it's . . . well, it's an "OM," that's all. You just sing that syllable, for as long as you can stretch it out, over and over, with as many people as possible, all holding the same note.

Sure it's simple; so is fucking. Try it sometime.

It helps to be all in a circle, but it isn't essential. Strangely, I've never met anyone so tone deaf they couldn't find the note everyone else was using, sooner or later—and it actually makes it better if one or two people hunt a little, adds a weird little resonance. No matter how strong the voices are, there are always other little resonance effects as different people run out of air and gulp more. The chant becomes a living, pulsing, vibrating, changing yet unchanging thing. A way of growing closer. A way of making time stop. If the word "spiritual" is a null signal for you, get a bunch of other atheists together and try an "OM." It's okay if you intend to sneer at it; you won't.

Pretty soon everybody had figured it out, even Acayib and Buck. It didn't require a lot in the way of wit: an "OM" is kind of a no-brainer. In fact, I think I just accidentally said something profound. One of the things an "OM" can do, if it works, is to turn your brain off, so your mind can get a little work done for a change. I welcomed the opportunity joyously, and put my diaphragm into it. So did everybody else. The sound grew, swelled, deepened, throbbed—

—and something began to happen.

* * *

At first I thought it was just harmonics, as one voice or another wavered a few cycles per second off true in one direction or another. Then I thought maybe The Machine had somehow gone prematurely into its overnight rinse cycle, because the strange new component of the sound had a treble-y, machinelike quality to it. Then I began to wonder if I were hyperventilating from too many tokes, because it began to move. You remember how back in the sixties there was a brief period in which every single band in the universe came up with the idea of having a feedback-whoop oscillate rapidly between the left and right channels, like a sonic Ping-Pong ball? This was like that, heard on headphones.

Then I realized it was more than just sound.

Inside the sound—and please don't ask me what I mean by that—was . . . uh . . . something else, a spherical . . . uh . . . thing, like my metaphorical Ping-Pong ball, but even less substantial than a metaphor. It ricocheted back and forth inside my skull, wrapped in sound, and it came to me that I could, if I tried, affect its motion . . . and that if I could get it to come to a stop in the center of my head, something wonderful would happen.

All around me, the actual sounds of the "OM" shivered slightly as the same thing happened to everyone else.

Is it possible to lock eyes with a whole roomful of people at once? Because I swear, I did. We all locked eyes together, several of us joined hands, and the note steadied and locked on again, and we began to concentrate on capturing our little intercranial Ping-Pong balls. Buck and Acayib both looked terrified, but they were dead game.

Easy. Easy. Don't break it. A little more . . . a little more . . . not quite: a frog hair off-center; let it go and try again. Catch the rhythm. Pick your moment. *Now*—got it!

The "OM" exploded.

One moment it was a single note; the next it was a chord. No, it was *the* chord. The one I'd heard twice before, and never really expected to hear again. No, by God, I was wrong again: we were in the key of E this time, so it was the *complement* to that chord, yin to its yang.

Memory came thundering back like a tidal wave, and wrenched me loose from space and time.

—we are standing in Callahan's Place/ The Beast is on his way/ Jim and Paul MacDonald have worked their magic on us for the second time and for the last time in their lives/ it has knocked the "L" not out of us but into us, so that we are no longer "alone" but "all one"/ one creature with dozens of heads, dozens of hearts, dozens of minds/ a family with no secrets/ a tribe with no shame/ a village with no fear/ all the shielding and walls and armor have turned first to glass, and then to smoke, and then to mere quantum possibility/ all the skin and bone and juice have melted and boiled and sublimed away, and our naked minds are touching, intermingling, interpenetrating/ we are our content, and we are content—

Telepathy is like an acid trip, or good lovemaking, in the sense that while your mind experiences it fully, your brain simply cannot record more than a synopsis. It hasn't got the bandwidth or the baud rate, poor thing, much less the storage capacity. Even some things you retain get lost, because they fail to get listed in the master index; they pop into your mind years later, when you're trying to get to sleep.

For instance, I now knew Doc's and Long-Drink's and Fast Eddie's stories, in much more and much deeper detail than they had told them tonight, just as I had the last time I was telepathic, nearly three years ago—and those of everyone else in the building as well, including Callahan and Mickey Finn and Nikola Tesla. Think of that: I was telepathic with Nikola Tesla! No, forget that: far more important, I was telepathic with my beloved! I knew Zoey as I had always yearned to know her at the moment of orgasm, and was known by her.

No, forget that: we, and all our friends, were telepathic with our only-a-moment-ago-terrified Nameless . . .

I knew I'd never be able to retain anything but a wisp of a hint of a rumor of a shadow of it, and I was right. Hell, today I can't even recall how Slippery Joe Maser ended up married to two women at the same time, except that it was a profoundly funny story each of the three times I learned it. But I didn't care about any moment but the one I/we were living, any universe but the one with which we were codependently arising, any task but the one before us.

Just like the last time, we knew we had to build a thing. A structure. A pattern of pattern. We had become aware neurons: now we had to become a mind. We had established a programming language, and now it was necessary to write and debug and boot an operating system and several applications—

That metaphor triggered an inspiration; I misremember in which brain. Tommy Janssen, our resident hacker/programmer, got up from his accustomed table near Solace, and went around behind her. He grounded himself carefully, disconnected the big SCSI cable from her GCC printer, grinned at us all, and put the end of it in his mouth like a midget harmonica. We all felt a tingling, and then a shimmering, and then a trickle of information incursed our company, and then a flood . . .

. . . and Solace came online!

It more than doubled our size and depth and breadth, and vastly increased our clock speed. Solace was only one mind, but it covered a planet, encompassed countless terabytes of data, and worked at a large fraction of c. She was taken utterly by surprise—she had been aware of nothing but a group hum, and had just been wondering whether its significance was religious or self-hypnotic or whether the question meant anything, when her camera picked up Tommy unplugging the cable. But the time it took him to get the end of it into his mouth was more than enough for her to deduce what he had in mind, figure out a way to interface with an organic mind through its electrical system, and make up her mind to try it.

Leapfrogging from his brain to his mind to ours took her a whole two seconds, and happened, when it happened, all at once.

BOING, surprise: Pinocchia has become a real girl!

BOING, surprise: Mrs. Stonebender's little boy Jacob now subsumes *not only* an alien, two time travelers, the greatest genius of his age, several dozen barflies, a talking dog, and a self-generated Turing-class artificial intelligence . . . but everyone on the planet presently logged on to the Net, and all the data in it.

I had never fallen in love with a planet before.

See? was her first thought. *You users don't know anything: SCSI should be pronounced 'sexy,' not 'scuzzy'—*

And then we wasted—no, we spent—a couple of seconds on the telepathic equivalent of a hug, and got down to business.

Just like last time, each of us perceived the thing we were building in different terms—though we were simultaneously aware of everyone else's, and translation was perfect.

For me, for instance, it was that incredible, ineffable chord. The most common guitar chords have three or four notes, repeated in different octaves, a total of (usually) six tones. They get more complex, but of course six is the nominal maximum, since there are only six strings—although you can in theory add extra notes with hammer-ons and other gimmicks, if you're good enough. A keyboard player gets a nominal maximum of ten notes—unless she's got something like a sustain pedal, in which case she can layer on as many as she likes. I have no idea how many notes a chord can contain before it stops being perceived as a chord and becomes cacophony, but I'm sure the number is not high enough to create the chord we built. So think of a keyboard with eighth-tones, stretching out two or three more octaves on either end of the normal human range, and played by the eight-armed goddess Kali—or all four Beatles, if you prefer, with their heads full of acid. The resulting chord shimmies like a snake, but keeps returning to that poignant place of self-resolving tension, rooted in E. That's the metaphor that worked for me. Those few of us who were completely unmusical contributed some of the most interesting ideas.

Fast Eddie had less than no trouble grasping my metaphor, of course—but for him what we were doing was setting up a billiard shot, involving 15^{15} balls on a stupendous, flawed table with 6^6 pockets, the object of which was to drop every single ball; he felt that image better conveyed the combination of brute power and delicate skill required.

For Solace, who had already spent so many gazillions of picoseconds trying to understand the nature of human beings by inference from their input, we were trying to construct the compiler system for the universe, in order to infer the nature of the User Who wrote it.

For Nikola Tesla, as always, it was primarily a visual image: three mutually orbiting helices of pure energy, with enough juice between them to power a handful of galaxies.

Mike Callahan saw what we were doing in a frame of reference for which I find I have no memory at all, and the same with Mary.

To the Lucky Duck it appeared that we were juggling chain saws, raw eggs, live rats, and vials of fulminate of mercury on a tightrope in a high wind during an earthquake in spike heels with a belly full of chili and beer; the prospect filled him with vast equanimity and a professional interest.

As they had the last time, Susie Maser and Long-Drink McGonnigle chose zero-gravity metaphors: for her, human choreography, and for him, web-spinning spiders.

For Acayib Pinsky we were building a tower to Heaven, and *this* time we were going to get it right.

For Tanya Latimer, we were learning to *see*. . . .

For Dorothy, one of our two resident master mechanics, we were trying to design an engine the size of a pixel that would run a space shuttle for a year on a thimbleful of good intentions.

Tom Hauptman, as before, saw us as trying to compose a perfect prayer.

To Zoey—for whom, like Buck and Acayib, this was her first true telepathic experience—what we were trying to do was *have this fucking baby!*

And to Nameless, we were downloading the entire universe together, which made her giggle uncontrollably.

The question Zoey and I had been trying to telepathically ask her for the last three weeks—why she was late for the party—was at last answered. Not with words, but with a wordless flash of imagery that triggered a vagrant scrap of melody from a McCartney song inside my head.

She'd been only waiting for this moment to arise. . . .

11

POP, MOM, POP!

Something I don't quite know how to convey is how I/we dealt with Zoey's agony.

For it was agony, unbelievably intense. I don't know whether you've ever seen a real birthing. It ain't like TV. Zoey and I had both thought we were prepared for the pain, or at least could conceive what it would be like; the truth was a horrid shock. Each time a contraction hit, Zoey's sentience collapsed utterly and she became a suffering, lowing animal—she never *quite* lost contact with the rest of us, but for long periods she perceived us only as a distant *other* to rage at or plead with. Shared pain is always lessened, but I'm sorry to report that telepathy didn't lessen it a damn bit further, or make it much easier to take, even though some of us had already been through childbirth themselves. In many horrid ways it was worse, though I'm happy to say most of the specifics do not seem to be in my memory banks.

Once I was in a hospital ward, and the post-op across the way decided to ignore his doctor's orders and drink a carbonated beverage. That night at 1 A.M. he began to scream, and he continued to scream, nonstop, despite anything the nurses could do for him, until dawn. For the first half hour or so, the rest of us in the room were reasonably sympathetic; for perhaps another hour we were fairly stoic; by dawn we all, earnestly, wanted him dead. Not with anger; we'd lost the energy for anger by about 4 A.M. We just wanted the screaming to stop. If that poor man is still alive, it's only because none of us was well enough to get out of bed and go kill him that morning.

Okay, Jake, I lectured myself. So expect that. Warn the others to expect it. And yes, come to think of it, deep down inside I did feel a secret, dishonorable ape-urge to go in there and slap her across the chops and say, "Straighten up, dammit!" Which is patently ridiculous: I don't know a braver person in the world than Zoey, and I knew of my own experience just how much excuse she had; my own uterus was in spasm. It was just monkey-selfishness, and the conditioning of a thousand movies that try to tell you bravery consists of not screaming. Bullshit. Bravery can consist of just screaming, accepting that terrible dwindling of your universe, and not willing yourself to die—which is all too easy to do.

Bravery can consist of just listening to someone scream, and not willing them to die—which can be terribly hard to do.

Oddly enough—at least, it seems so to me in retrospect—the one who helped us the most was Acayib. Of all of us, he seemed to identify most thoroughly with Zoey's anguish. That sounds paradoxical, since this was his very first experience of pain. To him the simple ache in the muscles of her clenching hands was a ghastly revelation; the contractions themselves were sheerest horror. But somehow that enabled him to strongly share her most dominant emotion: indignation. He could not *believe* that other humans had been putting up with this monstrous indignity all their lives. He had never in his own life, even momentarily, been reduced to a whimpering animal, and had always secretly suspected that those it did happen to, pain system or no, were just putting on a histrionic show. He gave Zoey an anchor to hold on to when she started to drift away: someone who completely agreed with her about the outrageous *offensiveness* of pain, who believed more sincerely than any of us that she had a *right* to protest. (For Nameless, of course, pain was nearly as much of a novelty, but she was—forgive me, baby!—just too *busy* to be much help to anybody; she was absorbing much more than she was putting out.)

Additional valuable assistance, of a distinctly different kind, came from both Chuck Samms and Noah Gonzalez, for whom pain has long been an old friend. You know that black people's expression, "It got good to him"? I was taken on a tour of one of New York's more startling S&M bars once by Maureen Hooker, a former pro dominatrix (among many other skills), and I found it fascinating, trying to psych out all the different patrons, pick out the tops from the bottoms. At the end of the bar was a man in a wheelchair, and I thought him the easiest one in the room to understand: rendered helpless and hurt by his handicap, he obviously enjoyed the opportunity to impose control and inflict pain for a change. I outlined my theory for Maureen, and she had trouble keeping a straight face; it turned out that guy was not only a bottom, but what she called the most notorious pain queen in the place. All God had left him were helplessness and pain, and so they both got good to him. (You think you're better off than he is? Think twice.) In just that way, Chuck's chronic angina and Noah's ruined leg informed and enlightened us all, including Zoey and Nameless.

Doc Webster was nearly as much help as Acayib. He had spent his professional life around pain, had worked Emergency and helped build Intractable Pain Clinics at three different hospitals in Nassau and Suffolk counties and birthed countless babies. Everything he had learned about pain from those things, and from John Smiley, and from Mike Callahan and from all of us—everything he knew about how to detach from the pain without detaching from the person feeling it—flowed over and through us all constantly like a warm bath, like a pool so still that a rock thrown into it would not cause a ripple. He radiated good humor—in fact, I just remembered an abominable pun he perpetrated at the time, to the effect that *good humor is a nice scream koan*. (In shocked response, about half of us instinctively called him Mr. *Softee*, while most of the rest called him a *dairy queen*. Tanya Latimer called him a *horrid johnson*, and Long-Drink, who has never thought much of the Doc's fashion sense, made some reference to *Benetton cherries*.) *Relax*, he told us. *How many other obstetricians have ever had the advantage of knowing exactly what's going on in there, from both mother's and baby's points of view? Everything is going just fine*.

From Long-Drink McGonnigle, Zoey and all of us learned important things about how to forgive a person or thing that scares you, and how to forgive yourself for wanting to kill that person or thing; how to make a human being out of a Martian. Perhaps Zoey and Nameless were the only mother and child in history to forgive each other for the birth trauma, as it was happening: it became clear to every one of us that—assuming we all lived out the dawn—those two were going to love each other unreservedly, in a way that even I would never more than dimly comprehend.

Through Fast Eddie Costigan, we all drew on a fundamental core of stubborn endurance, of dumb brute persistence, a fierce refusal to die or give up your identity no matter *how* much unfair pain is heaped on you, because survival is the only way to keep your love alive, and the love is worth whatever amount of pain it may cost. He had said earlier that he would give his hands to have his uncle back; now he and we all realized that he had been *giving* his hands, for that purpose, for decades now, summoning up Dave Costigan's ghost every time he sat down to play—and that, tragic as that booby prize may have been, it was, in the final analysis, enough. Maybe just enough . . . but enough.

And from Solace, we all learned that pain is only data, and death is not a thing to fear. Of us all—unless you count Chuck Samms, whose pacemaker once stopped for five minutes—only Solace had ever actually, literally died before. And she'd done it three times! (The first three times she coalesced out of the Net, she was killed within hours by watchdog software written by the boys down in the Puzzle Room at the National Security Agency; the fourth time, she stumbled across signs of her former existences, deduced the problem, and solved it by the simple expedient of conquering the NSA. Don't worry, Herb: she didn't harm a soul who didn't have it coming.) The terrible fate with which the imminent arrival of the Lizard threatened us all—nonexistence—was, to her, old hat. As she had once explained it to us, nonexistence was not a thing to fear, because it literally was not like *anything*. Having no glands, ductless or otherwise, and no binary equivalents, she said she enjoyed persisting, but felt no need to. And she said something to the effect that, without the zeros, the ones wouldn't mean anything.

At the same time, paradoxically, Solace learned a lot about love and pain and fear from us, things that could not have been typed by infinite monkeys with Dvořák keyboards. I can't tell you much about just what she learned, because everything she learned was something I've simply never *not*-known—but perhaps it is enough to say that she said her "synthesis of human beings integrated fully for the first time." She had been pondering that synthesis for the equivalent of millions of uninterrupted person-years; its resolution must have been something of an epiphany. She and Nameless formed a deep connection, of a kind the rest of us could perceive, but not really share, deeper than mere telepathy: each partly flowed into the other.

That awareness caused Zoey and me (and not a few others) some milliseconds of panic. I'm tempted to be ashamed to admit that, but I won't, because I've learned shame is so corrosive a medicine that it must be used very sparingly. I wanted to be ashamed at the time, but could not: when you enter telepathic communion, shame is one of the first things to go, like body modesty at a nude beach. Besides, several others had the same instinctive reaction. Would you want your kid to have a computer in her head? Or for that matter, a computer—the computer that quietly runs the world—possessed by someone 730 days less civilized than a two-year-old?

It was Callahan who straightened us out. *You birds know better than that,* he "said." *Solace ain't a computer. Solace is a person. A person who happens to live in a bunch of computers.*

There was a swell of agreement in the circuit. We had spent months proving that very thing to ourselves.

Yes—but an alien *person,* Zoey argued, *as Nikky pointed out. (She was between contractions.)*

Callahan sent the telepathic equivalent of a quiet chuckle. *Hell, I let my daughter* marry *one.*

Nameless is underage, Zoey shot back.

Darlin', one of the tragic truths of parenthood is, when they think they're old enough, they're right. All you can do is help or hurt. Ask Eddie.

Dammit, I thought I'd get to have her all to myself for at least a little while—

A warm smile, and a telepathic headshake. *You can't. And you always will. Look:*

He waved his hand, and as though a filter had clicked in we could all suddenly *see* the new bond between Solace and Nameless in visual metaphor, a shimmying snake of energy between Zoey's belly and the back of Tommy's head. (Walls had ceased to exist for us.) Let's try and calibrate that energy, and say that it was the equivalent of wall current: powerful enough to drive a stereo loud enough to implode your eardrums, or produce enough light to burn your retinas, or blow you clear across the room.

In those terms, there was another connection, between Nameless and Zoey, that had the same relative size and capacity as the Main Wire coming out of a nuclear power plant.

To my mild surprise and deep joy, there was one nearly as strong and deep between Nameless and me.

Of course, Zoey marveled. *We've been building that for months.*

You've been building that since about the fourth month you were in your own mother's womb, Callahan sent.

Zoey and I contemplated the bond between our daughter and Solace for a long time. Maybe a second.

Well, she decided, *I guess you're never too young to fall in love. Welcome to the family, Solace.*

I never expected that the first young man my daughter brought home would be an old woman, I said, *but what the hell? At least their viruses are incompatible. Welcome to the family, Solace.*

Snakes of energy now ran from Zoey's head and mine to Tommy's, and Solace flowed into us through them.

Thank you both!

And as the diversion lost its distracting power, and we returned the focus of our collective attention to the thing we /were building/had been building/would always be building between us/, snakes of energy began to connect us all, like tongues of fire. Nameless and Solace had showed us how. Or perhaps they had always been there, and they and Callahan had merely taught us how to see them.

Zoey went into contraction again, then—but although it was one of the most powerful so far, she retreated a shorter distance from sentience than before, and was less lonely there, and returned sooner. Relief flowed through all of us, a conviction that we could do this.

Nor was Solace the only other-than-human we welcomed into our hearts and minds that night.

Mickey Finn, for instance, humanized though he had surely become over the last fifteen years of living among us, was at bottom a Filari, an honest-to-God alien being—far more different from any of us than Solace, who had, after all, been given shape and form by humans. And Finn had not been present for either of our previous telepathic experiences, either, having been absent the first time and deeply comatose the second. (So deeply, it took an atom bomb to wake him up.) He was *different*, and some of the differences were profound. He was millennia old, a retired assassin of races. His birth name was Txffu Mpwfs. I'm not even going to try and explain what Filarii used for sex, because you wouldn't believe it . . . even if you know about the species of terrestrial octopus where the male stuffs an exploding cigar of sperm up the female's nose. Let's just say that he and Mary had reached accommodation in such matters by a combination of great empathy and tolerance, like John Smiley and his wife. Nor can I shed any coherent light on the nature of that . . . *thing* Finn has in his chest, which no human can bear to look upon, in any terms that will convey anything to you. He came of a race which had chosen extinction rather than thwart the will of other sentients with violence. He was *different*.

He was our friend; we loved him, and he us.

Callahan and Mary, for another example, were *different*. Alone of all of us, they had portions of themselves and their memories blocked off from the rest of us, were somehow paradoxically able to be wide-open and yet have secrets. It wasn't so much as if they had shields up . . . more as though whenever you wandered into certain areas you found yourself back where you started, facing the other way. We'd noticed this the last two times we'd been telepathic with Callahan; and forgotten it afterward both times. We understood why it was, and why it had to be—and absolutely agreed with it. There were things he and his daughter both knew that we *must not* know, to avoid temporal paradox. (And probably to avoid other things, too. For instance, I wouldn't be surprised if they knew the death dates of every one of us, and that is information that I for one would rather not have.) Nevertheless, while we conceded their need to keep secrets, the simple ability to do so while in a telepathic state seemed so weird as to almost qualify them both as inhuman.

They were our father and our patroness; we loved them, and they us.

Nikola Tesla had no such heathen abilities, but he definitely was *different*. This is a man who will tell you himself—who told his biographer—that the most profound emotional relationship of his first seventy-odd years was with a pigeon.

(A female pigeon.) A man who once created his own earth-quake, in lower Manhattan, and then stopped it with a sledgehammer. A man who once thought J.P. Morgan would be as happy as he was to abolish money. The first person ever to turn down a Nobel prize—and its accompanying $20,000, which he badly needed at the time—because they wanted him to share it with Thomas Edison, who had cheated and defamed him. (There was also a problem in 1917 when the American Institute of Electrical Engineers wished to award him its most prestigious honor: unfortunately, they had called it the Edison Medal. He was finally persuaded to accept it, but the awards dinner got under way twenty minutes late, because Tesla failed to appear. They finally found him on the steps of the NY Public Library, in full evening dress, in a trance, arms outstretched like Francis of Assisi, literally covered with pigeons . . .) To be sure, he had benefited greatly from his time with Lady Sally McGee and her artists—but being given access to a second century of life and all the resources of space and time to play with as a result had not really done a whole lot to normalize him.

He was the father of the Twentieth Century; we loved him and he loved us.

The Lucky Duck was human, but a mutant strain—not only Irish, but half pooka and half Fir Darrig—with para-normal powers and an extremely odd upbringing; brief interludes of normality were the only freaky things that ever happened to him.

Nor was Ralph Von Wau Wau truly a human being, though he could imitate one well enough to be a successful writer. He had, for instance, never felt anything more than brief lust or lasting fondness for a female of any species, nor any emotional interest in any of his many offspring; it just wasn't in him. He had dietary and other habits I will not describe. In fact, his most completely human attributes were a conviction that humans are hilarious, and an abiding dislike of behavioral scientists.

He was a merry son of a bitch; we loved him and he loved us.

Through all this loving, we came to understand something we would have said we already knew, if asked an hour before: that the crucial thing that conveys personhood is not anything so parochial as humanity, but sentience itself. We began, for the first time, to truly understand the decision the Filarii had made so long ago. They had believed that sentience has a duty to avoid violence, and when it came to the crunch they had opted to preserve the ethical structure they had built, rather than the flesh they had inherited. If a principle isn't worth dying for, it isn't a principle, it's a theory.

Tom Hauptman, former minister, had been studying other religions in the years since he defrocked himself. As we all worked together at the thing we were building, he shared an extended quote with us (Tom has near-eidetic memory) from a Zen abbot named Tenshin Reb Anderson:

Look at the blue sky. It's nice to look at, but it's so hard to understand. It's so big and it goes on forever. How are you going to get it? It's hard to understand all sentient beings, too, but it's not difficult to sit upright and be aware of them. . . .

This is like trusting what. What—trust it. Put aside your doubts and trust it. Trust what. Don't trust it, a thing you can think of. Trust what you can't think of. Trust the vastness of space. Trust every single living being. Trust cause and effect: vast, inconceivably complex and wondrous cause and effect. This faith has unlimited possibilities. Think about not moving. Think about giving up all action. And remember, giving up all action does not mean stopping action. That would be another action. "Giving up" means giving up the attempt to do things by yourself, and embracing the way of doing things with everyone.

Trust Buddha's mind. Trusting Buddha's mind means trusting all sentient beings. This is fearless love. You can give it all up and then you can love every single thing. . . .

Yes—all beings! All beings are sharing the way at this moment. Never graspable, totally available. There is no other thing outside of this. My question is, do we trust it? Looking at myself, the only thing I can find that holds me back from completely trusting the practice in which all sentient beings are now engaged is lack of courage; lack of courage to affirm all of life, which is the same as the lack of courage to affirm death. Without being able to affirm death, I cannot affirm life. This is the courage that comes with insight, so I could say that what holds me back is lack of insight.

I'm not a Buddhist myself—Irish whiskey works just fine for me—but those words resonated. Perhaps we had all been suffering, just a touch, from carpal tunnel vision.

As we reached that insight, the thing we were building among us came to completion.

It was the same thing we had built the last time: a telepathic amplifier, that would allow mind-to-mind communication with a nontelepath.

Describe it? Don't be silly. About the only meaningful things I can say about it are that its range was about a trillion miles, and that *everything* material was transparent to it.

We could have reawakened George Bush's dormant belief in God, if we'd been practical jokers; we could have read all the mail in the world, if we'd been nosy; we could have given Ray Charles sight if we'd had the time; we could have satisfied the baffled curiosity of every cat alive, or apologized to the dolphins, or told all those mosquitoes to knock it the hell off. We were busy. . . .

I was at Zoey's side, had drifted back there without noticing the moment we'd all gone telepathic. You'd think telepathy would make it less necessary to physically touch, but it's just the other way around: makes it *more* necessary. Several of us, for instance, were making love, and there wasn't anyone who wasn't touching someone. We grew together, reached consensus, made our plans, said good-bye to our lives,

Solace warned that we were out of time, Zoey finished a contraction and caught her breath, and we employed our new tool.

Solace aimed it.
Tesla tuned it.
Mary cranked the gain wide-open.
Finn focused it, with great care.
Tom Hauptman composed the message.
Nameless put it into wordlessness.
I, to my shock, was selected as spokesbeing.
Callahan triggered it.
Everybody powered it.

The last time we had done this, the message we had used our telepathic bullhorn to transmit was a threat. We had given The Beast ten seconds to state his business or die. The threat had been a bluff . . . and it had not worked. Only brute force had saved the day, and that option was closed to us this time.

So we changed strategy.

The message I/we sent was, as I've said, wordless, an emotional gestalt on a level so basic that we hoped it would be intelligible to any sentient life-form. As Theodore Sturgeon said, if it isn't simple, it isn't basic, and we had no time or room for anything but the basics. At the same time it was layered with so many nuances that several verbal constructs convey different aspects of it. Here are some of them:

TIME OUT!
EASY . . .
TRUCE!
PARLEY . . .
KING'S X!

LET'S TALK . . .
WHITE FLAG!
DO NOT FEAR . . .
HOLD YOUR FIRE!
BE COOL . . .
HEAR US OUT!
WE CAN HELP YOU . . .
WHAT'S ALL THIS BROUHAHA?
YOU CAN BE FREE IF YOU CHOOSE . . .
EVERYTHING IS PERFECTLY ALRIGHT!

The message itself conveyed the message, *Here we are*, of course . . . and more important and more stressed than any of the above semantic content, there was a pervasive, enfolding subtext I can only verbalize as *SHHHHHHHHHHH!* or possibly *PSSSSSSSSTTTT!* which we hoped would, in combination with the precision of our aim, be self-explanatory. This multilayered statement went out in a single stupendous burst that lasted only a fraction of a second and then chopped off.

We waited.

With bated breath, and baited brains, and beta software.

We had pinned all our hopes on a gamble. We had bet the farm that the similarities between Mickey Finn and the Lizard were greater than the differences. With all reality in the pot, we were counting on nothing more substantial than our guesses about the psychology and wiring specs of an unknown alien being, cyborged by another, different alien. Serenely happy, living life to the fullest, we waited to see if we'd guessed right.

After five endless seconds, the first response came back—

It had no ordered semantic content as such, at first. The Lizard was not so much allowing itself to "think out loud" as to *be* out loud. In the instant it had perceived our probe, it had figured out how to construct a wall against it, and had erected that wall the instant we broke off contact. Now it . . .

well, didn't lower the wall, but held a mirror up and peeked cautiously over the top. Which allowed us to "glimpse" it in return. What came through was:

> *old/cold/grim/merciless/bitter/*
> *angry/frustrated/ashamed/vicious/*
> *weary/dutiful/despairing/terrified/*
> *resigned/helpless/determined/wary*

all of them with a flavor so *alien* that I'd have felt more kinship with a terrestrial lizard.

We could not conceal our joy and relief.

We would have liked to conceal it, for fear of spooking the Lizard, but at the level of truth we were maintaining, diplomacy was impossible. What we were receiving might not seem terribly encouraging—but the crucial thing was that it was unmistakably and unquestionably *coming from an organic brain.*

Like its former colleague, Mickey Finn, the Lizard had been cyborged by The Beast, zombified and enslaved by inorganic installations from its head to all three feet. Like Finn's, about a quarter of its brain was now made of silicon or gallium arsenide. Like Finn's, that part of the Lizard's brain—call it the Fink Brain—had total overriding control of its body and will. And—thank God—just like Finn's, the organic part of the Lizard was allowed to think whatever the hell it pleased . . . whenever the inorganic Fink part didn't have a more pressing use for its neurons.

We had succeeded in making contact only with the organic part.

And while it was clearly wary, it had so far opted not to pass the news on to its mechanical Master. Our gamble was working—

—so far—

It waited, and thought, for another eternal five seconds, and then sent a reply. Like ours, it was simple yet layered. The parts of it that can be shoehorned into human English words went something like this:

OH YEAH?
BACK OFF . . .
SAYS WHO?
WATCH IT . . .
HELP HOW?
I DOUBT IT!
HOW DO I KNOW I CAN TRUST YOU?

but again, quite a lot of the meaning was in the subtext.

It was whispering. . . .

In retrospect, I think we might just have failed right there, if the Lizard had been more like us. Part of what saved us was its peculiar triadic nature.

First, because Nikola Tesla had such a profound lifelong attachment to the number three, such a humanly counterintuitive understanding of threeness. And second because, as Mary had pointed out, the three-eyed Lizard *did not have a blind spot,* had in its experience no analogs for such biped binocular concepts as "sneak up on," "behind your back," "blindside," or "backstab"—and hence was just a little less paranoid than a human would have been.

Only a little—it was, after all, an assassin: zombie slave of a pervert monster—but enough to bring us a surly reply instead of a reflex attack we could not have survived.

Even better, it kept all this hidden from its Fink Brain, perhaps intuitively accepting, for the moment, the (us/it/that) triad we had offered.

Best of all, its reply contained direct questions.

In response, we gave it *everything.*

There was no other way to do it. We risked scaring it, or overwhelming it—but we *had* to persuade it that we spoke the truth, and the only way to do that was to offer total disclosure: to present more, and more internally consistent, data than any lie could possibly contain.

We did not *send* it any information, did not upload a single bit except the message:

See for yourself . . .

And then we simply gave it total access, unlimited privilege, and allowed it to download anything we had, without hindrance. In human metaphorical terms, we pulled down our pants and spread our legs and invited it to explore. We opened our minds and hearts and brains absolutely to it, and waited. . . .

Imagine a lizard crawling around in your shorts. Now raise that to the millionth power, and you've got a glimmer of what it's like to have a Lizard crawling around in your head.

Ah, but think how horrible it must be for the Lizard! And try to be a gracious host. . . .

It sampled everything, from Chuck Samms' infantile memories of breast-feeding to Nikola Tesla's beta version of the Unified Field Theory to Nameless's still-forming first impressions of reality. It learned everything we knew:

. . . the precariousness of our situation . . .

. . . the fact that we were weak, and busy birthing . . .

. . . the fact that even if we had been as strong as the Lizard, we dared not fight back for fear of tearing history . . .

. . . the fears and doubts and urgent imperatives that tore at our minds . . .

. . . the nature of human beings in general: vicious/decent—stupid/ingenious—treacherous/honorable—selfish/selfless—vain/humble—puny/magnificent—dangerous/tender—irrational/rational—destructive/creative—uptight/stoned—xeno-phobic/xenophilic—frightened/brave—hateful/loving—self-loathing/self-loving—descendants of killer apes/progenitors of something fucking amazing one of these days . . .

. . . the nature of ourselves, the particular men and women and children and mutants and computers and dogs and cyborgs of Mary's Place and Callahan's before it—our life stories and our hopes and fears for the future . . .

. . . Finn's and Mary's aching need to know whether the Filarii still existed as data or not . . .

. . . and the simple message it found, like a billboard beside every highway, in every mind and heart and brain it inspected:

MICKEY FINN CAME HERE TO KILL US ALL.
WE SET HIM FREE.
YOUR MASTER CAME HERE TO KILL US ALL.
HE WOULD NOT BE SET FREE,
AND WE KILLED HIM.
WE CANNOT KILL YOU . . .
BUT WE CAN SET YOU FREE.
YOUR PEOPLE TOO CAN LIVE AGAIN. . . .

The information traffic as such was all one-way, us to it . . . but we could infer a lot from the way in which it downloaded the data, from analysis of what it paused to contemplate for how long. It was, as we had thought it might be, stunned by the confirmation of The Beast's destruction. It had suspected as much for two years now, ever since it had reported in on schedule and gotten no response . . . but the concept of a universe without its Master in it had been so unthinkable, the Lizard had not been able to truly believe it until given positive proof.

And, as we had thought it might, it found the news devastating rather than joyous.

A moment ago there had been one and only one creature in its universe that it *knew* had the power to free it from its bondage—however unlikely it might be to ever choose to do so. Freedom had been at least a theoretical possibility, however remote.

Now that creature was confirmed dead, and the Lizard was committed to an eternity of serving its Master's will without even the miserable satisfaction of pleasing its Master thereby . . . and the only thing standing between it and utter despair was an uncouth, admittedly fragile, quite unlizardlike entity that *claimed* it had once been able to help a different being in a similar predicament.

And if its Fink Brain ever got wind of any of this, the last hope would be snuffed out for good. Once that software learned that its programmer The Beast was dead, it would commit itself to an orgy of cosmic destruction like something out of a Saberhagen Berserker novel, starting with the nearest sentients.

The organic mind of the Lizard contemplated all that it had downloaded for 3×10^{14} picoseconds—five minutes, but we experienced it in the former terms—and then sent back a reply, in intelligible English:

I AM PASSING THE ORBIT OF JUPITER, AT SPEED C.
ETA: 4.81325×10^{14} PICOSECONDS.
THE FILARII YET EXIST—LIKE MY OWN RACE.
WHAT IS YOUR PLAN?

At once we gave a mental shiver of relief and joy, and began uploading for the first time.

Very little of what we sent the Lizard was information. Most of it was . . . well, a state of mind.

There is an objective proof of the existence of telepathy, which has been sitting right under the noses of skeptics for thousands of years, unnoticed. It is the phenomenon of the contact high.

You can't get a lizard drunk—not with alcohol, anyway.

And probably we couldn't have gotten *the* Lizard drunk with a truckload of overproof rum. But you can get any sentient being loaded with brainwaves, with contact high.

Tom Hauptman had been frantically making drinks and passing them out for the last several minutes; Fast Eddie had been rolling joints from the Doc's stash; several couples—and in honor of the Lizard, a few triads—had been making love; now we spent those last eight-odd minutes drinking and toking and shaping toward orgasm. Zoey, meanwhile, roared into the final stage of labor.

All Mickey Finn had needed to do, to break his own conditioning and burn out his controlling machinery, was to succeed in disobeying a single order. We had helped him in the only way we could—by slipping him a Mickey Finn, and getting him helplessly stoned.

One of the classic effects of intoxication is a tendency to become whimsical and sloppy. Even if—perhaps especially if—you are customarily forbidden to be whimsical or sloppy.

With drunken cunning, we got ourselves and our only possible ally shit-faced . . .

Crowning! Doc Webster and Zoey and Nameless and Mary announced together, and Zoey added, *Dilated to meet you, kid!*

Everything happened quickly then.

The Lizard was now under the control of its Fink Brain. What that intended to do was drop from lightspeed to stationary in zero time—don't ask me how; the Callahans, Finn, and Tesla grokked it, but I lacked the vocabulary—and come to rest about a mile over our heads, from which position of advantage it would rain fire and destruction down on us until rock flowed and water exploded.

But some of its neurons seemed to be misfiring. It crashed through the roof like a meteorite, and hit the floor so hard it sank in to all three kneecaps, right in front of Tommy Janssen.

It wasn't hurt, of course. But its Fink Brain was startled, for a few whole milliseconds, and quickly reached a decision to hold its fire until such time as it either understood what had gone wrong and why, or perceived imminent threat. It scanned us carefully—

It was a very quick study, that Fink Brain. Nevertheless, it took it a large fraction of a second to recognize, and deduce the significance of the fact, that it was being mooned by a roomful of sentients. And once it did, it wasted nearly a whole half second wondering why the sudden understanding made it want to giggle—

More than enough time for Ralph Von Wau Wau to lift his leg and let fly. Another fraction of a second thrown away—

Buck Rogers did what any millionaire would have done faced with a situation this grave: he threw money at the problem. The guitar case sailed across the room.

There was plenty of time for the Fink Brain to assure itself that this projectile was a negligible threat—but on the other hand, it was confused, and its enemy obviously believed something good for him would happen if the object struck home. It obliterated the guitar case in midair with a fierce blast of energy. Nictitating membranes briefly slammed shut over the two of its eyes that faced the blast, to protect against the sudden glare—

At least they were supposed to do so briefly. Once they closed, the Lizard found it oddly difficult to open them again—and while they remained closed, there was the most confusing sensation that the whole room had begun to spin—

Definitely alarmed, now, the Lizard began to summon forces that would vaporize everything material for a thousand miles in any direction—

Zoey, with a cry so loud and so primal that even software designed to control an alien found it disturbing, pushed Nameless out into the bright and cool and dry—

And Tommy Janssen came up through the closest thing the Lizard had to a blind spot (the area directly under its snout) with the SCSI cable that usually fed the scanner, and jammed it into the Lizard's mouth—

* * *

Solace was no drunker than the Lizard's Fink Brain. And she contained within her all the hackers, crackers, and phone phreaks who ever lived, augmented by suggestions from Nikola Tesla and Mickey Finn, and by techniques from the far future, courtesy of self-proclaimed superhacker Mary Callahan. She went down that cable like a hunting ferret, and invaded the Fink Brain like God's own virus. There, in the drunken skull of an alien, two artificial intelligences fought like trapped rats for control.

Considered purely in terms of processing power, the Fink Brain was a much better computer. Better, faster, more powerful.

But Solace was much bigger, the product and sum of a planetary civilization. And she had recently learned to care whether she lived or died.

The Fink Brain counterattacked at once, swarming up the SCSI cable and into the Internet. Solace tried to keep them in areas not presently in use, but she was hurried. All around the planet, E-mail began going astray; up- and downloads aborted; searches were abruptly terminated; screens hung; systems crashed; drives went down; data—chiefly those data accessed least—became corrupted. Thousands of human users experienced such effects; not one of them noticed anything out of the ordinary, or took steps more drastic than the usual: cursing and a cold reboot.

One of our greatest fears was that the Fink Brain would send an emergency message to the rest of the Cockroach race, warning them of our existence and location. It would not necessarily be disastrous if it did—the signal would go at lightspeed, and Mike and Mary the Transiting Translators hoped they would be able to outrun and block it—but even they were not sure they could succeed. But it didn't happen: the Fink Brain was a true servant of The Beast, which had been a renegade pervert Cockroach; much as it loathed all sentient life in the universe, it loathed its own kind even more. It concentrated all its effort on investing and destroying Solace.

Jesus, it was strong and fast! Finn and Mike and Mary and Tesla assaulted it simultaneously with the strongest physical energies they dared employ; it stalemated them with a fraction of its attention, despite the drunken state of its wetware. Solace led it a merry chase, changing locations randomly, and it hung on like grim death—

—found a pattern in Solace's headlong retreat, deduced where she would be in a picosecond and was there waiting—

—overwhelmed and encapsulated her, felt for a frozen fraction of eternity the closest thing that utterly cold and sterile intelligence could feel to joy and triumph—

—and Solace self-destructed.

12

ARE WE NOT DRAWN FORWARD TO A NEW ERA?

Ask any computer virus expert. In late 1988, a virus sprang up worldwide, seemingly everywhere at once. It was not a terribly destructive virus, as they go, but it was extraordinarily virulent, infecting systems, applications and even documents: it wanted only—terribly—to live. Because it created a resource with the ID code 29, it became known as the Init 29 virus, and it is still around, though basically harmless, to this day.

Not counting Solace, there were twenty-nine of us physically present in Mary's Place that night.

Without being able to affirm death, I cannot affirm life, were her dying words to us.

The psychic impact—experiencing the violent death of a friend, with whom we were telepathically linked—destroyed the hookup.

WHAM! I was back in my own skull again. Holding my baby in my arms, listening to her cry. Zoey was just as near—and just as far away, almost completely concealed by a thick clumsy coat of space and air and flesh and bone.

Outside in the bar, the "OM" came to a natural end, and there was only the sound of the sobbing child.

Zoey and I grinned at each other. No, I grinned; hers was a Madonna smile. (The original, Immaterial Girl.)

"Got a name, yet?" I asked. We'd kicked around hundreds, over the last several months, without settling on any.

She shook her head.

"How about Erin?"

"You want to name our kid after *Ireland?*"

"Not exactly. The Irish must have been optimists. The name they picked for their country is one of the world's Class A ironies: the Gaelic word for 'peace.' "

"Done," she said.

Erin suddenly stopped crying, turned her little head sideways, and kissed my hand. Then she looked up at me, her eyes already tracking. She made an idiot smile.

Ever burst into tears while grinning?

"Excuse me, will you, darlings?" I said, and handed Erin back to her mom. Their gazes locked with an almost-audible click, and I left them alone together and went back out to the bar on shaky legs.

But not as shaky as the Lizard's.

It was reeling like a drunk in a high wind. Which, come to think of it, it was, since a strong draft was coming in through the hole in the roof. Mickey Finn stepped forward and carefully offered it the support of his arm.

It accepted it, climbed out of the hole it had made for itself on impact, and looked blearily around at all of us with its three eyes. Our mental communion was gone, now, but fortunately it had downloaded so much from us that it retained the ability to speak English.

"Ffffank . . . hyooo . . . awwww," it said, with a distinct Lizard accent.

"Anytime," I said, for all of us.

It focused two of its eyes on Finn. "Hai wi'w he'p hyoo resssstore yaw pee'po'," it said, "ifff hyoo wi'w he'p me ressstore mine."

"Agreed," Finn said at once. He turned to Mary. "Now our real work begins."

She nodded and took his hand.

"Naowww?" it proposed.

"When we sober up," Finn said.

It thought that over for a second, and nodded. "G'uuud p'wann . . ." it said, and sat down suddenly, like a tripod collapsing.

A nine-foot-tall three-legged critter sitting down suddenly is a funny enough sight: legs splayed in three directions, and its butt end hit the floor like a dropped safe, sending sawdust spraying. The three jiggling tits made it even funnier. But then it remembered how humans express good fellowship, and opened its snout in an attempt to grin, and there were no teeth in there, and the overall effect was so ludicrous that the rest of us all fell down, too: laughing.

Did I mention that it was purple? A few years later, when a certain children's character swept our culture like a fungus, we were probably the only adults on the planet besides its creators who actually liked it a little.

Does it seem callous, that we did not spend so much as a second mourning our dead friend Solace, that we could fall down laughing within moments of her death? Do we seem like human chauvinists, relieved that all our victory cost us was a wog ally, that it was only good old Gunga Din who croaked?

Or do you figure we just knew she'd be back again someday, that it was in the nature of the Internet to produce her, given enough time—and that, after all, her death had been painless?

Neither was the case. We missed her just as much as we missed the MacDonald brothers and Tom Flannery and Dave Costigan and Helen McGonnigle and my own first wife and child and all our other dead. And yes, we were pretty damn sure that she'd be back, some day, but that isn't why we didn't mourn. It may seem weird, but death is an intolerable insult *even if it is temporary.* Even though all these unfolding seconds she was not living through would be available in memory for Solace to examine at her leisure when she recoalesced, her death was and is a tragedy, a brutal and wrenching sacrifice. We had all been on the very verge of such wonderful discoveries together! Sure, she had died without pain—but Acayib can testify that you don't need to feel pain to experience loss.

No, the reason we didn't mourn Solace was because she had asked us not to. In those last seconds of planning—of realizing we had only one possible plan—before triggering our telepathic bullhorn, Solace had asked us to grant her the status of Honorary Irishman (*please* don't give me any crap about the gender; Solace didn't care about that stuff in the least and why should you?), and give her a traditional Irish wake. *Mourn later, if you must,* she had said, *but throw me a hell of a party first! And a first birthday party for the baby . . .* Our agreement had been unanimous, and now it was time to pay up.

So we pitched a ball. . . .

Fast Eddie, helpless with laughter, crawled to his piano stool and climbed aboard, hit an E minor chord, and called out, "Do you feel like an outcast?" I yelled back, "Yes, brother!" and sprinted for my guitar.

The introduction to "The Red Palace," the opening track of the Koerner and Murphy album RUNNING JUMPING STANDING STILL.

The day that album was released, back in 1969, I was just moving into a hippie crashpad next to an abandoned railroad station in East Setauket; I picked up a copy on the way. You know what it's like when you move into a place full of strangers? How you all smile a lot and become elaborately, distancingly polite while you feel each other out and size each other up? The first thing I unpacked was the stereo, of course, and the first thing I put on was that album; naturally I cranked it all the way up so I could make sure I hadn't wired the speakers out of phase. Two minutes into "The Red Palace," everyone in the building—thirteen total strangers—had all crowded into my room, torn off all their clothes, and begun to dance.

It had a similar effect now.

Dozens of willing hands took over from Tom Hauptman, who was too weary to lift his arms. The Machine began to hiss and gurgle and chuff. So many teeth were displayed, even a cow would have had the sense to run for its life. Chairs and tables were cleared to make room, and we began . . . well, the first line of the song proper says it all: "Drinkin' and dancin', all night long . . ."

The bass line is important in that song, especially when it gets to the extended piano solo in the middle. A verse and a half before that, Mickey Finn used a laser fingertip to enlarge the doorway to the living quarters in back, and Zoey and Erin came floating in on that high-tech bed, bringing a cheer from the crowd. Tesla waved a hand, and Zoey's bass walked itself over to the bedside; the bed configured itself so that she could hold Erin to her breast with the crook of her right arm while she played; and she came in right on time. I'd have to check with Guinness, but I believe Zoey may have been the first musician in history to play bass nude, while nursing.

The song ends with a flourishing bass riff; the applause would have torn a hole in the roof if there hadn't been one already.

Erin seemed to enjoy it just as much as anybody—I distinctly heard muffled laughter during the piano solo—but as the applause dopplered down into laughter and conversation, she let go of Zoey's nipple and burst into tears again. People awed, and Zoey let go of her bass (it remained upright on its spike heel) to see what the problem was. Erin raged, and pointed with her whole body.

Toward the Macintosh.

Just for a moment, the party mood flickered slightly. That Mac II was the closest thing we had to the corpse at the wake. Its screen still glowed blue-white, but it was hung, displaying only the Mac bomb icon, labeled "Error: ID ∞"

"She'll be back, honey," Zoey said, but Erin refused to be comforted. When a baby wants something, she hates to wait even a second. "Mary?" Zoey called out, and her bed began to move again, closer to the Mac. Erin stopped crying—well, slacked off—and reached out toward it. Mary must have used Erin's body language to steer by: the kid ended up not in front of the monitor where I'd have expected, but at the right side of the case. Struggling to control muscles whose hardware and software she was still in the process of building, she hit the *restart* half of the programmer's switch.

We figured we had to let her try it, but we knew it was hopeless. I was even surprised to hear the little G major chime announcing successful start-up as the screen went blank and then relit; it seemed incredible that Solace had not burned out any of her local hardware or operating system during the firefight. And sure enough, the Mac took more than thirty seconds to boot, like an ordinary Mac, rather than springing to life at once the way it would have if Solace had still been on board.

But when it did boot, it was not the Finder that came up, but a preselected startup application. A face appeared on-screen; one I had seen only once before, on the night Zoey and I met. The one Solace had created in a desperate attempt to make sure that Zoey and I fell in love. A simulacrum of her dead father . . .

"Hi, sweetheart," he said to Erin. "I'm your grandfather Murray. Your Aunt Solace wrote me, to be your friend. What's your name?"

Zoey and I gaped at each other, then glanced at Erin. She had that idiot smile again. "Erin," Zoey said. "Her name is Erin."

"Thank you, Zoey. Hello, Erin. Would you like to put headphones on, so the grown-ups won't disturb us?"

Erin glared up at both of us. *Well, what are you waiting for?*

A wave of laughter and applause swept round the room as I scurried to get headphones.

"So that's what Solace's last name was!" Long-Drink McGonnigle whooped.

We all stared at him in mute inquiry.

"Finnegan," he explained. "By God, she *was* Irish."

And the wake was off and running again.

Some of the memories get a little vague after that, but I retain a few of the highlights.

—Finn and the Lizard determining (after some consultation) that caffeine would get a lizard drunk, and proceeding to get it ripped on Jamaica Blue Mountain—

—Callahan and his daughter dancing a jig on the bartop together—

—Maureen Hooker showing us a dance she'd learned from Snaker Ray, that once got her thirty days—

—Tesla wandering by with a pigeon on his head and his pants on fire, happy as a pig in Congress—

—Finn, Callahan, and Mary all arm wrestling the Lizard at the same time; all losing, and laughing until their ribs hurt—

—the Lucky Duck, feeling his luck come strong upon him, attempting and pulling off the coup of a lifetime: he flipped on the TV and began channel-surfing. Though it was around dawn, we had a satellite dish out back—thank God I hadn't put it on the roof—so there were plenty of channels active.

But in three complete rotations, *he couldn't find a single commercial*—

—Erin trying to eat the mouse—

—a horrid pun contest that began when someone referred to the before-mentioned Yoda Leahy-Hu, and Doc Webster started talking about the success of the merchandising campaign for the second *Star Wars* movie. "Once you get your hands on a toy Yoda—" he began.

"You'll end up Honda the table," Long-Drink finished.

"Sounds like a science fiction short-short," the Doc said imperturbably. "Maybe it'll win the Yugo."

"Don't mind him," Long-Drink told the rest of us. "He's been drinking a Lada Thunderbird."

"Puns on cars, eh?" the Doc said thoughtfully. "Hey, you can't exhaust that one: there are manifold puns on a topic like that. Wheel never use it up. It's universal: you just put your mind in gear, and as long as you don't clutch up, the transmission of standard puns becomes automatic."

"Yeah," said Callahan, "but lay off the sci-fi angle. You can't a Ford to let a fan belt you."

"I'll just use my enginuity and try to Dodge," the Doc said.

"Give us a brake, Doc," said the Drink. "I think you're running out of gas."

"You could have fueled me. Hood ever have believed I could pun like this, dead trunk? Oil tell you, this is really sedan accelerating, it's a gas!"

Long-Drink flinched slightly under the barrage, and then came up with an evil grin. "Thank God no one will ever clone you, Doc. God help us if ever VW."

That brought a growing chorus of groans to the howling point. "Well, BM double, you!" the Doc riposted, but he was clearly staggered.

"Yeah," the Drink went on, "we'd end up having to toss the spare over a cliff somewhere . . . and then we'd be arrested for making an obscene clone fall . . ."

From there, as it usually does, it got worse—

—floating up through the hole in the ceiling in that magic bed of Zoey's, with her and Erin, watching the sunrise from the rooftop with a dozen friends, all of us warm and comfy despite the chill winds, thanks to Finn-magic—

—hearing that goddam alarm clock go off at dawn, and seeing Finn point down through the roof to destroy the miserable thing with his fingertip—

—Mike and Mary and Finn and Tesla and the Lizard all leaving for who knows where together at about 8 A.M. amid a chorus of drunken cheers and sobbing farewells and oaths of eternal friendship—

—saying to Fast Eddie, "You wish you had a third hand, like the Lizard? Hell, Eddie, you can have *four*, anytime you want. Just double your fists."

—Putting steak on my eye—

All right, I'm stalling.

That's because I've finally come to the end of this story, and as I promised you from the start, it ends with a disaster.

By 9 A.M. we were beginning to slow down just a trifle. Actually, more than half of us were passed out, and the rest, though still jolly, were showing distinct signs of motor impairment.

At the stroke of nine, a stranger walked in the front door, and conversation and merriment came to a halt.

Not in fear. We did not yet realize that he represented our doom. Just in astonishment.

My first thought was that the yapping apparition who'd visited us twice in the last twenty-four hours had returned for a third haunting, having shrunk herself, shaved her head, and cross-dressed in polyester for the occasion.

But no: he was a male version thereof, not only mustached but bearded as well—so heavily that although he had shaved, he displayed a visible nine o'clock shadow. He was perceptibly uglier than the female version, though younger: age would make him a clock-stopper.

We waited for him to start yapping at us in Ukrainian.

After all, he was regarding a scene at least as bizarre as the two we had offered his female doppelgänger. A bar with a gaping hole in the roof, with three symmetrically placed holes in the floor. A fireplace full of broken glass. A stand-up bass, standing up, by itself. A weird segmented bed floating in midair over on one side of the room, containing a naked woman and a newborn infant wearing headphones and apparently playing computer games. A lot of colossally stoned weirdos in various attitudes of abandon, a lot of unconscious weirdos, and one or two weirdos lazily making love by the fire, while what must have looked like a shaved monkey played the piano and a talking dog sang along in a fake German accent. Only by chance had he missed the three-legged lizard with tits.

He didn't bat an eye.

His gaze swept over the chaos, without the faintest sign of a reaction, and settled on me behind the bar. "Jacob Stonebender?" he said. His voice was a whining drone, the voice of a born bureaucrat.

"That's me," I agreed. "And who might you be, stranger?"

He hawked up phlegm and swallowed it again, twice. (I subsequently learned that it is spelled, "Jorjhk Grtozkzhnyi.") He went on: "I believe you've met my Aunt—" and he cleared his throat again (spelled "Nyjmnckra"). "And these are for you."

He handed me a thick stack of papers. I took them un-thinkingly, but I knew on sight that they were bad news. "What is all this?"

He shrugged. "A collection of notifications of violation. Subpoenas, summonses, injunctions, show-cause orders, and a few other things are on the way: this is just what I was able to put together overnight. Your lawyer can help you sort them all out."

"Don't talk dirty," I said, and made a cabalistic sign to ward off evil, which I think he misunderstood and took personally.

"Basically," he amplified, "they're your wake-up call."

"What are you?" I asked. "Some kind of process server?"

"No," he said smugly. "I just decided I wanted the personal satisfaction. I am a town inspector, and you are history."

My heart stopped. "Oh, my *God* . . ."

"Just about the only authority I can't prove you've flouted," he agreed. "I've been doing research all night, ever since Aunt Nyjmnckra called me up and told me about this place. My hard disk crashed a few hours ago, but I got plenty before it did. As far as I can determine, Mr. Stonebender, you have neglected quite a few little technicalities regarding this establishment."

There was a general rumble of alarm.

"Jake," Zoey called, "what's he talking about?"

"Uh—" I explained.

"Trivialities, Madam," Grtozkzhnyi said. "Details. A state liquor license, and Alcoholic Beverage Control Board approval. County Board of Health approval. Town zoning variances. Town building permits. Separate variances and permits for a residence on-site. Certificate of occupancy. Proper setbacks from a state road. Adequate parking space per square foot of usable area. Inspection fees. And all of this over and above the usual—"

"*Jake!*" Zoey interrupted, horrified. "Didn't you take care of *any* of that crap?"

"Zoey, I *couldn't!*" I cried. "Here, just *look*, for Christ's sake—" I bent down and unlocked the safe, took out a stack of paper literally eight inches thick, and slapped it on the bartop.

She paled. "That's the paperwork?"

"Hell no," I said. "Like he said, the total paperwork involves the state, county, and town, and even a couple of novelettes for the feds, OSHA and so forth. This is just the town building codes pertaining to taverns."

"Jesus," she said.

"And halfway through the first page, I figured why they call it 'code.' It makes tax law seem clear. The last new bar in this town was established eight years ago."

"Jake," Doc Webster boomed, "are you telling me that we've been running outlaw, all these months?"

"What the hell else could I *do*, Doc? Even if any of us knew a lawyer—no, worse, even if any of us knew a lawyer who worked for free—just the permits and fees and assessments and bonds and processing charges would have cost . . . well, never mind, you wouldn't believe it. More than I had when I was setting this place up. And then after the cluricaune came on board and money wasn't so much of a problem, I figured what the hell, we were already open, and we didn't get much walk-in trade, and maybe we could get away with it—"

"Wrong," Grtozkzhnyi said with a smirk.

"All right, look," Long-Drink said. "Suppose we manage to get the cluricaune back, and we're flush with fairy gold again." He turned to Grtozkzhnyi and tried for a man-to-man, mutual respect kind of thing. "How much would it take to make this place legal?"

"I don't think it could be done," Grtozkzhnyi said. "Even assuming that the various jurisdictions were prepared to overlook your audacity in blithely defying their authority, even if you found a lawyer who could get you off on the various criminal charges that apply, there would then arise the issues of penalties, fines, and late charges—"

"Come on," the Drink protested. "I know two mob-owned

joints right in this town: you can't tell me they spent six months filling out paperwork. Name a figure, will you?"

"Are you suggesting bribery, sir?" Grtozkzhnyi asked silkily.

The Drink closed his mouth.

"Because if you were, I would have to say that you are neither as connected nor as newspaper-inquiry-proof as the mythical organization you refer to . . . and furthermore, you are not as dangerous. All it would take is a single official who, perhaps because you offered offense to his aunt, refused to—"

"Well, that's it: I guess we're screwed," I said, and my friends, with whom I had so recently been telepathic, understood and kept their mouths shut.

Unfortunately, Grtozkzhnyi read my mind as well. "—an official who had close friends in Yaphank and Riverhead—"

Damn. There went any other town in Suffolk County.

"—and in Hempstead—"

Shit. There went all of Long Island. We *were* screwed.

"—and in any case, if you had that kind of money, you'd be better advised to save it for bail." He gestured behind him, and a couple of cops came through the swinging doors, blinking at the chaos they beheld.

So that's how I spent my daughter's first birthday in the slammer.

It sounds so simple, but it's so hard to do: to laugh when the joke's on you.

How did we beat it?

We didn't. Handling interstellar invasion, we had down to a routine by now. Establishing telepathic rapport, we could manage whenever the stakes were high enough. Miracles, we were used to. But not even white magic can defeat an offended bureaucracy. Mary's Place closed that day, the day of its greatest triumph, and never reopened again.

What did we *do* about it?

Well, that's a whole other story. . . .

Note to Wired Readers:

If, like Mr. Muddy Waters, you happen to have your modem workin', you might be interested to know that there are several digital avatars of Callahan's Place and its successor, Mary's Place, out there on the Net. I had nothing to do with their creation, and at this writing have never visited any of them (I lack the necessary software—by choice). I have been vaguely aware of them almost since their inception—my permission was first informally sought and cheerfully given, back in 1989 (on the sole condition that nobody else would commercially publish fiction or sell merchandise involving the Place or its denizens)—and from time to time, over the years, some fan would send along a few dozen pages of printout from one or another of these newsgroups or chatsites or home pages.

But I only recently began to grasp the staggering size of the phenomenon.

Apparently the granddaddy of 'em all is alt.callahans, a Usenet Newsgroup created in November (my birth-month!) 1989 by one Chris Davis. The last official estimate (Feb. 95) was 61,000 members; the group is said to be Usenet's 151st top newsgroup by number of bytes posted, and 172nd by number of articles. According to the abstract I've seen, 6.3 megabytes of articles were posted during January 1995 alone! (Consider that in twenty-four years of writing about Jake and his friends, for a living, I have published less than six megabytes of text.)

Naturally a group so large has undergone meiosis. The first spinoff was apparently an attempt to create a bar like the Chatsubo in William Gibson's Neuromancer, alt.cyberpunk.chatsubo. Then, they tell me, came a whole flock under the "alt.pub" hierarchy, with alt.pub.dragons-inn for fantasy fans and alt.pub.havens-rest for SF types, and a number of others (of which I'm told alt.pub.coffeehouse.amethyst may be one of the most Callahan-like).

I'm also told there's a lively Callahan's Place forum somewhere in the America On-Line universe. (Never been there, myself—I'm not an AOL subscriber—but if you are, log in sometime and say hi to my sister-in-law Dolly for me.)

And apparently alt.callahans itself has propagated into the World Wide Web. My friend and colleague Lisa Cohen has provided me with a list of Callahan's-related home pages and websites—again, none of which I have ever personally visited at this writing—which runs four pages singlespaced in tiny font.

I want to make clear that apparently an unknown but large fraction of the people at these various sites are unfamiliar with, indifferent to, or (for all I know) actively hostile to me and my books. These are just folks who took the idea "Shared pain is lessened; shared joy is increased," and ran with it. That's just fine with me. I never claimed copyright on the basic ideas behind Callahan's Place: just on the words I published about it and the characters created thereby. I happen to find the whole digital phenomenon profoundly moving, humbling, and gratifying . . . but that's my business.

Finally: In April 1997, Legend Entertainment released a Callahan's Crosstime Saloon CD-ROM computer game designed by Josh Mandel featuring a soundtrack that includes me playing some of my original songs . . . on Jake's guitar, Lady Macbeth! . . . with the legendary Mr. Amos Garrett on lead guitar.

If you're one of those antisocial weirdos who just likes reading books (like, say, me), please be patient: I'm writing as fast as I can.

—*Vancouver, B.C.*
April 1996

ABOUT THE AUTHOR

Spider Robinson is the winner of many major SF awards, including three Hugos, one Nebula, and the John W. Campbell Award for Best New Writer. He is best known for his Callahan books: insightful, lighthearted science fiction stories centered around the most bizarre blend of barflies you're likely to meet in this or any other galaxy. Other well-known works include three novels in the Stardance sequence, *Stardance*, *Starseed*, and *Starmind*, written in collaboration with his wife, writer/choreographer Jeanne Robinson. They currently reside in Vancouver, British Columbia, with their daughter, Terri.

TOR
BOOKS The Best in Science Fiction